James George Frazer

The Golden Bough
Volume 6

James George Frazer

The Golden Bough
Volume 6

1st Edition | ISBN: 978-3-75239-009-4

Place of Publication: Frankfurt am Main, Germany

Year of Publication: 2020

Outlook Verlag GmbH, Germany.

The Golden Bough

By

James George Frazer

Vol. VI

Part IV: Adonis Attis Osiris.

Chapter I. The Myth Of Osiris.

yptian counterpart of Adonis and Attis.

In ancient Egypt the god whose death and resurrection were annually celebrated with alternate sorrow and joy was Osiris, the most popular of all Egyptian deities; and there are good grounds for classing him in one of his aspects with Adonis and Attis as a personification of the great yearly vicissitudes of nature, especially of the corn. But the immense vogue which he enjoyed for many ages induced his devoted worshippers to heap upon him the attributes and powers of many other gods; so that it is not always easy to strip him, so to say, of his borrowed plumes and to restore them to their proper owners. In the following pages I do not pretend to enumerate and analyse all the alien elements which thus gathered round the popular deity. All that I shall attempt to do is to peel off these accretions and to exhibit the god, as far as possible, in his primitive simplicity. The discoveries of recent years in Egypt enable us to do so with more confidence now than when I first addressed myself to the problem many years ago.

Osiris. The Pyramid Texts.

The story of Osiris is told in a connected form only by Plutarch, whose narrative has been confirmed and to some extent amplified in modern times by the evidence of the monuments.⌐ Of the monuments which illustrate [pg 004] the myth or legend of Osiris the oldest are a long series of hymns, prayers, incantations, and liturgies, which have been found engraved in hieroglyphics on the walls, passages, and galleries of five pyramids at Sakkara. From the place where they were discovered these ancient religious records are known as the Pyramid Texts. They date from the fifth and sixth dynasties, and the period of time during which they were carved on the pyramids is believed to have been roughly a hundred and fifty years from about the year 2625 B.C. onward. But from their contents it appears that many of these documents were drawn up much earlier; for in some of them there are references to works which have perished, and in others there are political allusions which seem to show that the passages containing them must have been composed at a time when the Northern and Southern Kingdoms were still independent and hostile states and had not yet coalesced into a single realm under the sway of one powerful monarch. As the union of the kingdoms appears to have taken place about three thousand four hundred years before our era, the whole period covered by the composition of the Pyramid Texts probably did not fall short of a thousand years. Thus the documents form the oldest body of religious literature surviving to us from the ancient world, and occupy a place in the history of Egyptian language and civilization like that which the Vedic hymns and incantations occupy in the history of Aryan speech and culture.[2]

Texts intended to ensure the blissful immortality of Egyptian kings.

The special purpose for which these texts were engraved on the pyramids was to ensure the eternal life and felicity of the dead kings who slept beneath these colossal monuments. [pg 005] Hence the dominant note that sounds through them all is an insistent, a passionate protest against the reality of death: indeed the word death never occurs in the Pyramid Texts except to be scornfully denied or to be applied to an enemy. Again and again the indomitable assurance is repeated that the dead man did not die but lives. "King Teti has not died the death, he has become a glorious one in the horizon." "Ho! King Unis! Thou didst not depart dead, thou didst depart living." "Thou hast departed that thou mightest live, thou hast not departed that thou mightest die." "Thou diest not." "This King Pepi dies not." "Have ye said that he would die? He dies not; this King Pepi lives for ever." "Live! Thou shalt not die." "Thou livest, thou livest, raise thee up." "Thou diest not, stand up, raise thee up." "O lofty one among the Imperishable Stars, thou perishest not eternally."[3] Thus for Egyptian kings death was swallowed up in victory; and through their tears Egyptian mourners might ask, like Christian mourners thousands of years afterwards, "O death, where is thy sting? O grave, where is thy victory?"

Osiris in the Pyramid Texts.

Now it is significant that in these ancient documents, though the myth or legend of Osiris is not set forth at length, it is often alluded to as if it were a matter of common knowledge. Hence we may legitimately infer the great antiquity of the Osirian tradition in Egypt. Indeed so numerous are the allusions to it in the Pyramid Texts that by their help we could reconstruct the story in its main outlines even without the narrative of Plutarch.[4] Thus the discovery of these texts has confirmed our belief in the accuracy and fidelity of the Greek writer, and we may accept his account with confidence even when it records incidents or details which have not yet been verified by a [pg 006] comparison with original Egyptian sources. The tragic tale runs thus:

of the earth-god and the sky-goddess.

Osiris was the offspring of an intrigue between the earth-god Seb (Keb or Geb, as the name is sometimes transliterated) and the sky-goddess Nut. The Greeks identified his parents with their own deities Cronus and Rhea. When the sun-god Ra perceived that his wife Nut had been unfaithful to him, he declared with a curse that she should be delivered of the child in no month

3

and no year. But the goddess had another lover, the god Thoth or Hermes, as the Greeks called him, and he playing at draughts with the moon won from her a seventy-second part[5] of every day, and having compounded five whole days out of these parts he added them to the Egyptian year of three hundred and sixty days. This was the mythical origin of the five supplementary days which the Egyptians annually inserted at the end of every year in order to establish a harmony between lunar and solar time.[6] On these five days, regarded as outside the year of twelve months, the curse of the sun-god did not rest, and accordingly Osiris was born on the first of them. At his nativity a voice rang out proclaiming that the Lord of All had come into the world. Some say that a certain Pamyles heard a voice from the temple at Thebes bidding him announce with a shout that a great king, the beneficent Osiris, was born. But Osiris was not the only child of his mother. On the second of the supplementary days she gave birth to the elder Horus, on the third to the god Set, whom the Greeks called Typhon, on the fourth to the goddess Isis, and on the fifth to the goddess Nephthys.[7] [pg 007] Afterwards Set married his sister Nephthys, and Osiris married his sister Isis.

uces the cultivation of corn and of the vine. His violent death. Isis searches for his body.

Reigning as a king on earth, Osiris reclaimed the Egyptians from savagery, gave them laws, and taught them to worship the gods. Before his time the Egyptians had been cannibals. But Isis, the sister and wife of Osiris, discovered wheat and barley growing wild, and Osiris introduced the cultivation of these grains amongst his people, who forthwith abandoned cannibalism and took kindly to a corn diet. Moreover, Osiris is said to have been the first to gather fruit from trees, to train the vine to poles, and to tread the grapes. Eager to communicate these beneficent discoveries to all mankind, he committed the whole government of Egypt to his wife Isis, and travelled over the world, diffusing the blessings of civilization and agriculture wherever he went. In countries where a harsh climate or niggardly soil forbade the cultivation of the vine, he taught the inhabitants to console themselves for the want of wine by brewing beer from barley. Loaded with the wealth that had been showered upon him by grateful nations, he returned to Egypt, and on account of the benefits he had conferred on mankind he was unanimously hailed and worshipped as a deity.[8] But his brother Set (whom the Greeks called Typhon) with seventy-two others plotted against him. Having taken the measure of his good brother's body by stealth, the bad brother Typhon fashioned and highly decorated a coffer of the same size, and once when they were all drinking and making merry he brought in the coffer and jestingly promised to give it to the one whom it should fit exactly. Well, they all tried one after the other, but it fitted none of them. Last of all Osiris stepped into it and lay down. On that the conspirators ran and slammed the lid

4

down on him, nailed it fast, soldered it with molten lead, and flung the [pg 008] coffer into the Nile. This happened on the seventeenth day of the month Athyr, when the sun is in the sign of the Scorpion, and in the eight-and-twentieth year of the reign or the life of Osiris. When Isis heard of it she sheared off a lock of her hair, put on mourning attire, and wandered disconsolately up and down, seeking the body.[9]

uge in the papyrus swamps. Isis and her infant son Horus.

By the advice of the god of wisdom she took refuge in the papyrus swamps of the Delta. Seven scorpions accompanied her in her flight. One evening when she was weary she came to the house of a woman, who, alarmed at the sight of the scorpions, shut the door in her face. Then one of the scorpions crept under the door and stung the child of the woman that he died. But when Isis heard the mother's lamentation, her heart was touched, and she laid her hands on the child and uttered her powerful spells; so the poison was driven out of the child and he lived. Afterwards Isis herself gave birth to a son in the swamps. She had conceived him while she fluttered in the form of a hawk over the corpse of her dead husband. The infant was the younger Horus, who in his youth bore the name of Harpocrates, that is, the child Horus. Him Buto, the goddess of the north, hid from the wrath of his wicked uncle Set. Yet she could not guard him from all mishap; for one day when Isis came to her little son's hiding-place she found him stretched lifeless and rigid on the ground: a scorpion had stung him. Then Isis prayed to the sun-god Ra for help. The god hearkened to her and staid his bark in the sky, and sent down Thoth to teach her the spell by which she might restore her son to life. She uttered the words of power, and straightway the poison flowed from the body of Horus, air passed into him, and he lived. Then Thoth ascended up into the sky and took his place once more in the bark of the sun, and the bright pomp passed onward jubilant.[10]

[pg 009]

Osiris floats to Byblus, where it is recovered by Isis. The body of Osiris dismembered by Typhon, and covered by Isis. Diodorus Siculus on the burial of Osiris.

Meantime the coffer containing the body of Osiris had floated down the river and away out to sea, till at last it drifted ashore at Byblus, on the coast of Syria. Here a fine *erica*-tree shot up suddenly and enclosed the chest in its trunk. The king of the country, admiring the growth of the tree, had it cut down and made into a pillar of his house; but he did not know that the coffer with the dead Osiris was in it. Word of this came to Isis and she journeyed to Byblus, and sat down by the well, in humble guise, her face wet with tears. To none would she speak till the king's handmaidens came, and them she greeted kindly, and braided their hair, and breathed on them from her own divine body

5

a wondrous perfume. But when the queen beheld the braids of her handmaidens' hair and smelt the sweet smell that emanated from them, she sent for the stranger woman and took her into her house and made her the nurse of her child. But Isis gave the babe her finger instead of her breast to suck, and at night she began to burn all that was mortal of him away, while she herself in the likeness of a swallow fluttered round the pillar that contained her dead brother, twittering mournfully. But the queen spied what she was doing and shrieked out when she saw her child in flames, and thereby she hindered him from becoming immortal. Then the goddess revealed herself and begged for the pillar of the roof, and they gave it her, and she cut the coffer out of it, and fell upon it and embraced it and lamented so loud that the younger of the king's children died of fright on the spot. But the trunk of the tree she wrapped in fine linen, and poured ointment on it, and gave it to the king and queen, and the wood stands in a temple of [pg 010] Isis and is worshipped by the people of Byblus to this day. And Isis put the coffer in a boat and took the eldest of the king's children with her and sailed away. As soon as they were alone, she opened the chest, and laying her face on the face of her brother she kissed him and wept. But the child came behind her softly and saw what she was about, and she turned and looked at him in anger, and the child could not bear her look and died; but some say that it was not so, but that he fell into the sea and was drowned. It is he whom the Egyptians sing of at their banquets under the name of Maneros. But Isis put the coffer by and went to see her son Horus at the city of Buto, and Typhon found the coffer as he was hunting a boar one night by the light of a full moon.[11] And he knew the body, and rent it into fourteen pieces, and scattered them abroad. But Isis sailed up and down the marshes in a shallop made of papyrus, looking for the pieces; and that is why when people sail in shallops made of papyrus, the crocodiles do not hurt them, for they fear or respect the goddess. And that is the reason, too, why there are many graves of Osiris in Egypt, for she buried each limb as she found it. But others will have it that she buried an image of him in every city, pretending it was his body, in order that Osiris might be worshipped in many places, and that if Typhon searched for the real grave he might not be able to find it.[12] However, the genital member of Osiris had been eaten by the fishes, so Isis made an image of it instead, and the image is used by the Egyptians at their festivals to this day.[13] "Isis," writes the historian Diodorus Siculus, "recovered all the parts of the body except the genitals; and because she wished that her husband's grave should be unknown and honoured by all who dwell in the land of Egypt, she resorted to the following device. She moulded human images out of wax and spices, corresponding to the stature of Osiris, round each one of the parts of his body. Then she called in the priests according to their families and took an oath of them all that [pg 011] they would reveal to no man the trust she was about to repose in them.

So to each of them privately she said that to them alone she entrusted the burial of the body, and reminding them of the benefits they had received she exhorted them to bury the body in their own land and to honour Osiris as a god. She also besought them to dedicate one of the animals of their country, whichever they chose, and to honour it in life as they had formerly honoured Osiris, and when it died to grant it obsequies like his. And because she would encourage the priests in their own interest to bestow the aforesaid honours, she gave them a third part of the land to be used by them in the service and worship of the gods. Accordingly it is said that the priests, mindful of the benefits of Osiris, desirous of gratifying the queen, and moved by the prospect of gain, carried out all the injunctions of Isis. Wherefore to this day each of the priests imagines that Osiris is buried in his country, and they honour the beasts that were consecrated in the beginning, and when the animals die the priests renew at their burial the mourning for Osiris. But the sacred bulls, the one called Apis and the other Mnevis, were dedicated to Osiris, and it was ordained that they should be worshipped as gods in common by all the Egyptians; since these animals above all others had helped the discoverers of corn in sowing the seed and procuring the universal benefits of agriculture."[14]

members of Osiris treasured as relics in various parts of Egypt.

Such is the myth or legend of Osiris, as told by Greek writers and eked out by more or less fragmentary notices or allusions in native Egyptian literature. A long inscription in the temple at Denderah has preserved a list of the god's graves, and other texts mention the parts of his body which were treasured as holy relics in each of the sanctuaries. Thus his heart was at Athribis, his backbone at Busiris, his neck at Letopolis, and his head at Memphis. As often happens in such cases, some of his divine limbs were miraculously multiplied. His head, for example, was at Abydos as well as at Memphis, and his legs, which were remarkably numerous, would have sufficed for several ordinary mortals.[15] [pg 012] In this respect, however, Osiris was nothing to St. Denys, of whom no less than seven heads, all equally genuine, are extant.[16]

ed by Isis and Nephthys.

According to native Egyptian accounts, which supplement that of Plutarch, when Isis had found the corpse of her husband Osiris, she and her sister Nephthys sat down beside it and uttered a lament which in after ages became the type of all Egyptian lamentations for the dead. "Come to thy house," they wailed, "Come to thy house. O god On! come to thy house, thou who hast no foes. O fair youth, come to thy house, that thou mayest see me. I am thy sister, whom thou lovest; thou shalt not part from me. O fair boy, come to thy house…. I see thee not, yet doth my heart yearn after thee and mine eyes desire thee. Come to her who loves thee, who loves thee, Unnefer, thou blessed one! Come to thy sister, come to thy wife, to thy wife, thou whose heart stands still. Come to thy housewife. I am thy sister by the same mother, thou shalt not be far from me. Gods and men have turned their faces towards thee and weep for thee together.... I call after thee and weep, so that my cry is heard to heaven, but thou hearest not my voice; yet am I thy sister, whom thou didst love on earth; thou didst love none but me, my brother! my brother!"[17] This lament for the fair youth cut off in his prime reminds us of the laments for Adonis. The title of Unnefer or "the Good Being" bestowed on him marks the beneficence which tradition universally ascribed to Osiris; it was at once his commonest title and one of his names as king.[18]

ht to life again, Osiris reigns as king and judge of the dead in the other world. The confession of the

The lamentations of the two sad sisters were not in vain. In pity for her sorrow the sun-god Ra sent down from heaven the jackal-headed god Anubis, who, with the [pg 013] aid of Isis and Nephthys, of Thoth and Horus, pieced together the broken body of the murdered god, swathed it in linen bandages, and observed all the other rites which the Egyptians were wont to perform over the bodies of the departed. Then Isis fanned the cold clay with her wings: Osiris revived, and thenceforth reigned as king over the dead in the other world.[19] There he bore the titles of Lord of the Underworld, Lord of Eternity, Ruler of the Dead.[20] There, too, in the great Hall of the Two Truths, assisted by forty-two assessors, one from each of the principal districts of Egypt, he presided as judge at the trial of the souls of the departed, who made their solemn confession before him, and, their heart having been weighed in the balance of justice, received the reward of virtue in a life eternal or the appropriate punishment of their sins.[21] The confession or rather profession which the *Book of the Dead* puts in the mouth of the deceased at the judgment-bar of Osiris[22] sets the morality of the ancient Egyptians in a very favourable light. In rendering an account of his life the deceased solemnly protested that he had not oppressed his fellow-men, that he had made none to weep, that he had done no murder, neither committed fornication nor borne false witness, that he had not falsified the balance, that he had not taken the milk from the mouths of babes, that he had given bread to the hungry and water to the thirsty, and had clothed the naked. In harmony [pg 014] with these professions are the epitaphs on Egyptian graves, which reveal, if not the moral practice, at least the moral ideals of those who slept beneath them. Thus, for example, a man says in his epitaph: "I gave bread to the hungry and clothes to the naked, and ferried across in my own boat him who could not pass the water. I was a father to the orphan, a husband to the widow, a shelter from the wind to them that were cold. I am one that spake good and told good. I earned my substance in righteousness."[23] Those who had done thus in their mortal life and had been acquitted at the Great Assize, were believed to dwell thenceforth at ease in a land where the corn grew higher than on earth, where harvests never failed, where trees were always green, and wives for ever young and fair.[24]

he wicked.

We are not clearly informed as to the fate which the Egyptians supposed to befall the wicked after death. In the scenes which represent the Last Judgment there is seen crouching beside the scales, in which the heart of the dead is being weighed, a monstrous animal known as the "Eater of the Dead." It has the head of a crocodile, the trunk of a lion, and the hinder parts of a hippopotamus. Some think that the souls of those whose hearts had been weighed in the balance and found wanting were delivered over to this grim monster to be devoured; but this view appears to be conjectural. "Generally the animal seems to have been placed there simply as guardian of the entrance to the Fields of the Blessed, but sometimes it is likened to Set. Elsewhere it is said that the judges of the dead slay the wicked and drink their blood. In brief, here also we have conflicting statements, and can only gather that there seems to have been no general agreement among the dwellers in the Valley of the Nile as to the ultimate lot of the wicked."[25]

[pg 015]

ection of Osiris the Egyptians saw a pledge of their own immortality.

In the resurrection of Osiris the Egyptians saw the pledge of a life everlasting for themselves beyond the grave. They believed that every man would live eternally in the other world if only his surviving friends did for his body what the gods had done for the body of Osiris. Hence the ceremonies observed by the Egyptians over the human dead were an exact copy of those which Anubis, Horus, and the rest had performed over the dead god. "At every burial there was enacted a representation of the divine mystery which had been performed of old over Osiris, when his son, his sisters, his friends were gathered round his mangled remains and succeeded by their spells and manipulations in converting his broken body into the first mummy, which they afterwards reanimated and furnished with the means of entering on a new individual life beyond the grave. The mummy of the deceased was Osiris; the professional female mourners were his two sisters Isis and Nephthys; Anubis, Horus, all the gods of the Osirian legend gathered about the corpse." In this solemn drama of death and resurrection the principal part was played by the celebrant, who represented Horus the son of the dead and resuscitated Osiris.[26] He formally opened the eyes and mouth of the dead man by rubbing or pretending to rub them four times with the bleeding heart and thigh of a sacrificed bull; after which a pretence was made of actually opening the mouth of the mummy or of the statue with certain instruments specially reserved for the purpose. Geese and gazelles were also sacrificed by being decapitated; they were supposed to represent the enemies of Osiris, who after the murder of the divine man had sought to evade the righteous punishment of their crime but had been detected and beheaded.[27]

[pg 016]

Egyptian identified with Osiris.

Thus every dead Egyptian was identified with Osiris and bore his name. From the Middle Kingdom onwards it was the regular practice to address the deceased as "Osiris So-and-So," as if he were the god himself, and to add the standing epithet "true of speech," because true speech was characteristic of Osiris.[28] The thousands of inscribed and pictured tombs that have been opened in the valley of the Nile prove that the mystery of the resurrection was performed for the benefit of every dead Egyptian;[29] as Osiris died and rose again from the dead, so all men hoped to arise like him from death to life eternal. In an Egyptian text it is said of the departed that "as surely as Osiris lives, so shall he live also; as surely as Osiris did not die, so shall he not die; as surely as Osiris is not annihilated, so shall he too not be annihilated." The dead man, conceived to be lying, like Osiris, with mangled body, was comforted by being told that the heavenly goddess Nut, the mother of Osiris, was coming to gather up his poor scattered limbs and mould them with her own hands into a form immortal and divine. "She gives thee thy head, she brings thee thy bones, she sets thy limbs together and puts thy heart in thy body." Thus the resurrection of the dead was conceived, like that of Osiris, not merely as spiritual but also as bodily. "They possess their heart, they possess their senses, they possess their mouth, they possess their feet, they possess their arms, they possess all their limbs."[30]

een Set and Horus, the brother and the son of Osiris, for the crown of Egypt.

If we may trust Egyptian legend, the trials and contests of the royal house did not cease with the restoration of Osiris [pg 017] to life and his elevation to the rank of presiding deity in the world of the dead. When Horus the younger, the son of Osiris and Isis, was grown to man's estate, the ghost of his royal and murdered father appeared to him and urged him, like another Hamlet, to avenge the foul unnatural murder upon his wicked uncle. Thus encouraged, the youth attacked the miscreant. The combat was terrific and lasted many days. Horus lost an eye in the conflict and Set suffered a still more serious mutilation. At last Thoth parted the combatants and healed their wounds; the eye of Horus he restored by spitting on it. According to one account the great battle was fought on the twenty-sixth day of the month of Thoth. Foiled in open war, the artful uncle now took the law of his virtuous nephew. He brought a suit of bastardy against Horus, hoping thus to rob him of his inheritance and to get possession of it himself; nay, not content with having murdered his good brother, the unnatural Set carried his rancour even beyond the grave by accusing the dead Osiris of certain high crimes and misdemeanours. The case was tried before the supreme court of the gods in the great hall at Heliopolis. Thoth, the god of wisdom, pleaded the cause of Osiris, and the august judges decided that "the word of Osiris was true." Moreover, they pronounced Horus to be the true-begotten son of his father. So that prince assumed the crown and mounted the throne of the lamented Osiris. However, according to another and perhaps later version of the story, the victory of Horus over his uncle was by no means so decisive, and their struggles ended in a compromise, by which Horus reigned over the Delta, while Set became king of the upper valley of the Nile from near Memphis to the first cataract. Be that as it may, with the accession of Horus began for the Egyptians the modern period of the world, for on his throne all the kings of Egypt sat as his successors.[31]

f their contest may be a reminiscence of dynastic struggles.

These legends of a contest for the throne of Egypt [pg 018] may perhaps contain a reminiscence of real dynastical struggles which attended an attempt to change the right of succession from the female to the male line. For under a rule of female kinship the heir to the throne is either the late king's brother, or the son of the late king's sister, while under a rule of male kinship the heir to the throne is the late king's son. In the legend of Osiris the rival heirs are Set and Horus, Set being the late king's brother, and Horus the late king's son; though Horus indeed united both claims to the crown, being the son of the king's sister as well as of the king. A similar attempt to shift the line of succession seems to have given rise to similar contests at Rome.[32]

ented as a king in tradition and art. The tomb of Osiris at Abydos.

Thus according to what seems to have been the general native tradition Osiris was a good and beloved king of Egypt, who suffered a violent death but rose from the dead and was henceforth worshipped as a deity. In harmony with this tradition he was regularly represented by sculptors and painters in human and regal form as a dead king, swathed in the wrappings of a mummy, but wearing on his head a kingly crown and grasping in one of his hands, which were left free from the bandages, a kingly sceptre.[33] Two cities above all others were associated with his myth or memory. One of them was Busiris in Lower Egypt, which claimed to possess his backbone; the other was Abydos in Upper Egypt, which gloried in the possession of his head.[34] Encircled by the nimbus of the dead yet living god, Abydos, originally an obscure place, became from the end of the Old Kingdom the holiest spot in Egypt; his tomb there would seem to have been to the Egyptians what the Church of the Holy [pg 019] Sepulchre at Jerusalem is to Christians. It was the wish of every pious man that his dead body should rest in hallowed earth near the grave of the glorified Osiris. Few indeed were rich enough to enjoy this inestimable privilege; for, apart from the cost of a tomb in the sacred city, the mere transport of mummies from great distances was both difficult and expensive. Yet so eager were many to absorb in death the blessed influence which radiated from the holy sepulchre that they caused their surviving friends to convey their mortal remains to Abydos, there to tarry for a short time, and then to be brought back by river and interred in the tombs which had been made ready for them in their native land. Others had cenotaphs built or memorial tablets erected for themselves near the tomb of their dead and risen Lord, that they might share with him the bliss of a joyful resurrection.[35]

f the old kings at Abydos. The tomb of King Khent identified with the tomb of Osiris. The sculptured ris. The hawk the crest of the earliest dynasties.

Hence from the earliest ages of Egyptian history Abydos would seem to have been a city of the dead rather than of the living; certainly there is no evidence that the place was ever of any political importance.[36] No less than nine of the most ancient kings of Egypt known to us were buried here, for their tombs have been discovered and explored within recent years.[37] The royal necropolis lies on the edge of the desert about a mile and a half from the temple of Osiris.[38] Of the graves the oldest is that of King Khent, the second or third king of the first dynasty. His reign, which fell somewhere between three thousand four hundred [pg 020] and three thousand two hundred years before our era, seems to have marked an epoch in the history of Egypt, for under him the costume, the figure drawing, and the hieroglyphics all assumed the character which they thenceforth preserved to the very end of Egyptian nationality.[39] Later ages identified him with Osiris in a more intimate sense than that in which the divine title was lavished on every dead king and indeed on every dead man; for his tomb was actually converted into the tomb of Osiris and as such received in great profusion the offerings of the faithful. Somewhere between the twenty-second and the twenty-sixth dynasty a massive bier of grey granite was placed in the sepulchral chamber. On it, cut in high relief, reposes a shrouded figure of the dead Osiris. He lies at full length, with bare and upturned face. On his head is the White Crown of Upper Egypt; in his hands, which issue from the shroud, he holds the characteristic emblems of the god, the sceptre and the scourge. At the four corners of the bier are perched four hawks, representing the four children of Horus, each with their father's banner, keeping watch over the dead god, as they kept watch over the four quarters of the world. A fifth hawk seems to have been perched on the middle of the body of Osiris, but it had been broken off before the tomb was discovered in recent years, for only the bird's claws remain in position. Finely carved heads of lions, one at each corner of the bier, with the claws to match below, complete the impressive monument. The scene represented is unquestionably the impregnation of Isis in the form of a hawk by the dead Osiris; the Copts who dismantled the shrine appear to have vented their pious rage on the figure of the hawk Isis by carrying it off or smashing it. If any doubt could exist as to the meaning of these sculptured figures, it would be set at rest by the ancient inscriptions attached to them. Over against the right shoulder of the shrouded figure, who lies stretched on the bier, are carved in hieroglyphics the words, "Osiris, the [pg 021] Good Being, true of speech"; and over against the place where the missing hawk perched on the body of the dead god is carved the symbol of Isis. Two relics of the ancient human occupants of the tomb escaped alike the fury of the fanatics and the avarice of the plunderers who pillaged and destroyed it. One of the relics is a human skull, from which the lower jawbone is missing; the other is an arm encircled by gorgeous jewelled bracelets of gold, turquoises, amethysts, and dark purple lapis lazuli. The former may be the head of King Khent himself; the latter is almost certainly the arm of his queen. One of the bracelets is composed of alternate plaques of gold and turquoise, each ornamented with the figure of a hawk perched on the top of it.[40] The hawk was the sacred bird or crest of the earliest dynasties of Egyptian kings. The figure of a hawk was borne before the king as a standard on solemn occasions: the oldest capital of the country known to us was called Hawk-town: there the kings of the first dynasty built a temple to the hawk: there in modern times has been found a splendid golden head of a hawk dating from the Ancient Empire; and on the life-like statue of King Chephren of the third dynasty we see a hawk with out-spread wings protecting the back of the monarch's head. [pg 022] From the earliest to the latest times of Egyptian civilization "the Hawk" was the epithet of the king of Egypt and of the king alone; it took the first place in the list of his titles.[41] The sanctity of the bird may help us to understand why Isis took the form of a hawk in order to mate with her dead husband; why the queen of Egypt wore on her arm a bracelet adorned with golden hawks; and why in the holy sepulchre the four sons of Horus were represented in the likeness of hawks keeping watch over the effigy of their divine grandfather.[42]

ion of Osiris with Byblus.

The legend recorded by Plutarch which associated the dead Osiris with Byblus in Phoenicia[43] is doubtless late and probably untrustworthy. It may have been suggested by the resemblance which the worship of the Egyptian Osiris bore to the worship of the Phoenician Adonis in that city. But it is possible that the story has no deeper foundation than a verbal misunderstanding. For Byblus is not only the name of a city, it is the Greek word for papyrus; and as Isis is said after the death of Osiris to have taken refuge in the papyrus swamps of the Delta, where she gave birth to and reared her son Horus, a Greek writer may perhaps have confused the plant with the city of the same name.[44] However [pg 023] that may have been, the association of Osiris with Adonis at Byblus gave rise to a curious tale. It is said that every year the people beyond the rivers of Ethiopia used to write a letter to the women of Byblus informing them that the lost and lamented Adonis was found. This letter they enclosed in an earthen pot, which they sealed and sent floating down the river to the sea. The waves carried the pot to Byblus, where every year it arrived at the time when the Syrian women were weeping for their dead Lord. The pot was taken up from the water and opened: the letter was read; and the weeping women dried their tears, because the lost Adonis was found.[45]

[pg 024]

Chapter II. The Official Egyptian Calendar.

a festival sometimes furnishes a clue to the nature of the god.

A useful clue to the original nature of a god or goddess is often furnished by the season at which his or her festival is celebrated. Thus, if the festival falls at the new or the full moon, there is a certain presumption that the deity thus honoured either is the moon or at least has lunar affinities. If the festival is held at the winter or summer solstice, we naturally surmise that the god is the sun, or at all events that he stands in some close relation to that luminary. Again, if the festival coincides with the time of sowing or harvest, we are inclined to infer that the divinity is an embodiment of the earth or of the corn. These presumptions or inferences, taken by themselves, are by no means conclusive; but if they happen to be confirmed by other indications, the evidence may be regarded as fairly strong.

he Egyptian calendar a vague or movable one.

Unfortunately, in dealing with the Egyptian gods we are in a great measure precluded from making use of this clue. The reason is not that the dates of the festivals are always unknown, but that they shifted from year to year, until after a long interval they had revolved through the whole course of the seasons. This gradual revolution of the festal Egyptian cycle resulted from the employment of a calendar year which neither corresponded exactly to the solar year nor was periodically corrected by intercalation.[46] [pg 025] The solar year is equivalent to about three hundred and sixty-five and a quarter days; but the ancient Egyptians, ignoring the quarter of a day, reckoned the year at three hundred and sixty-five days only.[47] Thus each of their calendar years was shorter than the true solar year by about a quarter of a day. In four years the deficiency amounted to one whole day; in forty years it amounted to ten days; in four hundred years it amounted to a hundred days; and so it went on increasing until after a lapse of four times three hundred and sixty-five, or one thousand four hundred and sixty solar years, the deficiency amounted to three hundred and sixty-five days, or a whole Egyptian year. Hence one thousand four hundred and sixty solar years, or their equivalent, one thousand four hundred and sixty-one Egyptian years, formed a period or cycle at the end of which the Egyptian festivals returned to those points of the solar year at which they had been celebrated in the beginning.[48] In the meantime they had been held successively on every day of the solar year, though always on the same day of the calendar.

Thus the official calendar was completely divorced, except at rare and long intervals, from what may be called the natural calendar of the shepherd, the husbandman, and the sailor—that is, from the course of the seasons in which the times for the various labours of cattle-breeding, tillage, and navigation are marked by the position of the sun in the sky, the rising or setting of the stars, the fall of rain, the growth of pasture, the ripening of the corn, the blowing of certain winds, and so forth. Nowhere, perhaps, are the events of this natural calendar better marked or more regular in their recurrence than in Egypt; nowhere accordingly could their divergence from the corresponding dates of the official calendar be more readily observed. The [pg 026] divergence certainly did not escape the notice of the Egyptians themselves, and some of them apparently attempted successfully to correct it. Thus we are told that the Theban priests, who particularly excelled in astronomy, were acquainted with the true length of the solar year, and harmonized the calendar with it by intercalating a day every few, probably every four, years.[49] But this scientific improvement was too deeply opposed to the religious conservatism of the Egyptian nature to win general acceptance. "The Egyptians," said Geminus, a Greek astronomer writing about 77 B.C., "are of an opposite opinion and purpose from the Greeks. For they neither reckon the years by the sun nor the months and days by the moon, but they observe a peculiar system of their own. They wish, in fact, that the sacrifices should not always be offered to the gods at the same time of the year, but that they should pass through all the seasons of the year, so that the summer festival should in time be celebrated in winter, in autumn, and in spring. For that purpose they employ a year of three hundred and sixty-five days, composed of twelve months of thirty days each, with five supplementary days added. But they do not add the quarter of a day for the reason I have given—namely, in order that their festivals may revolve."[50] So attached, indeed, were the Egyptians to their old calendar, that the kings at their consecration were led by the priest of Isis at Memphis into the holy of holies, and there made to swear that they would maintain the year of three hundred and sixty-five days without intercalation.[51]

The practical inconvenience of a calendar which marked true time only once in about fifteen hundred years might be [pg 027] calmly borne by a submissive Oriental race like the ancient Egyptians, but it naturally proved a stumbling-block to the less patient temperament of their European conquerors. Accordingly in the reign of King Ptolemy III. Euergetes a decree was passed that henceforth the movable Egyptian year should be converted into a fixed solar year by the intercalation of one day at the end of every four years, "in order that the seasons may do their duty perpetually according to the present constitution of the world, and that it may not happen, through the shifting of the star by one day in four years, that some of the public festivals which are now held in the winter should ever be celebrated in the summer, and that other festivals now held in the summer should hereafter be celebrated in the winter, as has happened before, and must happen again if the year of three hundred and sixty-five days be retained." The decree was passed in the year 239 or 238 B.C. by the high priests, scribes, and other dignitaries of the Egyptian church assembled in convocation at Canopus; but we cannot doubt that the measure, though it embodied native Egyptian science, was prompted by the king or his Macedonian advisers.[52] This sage attempt to reform the erratic calendar was not permanently successful. The change may indeed have been carried out during the reign of the king who instituted it, but it was abandoned by the year 196 B.C. at latest, as we learn from the celebrated inscription known as the Rosetta stone, in which a month of the Macedonian calendar is equated to the corresponding month of the movable Egyptian year.[53] And the testimony of Geminus, which I have cited, proves that in the following century the festivals were still revolving in the old style.

f the fixed Alexandrian year by the Romans.

The reform which the Macedonian king had vainly attempted to impose upon his people was accomplished by the practical Romans when they took over the administration [pg 028] of the country. The expedient by which they effected the change was a simple one; indeed it was no other than that to which Ptolemy Euergetes had resorted for the same purpose. They merely intercalated one day at the end of every four years, thus equalizing within a small fraction four calendar years to four solar years. Henceforth the official and the natural calendars were in practical agreement. The movable Egyptian year had been converted into the fixed Alexandrian year, as it was called, which agreed with the Julian year in length and in its system of intercalation, though it differed from that year in retaining the twelve equal Egyptian months and five supplementary days.[54] But while the new calendar received the sanction of law and regulated the business of government, the ancient calendar was too firmly established in popular usage to be at once displaced. Accordingly it survived for ages side by side with its modern rival.[55] The spread of Christianity, which required a fixed year for the due observance of its festivals, did much to promote the adoption of the new Alexandrian style, and by the beginning of the fifth century the ancient movable year of Egypt appears to have been not only dead but forgotten.[56]

[pg 030]

Chapter III. The Calendar of the Egyptian Farmer.

§ 1. The Rise and Fall of the Nile.

If the Egyptian farmer of the olden time could thus get no help, except at the rarest intervals, from the official or sacerdotal calendar, he must have been compelled to observe for himself those natural signals which marked the times for the various operations of husbandry. In all ages of which we possess any records the Egyptians have been an agricultural people, dependent for their subsistence on the growth of the corn. The cereals which they cultivated were wheat, barley, and apparently sorghum (*Holcus sorghum*, Linnaeus), the *doora* of the modern fellaheen.[57] Then as now the whole country, with the exception of a fringe on the coast of the Mediterranean, was almost rainless, and owed its immense fertility entirely to the annual inundation of the Nile, which, regulated by an elaborate system of dams and canals, was distributed over the fields, renewing the soil year by year with a fresh deposit of mud washed down from the great equatorial lakes and the mountains of Abyssinia. Hence the rise of the river has always been watched by the inhabitants with the utmost anxiety; for if it either falls short of or exceeds a certain height, dearth and famine are the inevitable consequences.[58] The water begins to rise early in [pg 031] June, but it is not until the latter half of July that it swells to a mighty tide. By the end of September the inundation is at its greatest height. The country is now submerged, and presents the appearance of a sea of turbid water, from which the towns and villages, built on higher ground, rise like islands. For about a month the flood remains nearly stationary, then sinks more and more rapidly, till by December or January the river has returned to its ordinary bed. With the approach of summer the level of the water continues to fall. In the early days of June the Nile is reduced to half its ordinary breadth; and Egypt, scorched by the sun, blasted by the wind that has blown from the Sahara for many days, seems a mere continuation of the desert. The trees are choked with a thick layer of grey dust. A few meagre patches of vegetables, watered with difficulty, struggle painfully for existence in the immediate neighbourhood of the villages. Some appearance of verdure lingers beside the canals and in the hollows from which the moisture has not wholly evaporated. The plain appears to pant in the pitiless sunshine, bare, dusty, ash-coloured, cracked and seamed as far as the eye can see with a network of fissures. From the middle of April till the middle of June the land of Egypt is but half alive, waiting for the new Nile.[59]

For countless ages this cycle of natural events has determined the annual labours of the Egyptian husbandman. The first work of the agricultural year is the cutting [pg 032] of the dams which have hitherto prevented the swollen river from flooding the canals and the fields. This is done, and the pent-up waters released on their beneficent mission, in the first half of August.[60] In November, when the inundation has subsided, wheat, barley, and sorghum are sown. The time of harvest varies with the district, falling about a month later in the north than in the south. In Upper or Southern Egypt barley is reaped at the beginning of March, wheat at the beginning of April, and sorghum about the end of that month.[61]

f the agricultural year were probably celebrated with religious rites.

It is natural to suppose that these various events of the agricultural year were celebrated by the Egyptian farmer with some simple religious rites designed to secure the blessing of the gods upon his labours. These rustic ceremonies he would continue to perform year after year at the same season, while the solemn festivals of the priests continued to shift, with the shifting calendar, from summer through spring to winter, and so backward through autumn to summer. The rites of the husbandman were stable because they rested on direct observation of nature: the rites of the priest were unstable because they were based on a false calculation. Yet many of the priestly festivals may have been nothing but the old rural festivals disguised in the course of ages by the pomp of sacerdotalism and severed, by the error of the calendar, from their roots in the natural cycle of the seasons.

[pg 033]

§ 2. Rites of Irrigation.

r Osiris at midsummer when the Nile begins to rise.

These conjectures are confirmed by the little we know both of the popular and of the official Egyptian religion. Thus we are told that the Egyptians held a festival of Isis at the time when the Nile began to rise. They believed that the goddess was then mourning for the lost Osiris, and that the tears which dropped from her eyes swelled the impetuous tide of the river.[62] Hence in Egyptian inscriptions Isis is spoken of as she "who maketh the Nile to swell and overflow, who maketh the Nile to swell in his season."[63] Similarly the Toradjas of Central Celebes imagine that showers of rain are the tears shed by the compassionate gods in weeping for somebody who is about to die; a shower in the morning is to them an infallible omen of death.[64] However, an uneasy suspicion would seem to have occurred to the Egyptians that perhaps after all the tears of the goddess might not suffice of themselves to raise the water to the proper level; so in the time of Rameses II. the king used on the first day of the flood to throw into the Nile a written order commanding the river to do its duty, and the submissive stream never failed to obey the royal mandate.[65] Yet the ancient belief survives in a modified form to this day. For the Nile, as we saw, begins to rise in June about the time of the summer solstice, and the people still attribute its increased volume to a miraculous drop which falls into the river on the night of the seventeenth of the month. The charms and divinations which they practise on that mystic night in order to ascertain the length of their own life and to rid the houses of bugs may well date from a remote antiquity.[66] Now if Osiris was in one of his aspects [pg 034] a god of the corn, nothing could be more natural than that he should be mourned at midsummer. For by that time the harvest was past, the fields were bare, the river ran low, life seemed to be suspended, the corn-god was dead. At such a moment people who saw the handiwork of divine beings in all the operations of nature might well trace the swelling of the sacred stream to the tears shed by the goddess at the death of the beneficent corn-god her husband.

ded as the star of Isis. The rising of Sirius marked the beginning of the sacred Egyptian year. The of the gradual displacement of Sirius in the calendar led to the determination of the true length of the

And the sign of the rising waters on earth was accompanied by a sign in heaven. For in the early days of Egyptian history, some three or four thousand years before the beginning of our era, the splendid star of Sirius, the brightest of all the fixed stars, appeared at dawn in the east just before sunrise about the time of the summer solstice, when the Nile begins to rise.[67] The Egyptians called it Sothis, and regarded it as the star of Isis,[68] just as the [pg 035]

Babylonians deemed the planet Venus the star of Astarte. To both peoples apparently the brilliant luminary in the morning sky seemed the goddess of life and love come to mourn her departed lover or spouse and to wake him from the dead. Hence the rising of Sirius marked the beginning of the sacred Egyptian year,[69] and was regularly celebrated by a festival which did not shift with the shifting official year.[70] The [pg 036] first day of the first month Thoth was theoretically supposed to date from the heliacal rising of the bright star, and in all probability it really did so when the official or civil year of three hundred and sixty-five days was first instituted. But the miscalculation which has been already explained[71] had the effect of making the star to shift its place in the calendar by one day in four years. Thus if Sirius rose on the first of Thoth in one year, it would rise on the second of Thoth four years afterwards, on the third of Thoth eight years afterwards, and so on until after the lapse of a Siriac or Sothic period of fourteen hundred and sixty solar years the first of Thoth again coincided with the heliacal rising of Sirius.[72] This observation of the gradual displacement of [pg 037] the star in the calendar has been of the utmost importance for the progress of astronomy, since it led the Egyptians directly to the determination of the approximately true length of the solar year and thus laid the basis of our modern calendar; for the Julian calendar, which we owe to Caesar, was founded on the Egyptian theory, though not on the Egyptian practice.[73] It was therefore a fortunate moment for the world when some pious Egyptian, thousands of years ago, identified for the first time the bright star of Sirius with his goddess; for the identification induced his countrymen to regard the heavenly body with an attention which they would never have paid to it if they had known it to be nothing but a world vastly greater than our own and separated from it by an inconceivable, if not immeasurable, abyss of space.

observed in Egypt at the cutting of the dams early in August. The Bride of the Nile. Sacrifices offered t the cutting of dams.

The cutting of the dams and the admission of the water [pg 038] into the canals and fields is a great event in the Egyptian year. At Cairo the operation generally takes place between the sixth and the sixteenth of August, and till lately was attended by ceremonies which deserve to be noticed, because they were probably handed down from antiquity. An ancient canal, known by the name of the Khalíj, formerly passed through the native town of Cairo. Near its entrance the canal was crossed by a dam of earth, very broad at the bottom and diminishing in breadth upwards, which used to be constructed before or soon after the Nile began to rise. In front of the dam, on the side of the river, was reared a truncated cone of earth called the 'arooseh or "bride," on the top of which a little maize or millet was generally sown. This "bride" was commonly washed down by the rising tide a week or a fortnight before the cutting of the dam. Tradition runs that the old custom was to deck a young virgin in gay apparel and throw her into the river as a sacrifice to obtain a plentiful inundation.[74] Certainly human sacrifices were offered for a similar purpose by the Wajagga of German East Africa down to recent years. These people irrigate their fields by means of skilfully constructed channels, through which they conduct the water of the mountain brooks and rivers to the thirsty land. They imagine that the spirits of their forefathers dwell in the rocky basins of these rushing streams, and that they would resent the withdrawal of the water to irrigate the fields if compensation were not offered to them. The water-rate paid to them consisted of a child, uncircumcised and of unblemished body, who was decked with ornaments and bells and thrown into the river to drown, before they ventured to draw off the water into the irrigation channel. Having thrown him in, his executioners shewed a clean pair of heels, because they expected the river to rise in flood at once on receipt of the water-rate.[75] In similar circumstances the Njamus of British East Africa sacrifice a sheep before they let the water of the stream flow into the ditch [pg 039] or artificial channel. The fat, dung, and blood of the animal are sprinkled at the mouth of the ditch and in the water; thereupon the dam is broken down and the stream pours into the ditch. The sacrifice may only be offered by a man of the Il Mayek clan, and for two days afterwards he wears the skin of the beast tied round his head. No one may quarrel with this man while the water is irrigating the crops, else the people believe that the water would cease to flow in the ditch; more than that, if the men of the Il Mayek clan were angry and sulked for ten days, the water would dry up permanently for that season. Hence the Il Mayek clan enjoys great consideration in the tribe, since the crops are thought to depend on their good will and good offices. Ten elders assist at the sacrifice of the sheep, though they may take no part in it. They must all be of a particular age; and after the ceremony they may not cohabit with their wives until harvest, and they are obliged to sleep at night in their granaries. Curiously enough, too, while the water is irrigating the fields, nobody may kill waterbuck, eland, oryx, zebra, rhinoceros, or hippopotamus. Anybody caught red-handed in the act of breaking this game-law would at once be cast out of the village.[76]

ptian ceremony at the cutting of the dams.

Whether the "bride" who used to figure at the ceremony of cutting the dam in Cairo was ever a live woman or not, the intention of the practice appears to have been to marry the river, conceived as a male power, to his bride the corn-land, which was soon to be fertilized by his water. The ceremony was therefore a charm to ensure the growth of the crops. As such it probably dated, in one form or another, from ancient times. Dense crowds assembled to witness the cutting of the dam. The operation was performed before sunrise, and many people spent the preceding night on the banks of the canal or in boats lit with lamps on the river, while fireworks were displayed and guns discharged at frequent intervals. Before sunrise a great number of workmen began to cut the dam, and the task was accomplished about an hour before the sun appeared on the [pg 040] horizon. When only a thin ridge of earth remained, a boat with an officer on board was propelled against it, and breaking through the slight barrier descended with the rush of water into the canal. The Governor of Cairo flung a purse of gold into the boat as it passed. Formerly the custom was to throw money into the canal. The populace used to dive after it, and several lives were generally lost in the scramble.[77] This practice also would seem to have been ancient, for Seneca tells us that at a place called the Veins of the Nile, not far from Philae, the priests used to cast money and offerings of gold into the river at a festival which apparently took place at the rising of the water.[78] At Cairo the time-honoured ceremony came to an end in 1897, when the old canal was filled up. An electric tramway now runs over the spot where for countless ages crowds of worshippers or holiday-makers had annually assembled to witness the marriage of the Nile.[79]

§ 3. Rites of Sowing.

The next great operation of the agricultural year in Egypt is the sowing of the seed in November, when the water of the inundation has retreated from the fields. With the Egyptians, as with many peoples of antiquity, the committing of the seed to the earth assumed the character of a solemn and mournful rite. On this subject I will let Plutarch speak for himself. "What," he asks, "are we to make of the gloomy, joyless, and mournful sacrifices, if it is wrong either to omit the established rites or to confuse and disturb our conceptions of the gods by absurd suspicions? For the Greeks also perform many rites which resemble those of the Egyptians and are observed about the same time. Thus at the festival of the Thesmophoria in Athens [pg 041] women sit on the ground and fast. And the Boeotians open the vaults of the Sorrowful One,[80] naming that festival sorrowful because Demeter is sorrowing for the descent of the Maiden. The month is the month of sowing about the setting of the Pleiades.[81] The Egyptians call it Athyr, the Athenians Pyanepsion, the Boeotians the month of Demeter. Theopompus informs us that the western peoples consider and call the winter Cronus, the summer Aphrodite, and the spring Persephone, and they believe that all things are brought into being by Cronus and Aphrodite. The Phrygians imagine that the god sleeps in winter and wakes in summer, and accordingly they celebrate with Bacchic rites the putting him to bed in winter and his awakening in summer. The Paphlagonians allege that he is bound fast and shut up in winter, but that he stirs and is set free in spring. And the season furnishes a hint that the sadness is for the hiding of those fruits of the earth which the ancients esteemed, not indeed gods, but great and necessary gifts bestowed by the gods in order that men might not lead the life of savages and of wild beasts. For it was that time of year when they saw some of the fruits vanishing and falling from the trees, while they sowed others grudgingly and with difficulty, scraping the earth with their hands and huddling it up again, on the uncertain chance that what they deposited in the ground would ever ripen and come to maturity. Thus they did in many respects like those who bury and mourn their dead. And just as we say that a purchaser of Plato's books purchases Plato, or that an actor who plays the comedies of Menander plays Menander, so the men of old did not hesitate to call the gifts and products of the gods by the names of the gods themselves, thereby honouring and glorifying the things on account of their utility. But in [pg 042] after ages simple folk in their ignorance applied to the gods statements which only held true of the fruits of the earth, and so they came not merely to say but actually to believe that the growth and decay of plants, on which they subsisted,[82] were the birth and the death of gods. Thus they fell into absurd, immoral, and confused ways of thinking, though all the while the absurdity of the fallacy was manifest. Hence Xenophanes of Colophon declared that if the Egyptians deemed their gods divine they should not weep for them, and that if they wept for them they should not deem them divine. 'For it is ridiculous,' said he, 'to lament and pray that the fruits would be good enough to grow and ripen again in order that they may again be eaten and lamented.' But he was wrong, for though the lamentations are for the fruits, the prayers are addressed to the gods, as the causes and givers of them, that they would be pleased to make fresh fruits to spring up instead of those that perish."[83]

ew that the worship of the fruits of the earth sprang from a verbal misunderstanding.

In this interesting passage Plutarch expresses his belief that the worship of the fruits of the earth was the result of a verbal misapprehension or disease of language, as it has been called by a modern school of mythologists, who explain the origin of myths in general on the same easy principle of metaphors misunderstood. Primitive man, on Plutarch's theory, firmly believed that the fruits of the earth on which he subsisted were not themselves gods but merely the gifts of the gods, who were the real givers of all good things. Yet at the same time men were in the habit of bestowing on these divine products the names of their divine creators, either out of gratitude or merely for the sake of brevity, as when we say that a man has bought a Shakespeare or acted Molière, when we mean that he has bought the works of Shakespeare or acted the plays of Molière. This abbreviated mode of expression was misunderstood in later times, and so [pg 043] people came to look upon the fruits of the earth as themselves divine instead of as being the work of divinities: in short, they mistook the creature for the creator. In like manner Plutarch would explain the Egyptian worship of animals as reverence done not so much to the beasts themselves as to the great god who displays the divine handiwork in sentient organisms even more than in the most beautiful and wonderful works of inanimate nature.[84]

an inversion of the truth: for fetishism is the antecedent, not the corruption, of theism. Lamentations of or the animals and plants which he kills and eats.

The comparative study of religion has proved that these theories of Plutarch are an inversion of the truth. Fetishism, or the view that the fruits of the earth and things in general are divine or animated by powerful spirits, is not, as Plutarch imagined, a late corruption of a pure and primitive theism, which regarded the gods as the creators and givers of all good things. On the contrary, fetishism is early and theism is late in the history of mankind. In this respect Xenophanes, whom Plutarch attempts to correct, displayed a much truer insight into the mind of the savage. To weep crocodile tears over the animals and plants which he kills and eats, and to pray them to come again in order that they may be again eaten and again lamented—this may seem absurd to us, but it is precisely what the savage does. And from his point of view the proceeding is not at all absurd but perfectly rational and well calculated to answer his ends. For he sincerely believes that animals and fruits are tenanted by spirits who can harm him if they please, and who cannot but be put to considerable inconvenience by that destruction of their bodies which is unfortunately inseparable from the processes of mastication and digestion. What more natural, therefore, than that the savage should offer excuses to the beasts and the fruits for the painful necessity he is under of consuming them, and that he should endeavour to alleviate their pangs by soft words and an air of respectful sympathy, in order that they may bear him no grudge, and may in due time come again to be again eaten and again lamented? Judged by the standard of primitive manners the attitude of the walrus to the oysters was strictly correct:—

[pg 044]

> " 'I weep for you,' the Walrus said:
>
> 'I deeply sympathize.'
>
> With sobs and tears he sorted out
>
> Those of the largest size,
>
> Holding his pocket-handkerchief
>
> Before his streaming eyes."

wn by savages for the fruits and the animals which they eat.

Many examples of such hypocritical lamentations for animals, drawn not from the fancy of a playful writer but from the facts of savage life, could be cited.[85] Here I shall quote the general statement of a writer on the Indians of British Columbia, because it covers the case of vegetable as well as of animal food. After describing the respectful welcome accorded by the Stlatlum Indians to the first "sock-eye" salmon which they have caught in the season, he goes on: "The significance of these ceremonies is easy to perceive when we remember the attitude of the Indians towards nature generally, and recall their myths relating to the salmon, and their coming to their rivers and streams. Nothing that the Indian of this region eats is regarded by him as mere food and nothing more. Not a single plant, animal, or fish, or other object upon which he feeds, is looked upon in this light, or as something he has secured for himself by his own wit and skill. He regards it rather as something which has been voluntarily and compassionately placed in his hands by the goodwill and consent of the 'spirit' of the object itself, or by the intercession and magic of his culture-heroes; to be retained and used by him only upon the fulfilment of certain conditions. These conditions include respect and reverent care in the killing or plucking of the animal or plant and proper treatment of the parts he has no use for, such as the bones, blood, and offal; and the depositing of the same in some stream or lake, so that the object may by that means renew its life and physical form. The practices in connection with the killing of animals and the gathering of plants and fruits all make this quite clear, and it is only when we bear this attitude of the savage towards nature in mind that we can hope to rightly understand the motives and purposes of many of his strange customs and beliefs."[86]

[pg 045]

entations of the sower become intelligible.

We can now understand why among many peoples of antiquity, as Plutarch tells us, the time of sowing was a time of sorrow. The laying of the seed in the earth was a burial of the divine element, and it was fitting that like a human burial it should be performed with gravity and the semblance, if not the reality, of sorrow. Yet they sorrowed not without hope, perhaps a sure and certain hope, that the seed which they thus committed with sighs and tears to the ground would yet rise from the dust and yield fruit a hundredfold to the reaper. "They that sow in tears shall reap in joy. He that goeth forth and weepeth, bearing precious seed, shall doubtless come again with rejoicing, bringing his sheaves with him."[87]

§ 4. Rites of Harvest.

s of the Egyptian corn-reapers.

The Egyptian harvest, as we have seen, falls not in autumn but in spring, in the months of March, April, and May. To the husbandman the time of harvest, at least in a good year, must necessarily be a season of joy: in bringing home his sheaves he is requited for his long and anxious labours. Yet if the old Egyptian farmer felt a secret joy at reaping and garnering the grain, it was essential that he should conceal the natural emotion under an air of profound dejection. For was he not severing the body of the corn-god with his sickle and trampling it to pieces under the hoofs of his cattle on the threshing-floor? [88] Accordingly we are told that it was an ancient custom of the Egyptian corn-reapers to beat their breasts and lament over the first sheaf cut, while at the same time they called upon Isis.[89] The invocation seems to have taken the form of a melancholy chant, to which the Greeks gave the name of Maneros. Similar plaintive strains were chanted by corn-reapers in [pg 046] Phoenicia and other parts of Western Asia.[90] Probably all these doleful ditties were lamentations for the corn-god killed by the sickles of the reapers. In Egypt the slain deity was Osiris, and the name *Maneros* applied to the dirge appears to be derived from certain words meaning "Come to thy house," which often occur in the lamentations for the dead god.[91]

monies observed by the Cherokee Indians in the cultivation of the corn. The Old Woman of the corn and or her death.

Ceremonies of the same sort have been observed by other peoples, probably for the same purpose. Thus we are told that among all vegetables corn (*selu*), by which is apparently meant maize, holds the first place in the household economy and the ceremonial observance of the Cherokee Indians, who invoke it under the name of "the Old Woman" in allusion to a myth that it sprang from the blood of an old woman killed by her disobedient sons. "Much ceremony accompanied the planting and tending of the crop. Seven grains, the sacred number, were put into each hill, and these were not afterwards thinned out. After the last working of the crop, the priest and an assistant—generally the owner of the field—went into the field and built a small enclosure in the centre. Then entering it, they seated themselves upon the ground, with heads bent down, and while the assistant kept perfect silence the priest, with rattle in hand, sang songs of invocation to the spirit of the corn. Soon, according to the orthodox belief, a loud rustling would be heard outside, which they would know was caused by the 'Old Woman' bringing the corn into the field, but neither must look up until the song was finished. This ceremony was repeated on four successive nights, after which no one entered the field for seven other nights, when the priest himself went in, and, if all the sacred regulations had been properly observed, was rewarded by finding young ears upon the stalks. The corn ceremonies could be performed by the owner of the field himself, provided he was willing to pay a sufficient fee to the priest in order to learn the songs and ritual. Care was always taken to keep a [pg 047] clean trail from the field to the house, so that the corn might be encouraged to stay at home and not go wandering elsewhere. Most of these customs have now fallen into disuse excepting among the old people, by many of whom they are still religiously observed. Another curious ceremony, of which even the memory is now almost forgotten, was enacted after the first working of the corn, when the owner or priest stood in succession at each of the four corners of the field and wept and wailed loudly. Even the priests are now unable to give a reason for this performance, which may have been a lament for the bloody death of Selu," the Old Woman of the Corn.[22] In these Cherokee practices the lamentations and the invocations of the Old Woman of the Corn resemble the ancient Egyptian customs of lamenting over the first corn cut and calling upon Isis, herself probably in one of her aspects an Old Woman of the Corn. Further, the Cherokee precaution of leaving a clear path from the field to the house resembles the Egyptian invitation to Osiris, "Come to thy house." So in the East Indies to this day people observe elaborate ceremonies for the purpose of bringing back the Soul of the Rice from the fields to the barn.[23] The Nandi of British East Africa perform a ceremony in September when the eleusine grain is ripening. Every woman who owns a plantation goes out with her daughters into the cornfields and makes a bonfire of the branches and leaves of certain trees (the *Solanum campylanthum* and *Lantana salvifolia*). After that they pluck some of the eleusine, and each of them puts one grain in her necklace, chews another and rubs it on her forehead, throat, and breast. "No joy is shown by the womenfolk on this occasion, and they sorrowfully cut a basketful of the corn which they take home with them and place in the loft to dry."[24]

s of Indians at cutting sacred wood.

Just as the Egyptians lamented at cutting the corn, so the Karok Indians of California lament at hewing the [pg 048] sacred wood for the fire in the assembly-room. The wood must be cut from a tree on the top of the highest hill. In lopping off the boughs the Indian weeps and sobs piteously, shedding real tears, and at the top of the tree he leaves two branches and a top-knot, resembling a man's head and outstretched arms. Having descended from the tree, he binds the wood in a faggot and carries it back to the assembly-room, blubbering all the way. If he is asked why he thus weeps at cutting and fetching the sacred fuel, he will either give no answer or say simply that he does it for luck.[25] We may suspect that his real motive is to appease the wrath of the tree-spirit, many of whose limbs he has amputated, though he took care to leave him two arms and a head.

ny of burying "the old man" at harvest.

The conception of the corn-spirit as old and dead at harvest is very clearly embodied in a custom observed by the Arabs of Moab. When the harvesters have nearly finished their task and only a small corner of the field remains to be reaped, the owner takes a handful of wheat tied up in a sheaf. A hole is dug in the form of a grave, and two stones are set upright, one at the head and the other at the foot, just as in an ordinary burial. Then the sheaf of wheat is laid at the bottom of the grave, and the sheikh pronounces these words, "The old man is dead." Earth is afterwards thrown in to cover the sheaf, with a prayer, "May Allah bring us back the wheat of the dead."[26]

[pg 049]

Chapter IV. The Official Festivals of Osiris.

§ 1. The Festival at Sais.

ption of the Alexandrian year in 30 B.C. the Egyptian festivals ceased to rotate through the natural year.

Such, then, were the principal events of the farmer's calendar in ancient Egypt, and such the simple religious rites by which he celebrated them. But we have still to consider the Osirian festivals of the official calendar, so far as these are described by Greek writers or recorded on the monuments. In examining them it is necessary to bear in mind that on account of the movable year of the old Egyptian calendar the true or astronomical dates of the official festivals must have varied from year to year, at least until the adoption of the fixed Alexandrian year in 30 B.C. From that time onward, apparently, the dates of the festivals were determined by the new calendar, and so ceased to rotate throughout the length of the solar year. At all events Plutarch, writing about the end of the first century, implies that they were then fixed, not movable; for though he does not mention the Alexandrian calendar, he clearly dates the festivals by it.[97] Moreover, the long festal calendar of [pg 050] Esne, an important document of the Imperial age, is obviously based on the fixed Alexandrian year; for it assigns the mark for New Year's Day to the day which corresponds to the twenty-ninth of August, which was the first day of the Alexandrian year, and its references to the rising of the Nile, the position of the sun, and the operations of agriculture are all in harmony with this supposition.[98] Thus we may take it as fairly certain that from 30 B.C. onwards the Egyptian festivals were stationary in the solar year.

gs of Osiris displayed as a mystery at Sais. The illumination of houses throughout Egypt on the night of uggests that the rite was a Feast of All Souls.

Herodotus tells us that the grave of Osiris was at Sais in Lower Egypt, and that there was a lake there upon which the sufferings of the god were displayed as a mystery by night.[99] This commemoration of the divine passion was held once a year: the people mourned and beat their breasts at it to testify their sorrow for the death of the god; and an image of a cow, made of gilt wood with a golden sun between its horns, was carried out of the chamber in which it stood the rest of the year.[100] The cow no doubt represented Isis herself, for cows were sacred to her, and she was regularly depicted with the horns of a cow on her head,[101] or even as a woman with the head of a cow.[102] It is probable that the carrying out of her cow-shaped image symbolized the goddess searching for the dead body of Osiris; for this was the native Egyptian interpretation of a similar ceremony observed in Plutarch's time about the winter solstice, when the gilt cow was carried seven times round the temple.[103] A great feature of the festival was the [pg 051] nocturnal illumination. People fastened rows of oil-lamps to the outside of their houses, and the lamps burned all night long. The custom was not confined to Sais, but was observed throughout the whole of Egypt.[104]

This universal illumination of the houses on one night of the year suggests that the festival may have been a commemoration not merely of the dead Osiris but of the dead in general, in other words, that it may have been a night of All Souls.[105] For it is a widespread belief that the souls of the dead revisit their old homes on one night of the year; and on that solemn occasion people prepare for the reception of the ghosts by laying out food for them to eat, and lighting lamps to guide them on their dark road from and to the grave. The following instances will illustrate the custom.

§ 2. Feasts of All Souls.

The Esquimaux of St. Michael and the lower Yukon River in Alaska hold a festival of the dead every year at the end of November or the beginning of December, as well as a greater festival at intervals of several years. At these seasons, food, drink, and clothes are provided for the returning ghosts in the *kashim* or clubhouse of the village, which is illuminated with oil lamps. Every man or woman who wishes to honour a dead friend sets up a lamp on a stand in front of the place which the deceased used to occupy in the clubhouse. These lamps, filled with seal oil, are kept burning day and night till the festival is over. They are believed to light the shades on their return to [pg 052] their old home and back again to the land of the dead. If any one fails to put up a lamp in the clubhouse and to keep it burning, the shade whom he or she desires to honour could not find its way to the place and so would miss the feast. On the eve of the festival the nearest male relation goes to the grave and summons the ghost by planting there a small model of a seal spear or of a wooden dish, according as the deceased was a man or a woman. The badges of the dead are marked on these implements. When all is ready, the ghosts gather in the fire-pit under the clubhouse, and ascending through the floor at the proper moment take possession of the bodies of their namesakes, to whom the offerings of food, drink, and clothing are made for the benefit of the dead. Thus each shade obtains the supplies he needs in the other world. The dead who have none to make offerings to them are believed to suffer great destitution. Hence the Esquimaux fear to die without leaving behind them some one who will sacrifice to their spirits, and childless people generally adopt children lest their shades should be forgotten at the festivals. When a person has been much disliked, his ghost is sometimes purposely ignored, and that is deemed the severest punishment that could be inflicted upon him. After the songs of invitation to the dead have been sung, the givers of the feast take a small portion of food from every dish and cast it down as an offering to the shades; then each pours a little water on the floor so that it runs through the cracks. In this way they believe that the spiritual essence of all the food and water is conveyed to the souls. The remainder of the food is afterwards distributed among the people present, who eat of it heartily. Then with songs and dances the feast comes to an end, and the ghosts are dismissed to their own place. Dances form a conspicuous feature of the great festival of the dead, which is held every few years. The dancers dance not only in the clubhouse but also at the graves and on the ice, if the deceased met their death

35

by drowning.[106]

The Indians of California used to observe annual ceremonies [pg 053] of mourning for the dead,[107] at some of which the souls of the departed were represented by living persons. Ten or more men would prepare themselves to play the part of the ghosts by fasting for several days, especially by abstaining from flesh. Disguised with paint and soot, adorned with feathers and grasses, they danced and sang in the village or rushed about in the forest by night with burning torches in their hands. After a time they presented themselves to the relations of the deceased, who looked upon these maskers as in very truth their departed friends and received them accordingly with an outburst of lamentation, the old women scratching their own faces and smiting their breasts with stones in token of mourning. These masquerades were generally held in February. During their continuance a strict fast was observed in the village.[108] Among the Konkaus of California the dance of the dead is always held about the end of August and marks their New Year's Day. They collect a large quantity of food, clothing, baskets, ornaments, and whatever else the spirits are supposed to need in the other world. These they hang on a semicircle of boughs or small trees, cut and set in the ground leafless. In the centre burns a great fire, and hard by are the graves. The ceremony begins at evening and lasts till daybreak. As darkness falls, men and women sit on the graves and wail for the dead of the year. Then they dance round the fire with frenzied yells and whoops, casting from time to time the offerings into the flames. All must be consumed before the first faint streaks of dawn glimmer in the East.[109] The Choctaws used to have a great respect for their dead. They did not bury their bodies but laid them on biers made of bark and supported by forked sticks about fifteen feet high. [pg 054] When the worms had consumed the flesh, the skeleton was dismembered, any remains of muscles and sinews were buried, and the bones were deposited in a box, the skull being reddened with ochre. The box containing the bones was then carried to the common burial ground. In the early days of November the tribe celebrated a great festival which they called the Festival of the Dead or of the Souls; every family then gathered in the common burial ground, and there with weeping and lamentation visited the boxes which contained the mouldering relics of their dead. On returning from the graveyard they held a great banquet, which ended the festival.[110] Some of the Pueblo Indians of New Mexico "believe that on a certain day (in August, I think) the dead rise from their graves and flit about the neighbouring hills, and on that day all who have lost friends carry out quantities of corn, bread, meat, and such other good things of this life as they can obtain, and place them in the haunts frequented by the dead, in order that the departed spirits may once more enjoy the comforts of this nether world. They have been encouraged in this belief by the

36

priests, who were in the habit of sending out and appropriating to themselves all these things, and then making the poor simple Indians believe that the dead had eaten them."[111]

val of the dead among the Miztecs of Mexico.

The Miztecs of Mexico believed that the souls of the dead came back in the twelfth month of every year, which corresponded to our November. On this day of All Souls the houses were decked out to welcome the spirits. Jars of food and drink were set on a table in the principal room, and the family went forth with torches to meet the ghosts and invite them to enter. Then returning themselves to the house they knelt around the table, and with eyes bent on the ground prayed the souls to accept of the offerings and to procure the blessings of the gods upon the family. Thus they remained on bended knees and with downcast eyes till the morning, not daring to look at the table lest they [pg 055] should offend the spirits by spying on them at their meal. With the first beams of the sun they rose, glad at heart. The jars of food which had been presented to the dead were given to the poor or deposited in a secret place.[112] The Indians of Santiago Tepehuacan believe that the souls of their dead return to them on the night of the eighteenth of October, the festival of St. Luke, and they sweep the roads in order that the ghosts may find them clean on their passage.[113]

val of the dead in Sumba.

Again, the natives of Sumba, an East Indian island, celebrate a New Year's festival, which is at the same time a festival of the dead. The graves are in the middle of the village, and at a given moment all the people repair to them and raise a loud weeping and wailing. Then after indulging for a short time in the national pastimes they disperse to their houses, and every family calls upon its dead to come back. The ghosts are believed to hear and accept the invitation. Accordingly betel and areca nuts are set out for them. Victims, too, are sacrificed in front of every house, and their hearts and livers are offered with rice to the dead. After a decent interval these portions are distributed amongst the living, who consume them and banquet gaily on flesh and rice, a rare event in their frugal lives. Then they play, dance, and sing to their heart's content, and the festival which began so lugubriously ends by being the merriest of the year. A little before daybreak the invisible guests take their departure. All the people turn out of their houses to escort them a little way. Holding in one hand the half of a coco-nut, which contains a small packet of provisions for the dead, and in the other hand a piece of smouldering wood, they march in procession, singing a drawling song to the accompaniment of a gong and waving the lighted brands in time to the music. So they move through the darkness till with the last words of the song [pg 056] they throw away the coco-nuts and the brands in the direction of the spirit-land, leaving the ghosts to wend their way thither, while they themselves return to the village.[114]

In Kiriwina, one of the Trobriand Islands, to the east of New Guinea, the spirits of the ancestors are believed to revisit their native village in a body once a year after the harvest has been got in. At this time the men perform special dances, the people openly display their valuables, spread out on platforms, and great feasts are made for the spirits. On a certain night, when the moon is at the full, all the people raise a great shout and so drive away the spirits to the spirit land.[115] The Sea Dyaks of Borneo celebrate a great festival in honour of the dead at irregular intervals, it may be one or more years after the death of a particular person. All who have died since the last feast was held, and have not yet been honoured by such a celebration, are remembered at this time; hence the number of persons commemorated may be great, especially if many years have elapsed since the last commemoration service. The preparations last many weeks: food and drink and all other necessaries are stored in plenty, and the whole neighbourhood for miles round is invited to attend. On the eve of the feast the women take bamboo splints and fashion out of them little models of various useful articles, and these models are hung over the graves for the use of the dead in the other world. If the feast is held in honour of a man, the things manufactured in his behoof will take the form of a bamboo gun, a shield, a war-cap, and so on; if it is a woman who is commemorated, little models of a loom, a fish-basket, a winnowing-fan and such like things will be provided for her spirit; and if it is a child for whom the rite is performed, toys of various kinds will be made ready for the childish ghost. Finally, to stay the appetite of ghosts who may be too sharp-set to wait for the formal banquet in the house, [pg 057] a supply of victuals is very considerably placed outside the house on which the hungry spirits may fall to without delay. The dead arrive in a boat from the other world; for living Dyaks generally travel by river, from which it necessarily follows that Dyak ghosts do so likewise. The ship in which the ghostly visitors voyage to the land of the living is not much to look at, being in appearance nothing but a tiny boat made out of a bamboo which has been used to cook rice. Even this is not set floating on the river but is simply thrown away under the house. Yet through the incantations uttered by the professional wailing-woman the bark is wafted away to the spirit world and is there converted into a large war-canoe. Gladly the ghosts embark and sail away as soon as the final summons comes. It always comes in the evening, for it is then that the wailer begins to croon her mournful ditties; but the way is so long that the spirits do not arrive in the house till the day is breaking. To refresh them after their weary journey a bamboo full of rice-spirit awaits them; and this they partake of by deputy, for a brave old man, who does not fear the face of ghosts, quaffs the beverage in their stead amid the joyful shouts of the spectators. On the morning after the feast the living pay the last offices of respect to the dead. Monuments made of ironwood, the little bamboo articles, and food of all kinds are set upon the graves. In consideration of these gifts the ghosts now relinquish all claims on their surviving relatives, and henceforth earn their own living by the sweat of their brow. Before they take their final departure they come to eat and drink in the house for the last time.[116]

Thus the Dyak festival of the dead is not an annual welcome accorded to all the souls of ancestors; it is a propitiatory ceremony designed to secure once for all the eternal welfare of the recently departed, or at least to prevent their ghosts from returning to infest and importune the living. The same is perhaps the intention of the "soul departure" (*Kathi Kasham*) festival which the Tangkul [pg 058] Nagas of Manipur, in Assam, celebrate every year about the end of January. At this great feast the dead are represented by living men, chosen on the ground of their likeness to the departed, who are decked with ornaments and treated as if they were in truth the deceased persons come to life again. In that character they dance together in the large open space of the village, they are fed by the female relations, and they go from house to house, receiving presents of cloth. The festival lasts ten days, but the great day is the ninth. Huge torches of pinewood are made ready to be used that evening when darkness has fallen. The time of departure of the dead is at hand. Their living representatives are treated to a last meal in the houses, and they distribute farewell presents to the sorrowing kinsfolk, who have come to bid them good-bye. When the sun has set, a procession is formed. At the head of it march men holding aloft the flaring, sputtering torches. Then follow the elders armed and in martial array, and behind them stalk the representatives of the dead, with the relations of the departed crowding and trooping about them. Slowly and mournfully the sad procession moves, with loud lamentations, through the darkness to a spot at the north end of the village which is overshadowed by a great tree. The light of the torches is to guide the souls of the dead to their place of rest; the warlike array of the elders is to guard them from the perils and dangers of the way. At the village boundary the procession stops and the torch-bearers throw down their torches. At the same moment the spirits of the dead are believed to pass into the dying flambeaux and in that guise to depart to the far country. There is therefore no further need for their living representatives, who are accordingly stripped of all their finery on the spot. When the people return home, each family is careful to light a pine torch and set it burning on a stone in the house just inside the front door; this they do as a precaution to prevent their own souls from following the spirits of the dead to the other world. The expense of thus despatching the dead to their long home is very great; when the head of a family dies, debts may be incurred and rice-fields and houses sold to defray the cost of carriage. Thus [pg 059] the living impoverish themselves in order to enrich the dead.[117]

val of the dead among the Oraons of Bengal.

The Oraons or Uraons of Bengal feast their dead every year on a day in January. This ceremony is called the Great Marriage, because by it the bones of the deceased are believed to be mysteriously reunited to each other. The Oraons treat the bones of the dead differently according to the dates of their death in the agricultural year. The bones of those who died before the seeds have sprouted in the fields are burnt, and the few charred bones which have not been reduced to ashes are gathered in an earthen pot. With the bones in the pot are placed offerings of rice, native gin, and money, and then they carry the urn to the river, where the bones of their forefathers repose. But the bones of all who die after the seeds have sprung up and before the end of harvest may not be taken to the river, because the people believe that were that to be done the crops would suffer. These bones are therefore put away in a pot under a stone near the house till the harvest is over. Then on the appointed day in January they are all collected. A banquet is given in honour of the dead, and then both men and women form a procession to accompany the bones to their last resting-place in the sands of the river. But first the relics of mortality are carried from house to house in the village, and each family pours rice and gin into the urn which contains the bones of its dead. Then the procession sets out for the river, men and women dancing, singing, beating drums, and weeping, while the earthen pots containing the bones are passed from hand to hand and dance with the jigging steps of the dancers. When they are yet some way from the spot, the bearers of the urns run forward and bury them in the sand of the river. When the rest come up, they all bathe and the Great Marriage is over.[118]

[pg 060]

val of the dead in Bilaspore.

In the Bilaspore district of the Central Provinces, India, "the festival known as the Fortnight of the Manes—*PitrPāk*—occurs about September. It is believed that during this fortnight it is the practice of all the departed to come and visit their relatives. The homes are therefore cleaned, and the spaces in front of the house are plastered and painted in order to be pleasing to those who are expected. It is believed that the departed will return on the very date on which they went away. A father who left on the fourth, be it the fourth of the dark half or the light half of the moon, will return to visit his family on the fourth

40

of the Fortnight of the Manes. On that day cakes are prepared, and with certain ceremony these are offered to the unseen hovering spirit. Their implicit belief is that the spirit will partake of the essence of the food, and that which remains—the material portion—may be eaten by members of the family. The souls of women, it is said, will all come on the ninth of the fortnight. On the thirteenth come those who have met with a violent death and who lost their lives by a fall, by snake-bite, or any other unusual cause. During the Fortnight of the Manes a woman is not supposed to put on new bangles and a man is not permitted to shave. In short, this is a season of sad remembrances, an annual festival for the departed."[119]

val of the dead among the Bghais and Hkamies.

The Bghais, a Karen tribe of Burma, hold an annual feast for the dead at the new moon which falls near the end of August or the beginning of September. All the villagers who have lost relatives within the last three years take part in it. Food and drink are set out on tables for the ghosts, and new clothes for them are hung up in the room. All being ready, the people beat gongs and begin to weep. Each one calls upon the relation whom he has lost to come and eat. When the dead are thought to have arrived, the [pg 061] living address them, saying, "You have come to me, you have returned to me. It has been raining hard, and you must be wet. Dress yourselves, clothe yourselves with these new garments, and all the companions that are with you. Eat betel together with all that accompany you, all your friends and associates, and the long dead. Call them all to eat and drink." The ghosts having finished their repast, the people dry their tears and sit down to eat what is left. More food is then prepared and put into a basket, and at cock-crow next morning the contents of the basket are thrown out of the house, while the living weep and call upon their dead as before.[120] The Hkamies, a hill tribe of North Aracan, hold an important festival every year in honour of departed spirits. It falls after harvest and is called "the opening of the house of the dead." When a person dies and has been burnt, the ashes are collected and placed in a small house in the forest together with his spear or gun, which has first been broken. These little huts are generally arranged in groups near a village, and are sometimes large enough to be mistaken for one. After harvest all the relations of the deceased cook various kinds of food and take them with pots of liquor distilled from rice to the village of the dead. There they open the doors of the houses, and having placed the food and drink inside they shut them again. After that they weep, eat, drink, and return home.[121]

val of the dead in Cambodia.

The great festival of the dead in Cambodia takes place on the last day of the month Phatrabot (September-October), but ever since the moon began to wane everybody has been busy preparing for it. In every house cakes and sweetmeats are set out, candles burn, incense sticks smoke, and the whole is offered to the ancestral shades with an invocation which is thrice repeated: "O all you our ancestors who are departed, deign to come and eat what we have prepared [pg 062] for you, and to bless your posterity and make it happy." Fifteen days afterwards many little boats are made of bark and filled with rice, cakes, small coins, smoking incense sticks, and lighted candles. At evening these are set floating on the river, and the souls of the dead embark in them to return to their own place. The living now bid them farewell. "Go to the lands," they say, "go to the fields you inhabit, to the mountains, under the stones which are your abodes. Go away! return! In due time your sons and your grandsons will think of you. Then you will return, you will return, you will return." The river is now covered with twinkling points of fire. But the current soon bears them away, and as they vanish one by one in the darkness the souls depart with them to the far country.[122] In Tonquin, as in Sumba, the dead revisit their kinsfolk and their old homes at the New Year. From the hour of midnight, when the New Year begins, no one dares to shut the door of his house for fear of excluding the ghosts, who begin to arrive at that time. Preparations have been made to welcome and refresh them after their long journey. Beds and mats are ready for their weary bodies to repose upon, water to wash their dusty feet, slippers to comfort them, and canes to support their feeble steps. Candles burn on the domestic altar, and pastilles diffuse a fragrant odour. The people bow before the unseen visitors and beseech them to remember and bless their descendants in the coming year. Having discharged this pious duty they abstain from sweeping the houses for three days lest the dust should incommode the ghosts.[123]

val of the dead in Annam.

In Annam one of the most important festivals of the year is the festival of Têt, which falls on the first three days of the New Year. It is devoted to the worship of ancestors. Everybody, even the poorest, must provide a good meal for the souls of his dead at this time and must himself eat and [pg 063] drink heartily. Some families, in order to discharge this pious duty, run into debt for the whole year. In the houses everything is put in order, washed, and scoured for the reception of the dear and distinguished guests. A tall bamboo pole is set up in the front of every house and allowed to stand there for seven days. A small basket containing areca, betel, and leaves of gilt paper is fastened to the pole. The erection of the pole is a sacred rite which no family omits to perform, though why they do so few people can say. Some, however, allege that the posts are intended to guide the ancestral spirits to their old homes. The ceremony of the reception of the shades takes place at nightfall on the last day of the year. The house of the head of the family is then decked with flowers, and in the room which serves as a domestic chapel the altar of the ancestors is surrounded with flowers, among which the lotus, the emblem of immortality, is most conspicuous. On a table are set red candles, perfumes, incense, sandal-wood, and plates full of bananas, oranges, and other fruits. The relations crouch before the altar, and kneeling at the foot of it the head of the house invokes the name of the family which he represents. Then in solemn tones he recites an incantation, mentioning the names of his most illustrious ancestors and marking time with the strokes of a hammer upon a gong, while crackers are exploded outside the room. After that, he implores the ancestral shades to protect their descendants and invites them to a repast, which is spread for them on a table. Round this table he walks, serving the invisible guests with his own hands. He distributes to them smoking balls of rice in little china saucers, and pours tea or spirits into each little cup, while he murmurs words of invitation and compliment. When the ghosts have eaten and drunk their fill, the head of the family returns to the altar and salutes them for the last time. Finally, he takes leaves of yellow paper, covered with gold and silver spangles, and throws them into a brazier placed at the foot of the ancestral tablets. These papers represent imaginary bars of gold and silver which the living send to the dead. Cardboard models of houses, furniture, jewels, clothes, of everything in short that the [pg 064] ghosts can need in the other world, are despatched to them in like manner in the flames. Then the family sits down to table and feasts on the remains of the ghostly banquet.[124]

val of friendless ghosts in Annam.

But in Annam it is not merely the spirits of ancestors who are thus feasted and supplied with all the necessaries of life. The poor ghosts of those who died without leaving descendants or whose bodies were left unburied are not forgotten by the pious Annamites. But these spirits come round at a different time of year from the others. The seventh month of the year is set apart for expiatory sacrifices destined to benefit these unhappy beings, and that is why in Annam nobody should marry or be betrothed in that month. The great day of the month is the fifteenth, which is called the Festival of the Souls. On that day the ghosts in question are set free by the lord of the underworld, and they come prowling about among the living. They are exceedingly dangerous, especially to children. Hence in order to appease their wrath and prevent them from entering the houses every family takes care to put out offerings for them in the street. Before every house on that night you may see candles lighted, paper garments of many colours, paper hats, paper boots, paper furniture, ingots of gold and silver paper, all hanging in tempting array from a string, while plates of food and cups of tea and rice-spirit stand ready for the use of hungry and thirsty souls. The theory is that the ghosts will be so busy consuming the victuals, appropriating the deceitful riches, and trying on the paper coats, hats, and boots that they will have neither the leisure nor the inclination to intrude upon the domestic circle indoors. At seven o'clock in the evening fire is put to the offerings, and the paper wardrobe, furniture, and money soon vanish crackling in the flames. At the same moment, peeping in at a door or window, you may see the domestic ancestral altar brilliantly illuminated. As for the food, it is supposed to be thrown on the fire or on the ground for the [pg 065] use of the ghosts, but practically it is eaten by vagabonds and beggars, who scuffle for the booty.[125]

vals of the dead in Cochinchina, Siam and Japan.

In Cochinchina the ancestral spirits are similarly propitiated and fed on the first day of the New Year. The tablets which represent them are placed on the domestic altar, and the family prostrate themselves before these emblems of the departed. The head of the family lights sticks of incense on the altar and prays the shades of his forefathers to accept the offerings and be favourable to their descendants. With great gravity he waits upon the ghosts, passing dishes of food before the ancestral tablets and pouring out wine and tea to slake the thirst of the spirits. When the dead are supposed to be satisfied with the shadowy essence of the food, the living partake of its gross material substance.[126] In Siam and Japan also the souls of the dead revisit their families for three days in every year, and the lamps which the Japanese kindle in multitudes on that occasion to light the spirits on their way have procured for the festival the name of the Feast of Lanterns. It is to be observed that in Siam, as in Tonquin and Sumba, the return of the ghosts takes place at the New Year.[127]

vals of the dead among the Chewsurs and Armenians.

The Chewsurs of the Caucasus believe that the souls of the departed revisit their old homes on the Saturday night of the second week in Lent. This gathering of the dead is called the "Assembly of Souls." The people spare no expense to treat the unseen guests handsomely. Beer is brewed and loaves of various shapes baked specially for the occasion.[128] The Armenians celebrate the memory of the dead on many days of the year, burning incense and lighting tapers in their honour. One of their customs is to keep a "light of the dead" burning all night in the house in order that the ghosts may be able to enter. For if the [pg 066] spirits find the house dark, they spit down the chimney and depart, cursing the churlish inmates.[129]

vals of the dead in Africa.

Early in April every year the Dahomans of West Africa "set a table, as they term it, and invite friends to eat with the deceased relatives, whose spirits are supposed to move round and partake of the good things of this life. Even my interpreter, Madi-Ki Lemon, who pretends to despise the belief in fetish, sets a table to his ancestors, and will tell you that his grand- or great-grandfather,

Corporal Lemon, makes a meal on this occasion which will last him till the next annual feast."[130] The Barea and apparently the Kunama, two heathen tribes who lead a settled agricultural life to the north of Abyssinia, celebrate every year a festival in the month of November. It is a festival of thanksgiving for the completion of the harvest, and at the same time a commemoration and propitiation of the dead. Every house prepares much beer for the occasion, and a small pot of beer is set out for each deceased member of the household. After standing for two days in the house the beer which was devoted to the dead is drunk by the living. At these festivals all the people of a district meet in a special place, and there pass the time in games and dances. Among the Barea the festive gatherings are held in a sacred grove. We are told that "he who owes another a drubbing on this day can pay his debt with impunity; for it is a day of peace when all feuds are in abeyance." Wild honey may not be gathered till the festival has been held.[131] Apparently the festival is a sort of Saturnalia, such as is celebrated elsewhere at the end of harvest.[132] At that season there is food and to spare for the dead as well as the living.

[pg 067]

vals of the dead among peoples of the Aryan stock. Annual festival of the dead (the Fravashis) among ans. Annual festival of the dead among the Persians.

Among peoples of the Aryan stock, so far back as we can trace their history, the worship and propitiation of the dead seem to have formed a principal element of the popular religion;[133] and like so many other races they appear to have believed that once a year the souls of their departed kinsfolk revisited their old homes and expected to be refreshed with abundance of good cheer by their surviving relations. This belief gave rise to the custom of celebrating an annual Feast of All Souls, which has come down to us from a dateless antiquity and is still observed year by year, with rites of primitive simplicity, in some parts of Europe. Such a festival was held every year in spring by the old Iranians. The celebration fell at the end of the year and lasted ten days, namely the last five days of the last month and the five following supplementary days, which were regularly inserted to make up a year of three hundred and sixty-five days; for the old Iranian, like the old Egyptian, year was a vague year of twelve months of thirty days each, with five supplementary days added at the end for the sake of bringing it into apparent, though not real, harmony with the sun's annual course in the sky. According to one calculation the ten days of the festival corresponded to the last days of February, but according to another they fell in March; in later ages the Parsees assigned them to the time of the spring equinox. The name of the festival was Hamaspathmaedaya.[134] From a passage in the *Zend-Avesta*, the [pg 068] ancient sacred book of the Iranians, we learn that on the ten nights of the festival the souls of the dead (the Fravashis) were believed to go about the

45

village asking the people to do them reverence, to pray to them, to meditate on them, and to furnish them with meat and clothes, while at the same time they promised that blessings should rest on the pious householder who complied with their request.[135] The Arab geographer Albiruni, who flourished about the year one thousand of our era, tells us that among the Persians of his time the last five days of the month Aban were called Farwardajan. "During this time," he says, "people put food in the halls of the dead and drink on the roofs of the houses, believing that the spirits of their dead during these days come out from the places of their reward or their punishment, that they go to the dishes laid out for them, imbibe their strength and suck their taste. They fumigate their houses with juniper, that the dead may enjoy its smell. The spirits of the pious men dwell among their families, children, and relations, and occupy themselves with their affairs, although invisible to them." He adds that there was a controversy among the Persians as to the date of this festival of the dead, some maintaining that the five days during which it lasted were the last five days of the month Aban, whereas others held that they were the five supplementary days which were inserted between the months Aban and Adhar. The dispute, he continues, was settled by the adoption of all ten days for the celebration of the feast.[136]

[pg 069]

Souls in Brittany and other parts of France.

Similar beliefs as to the annual return of the dead survive to this day in many parts of Europe and find expression in similar customs. The day of the dead or of All Souls, as we call it, is commonly the second of November. Thus in Lower Brittany the souls of the departed come to visit the living on the eve of that day. After vespers are over, the priests and choir walk in procession, "the procession of the charnel-house," chanting a weird dirge in the Breton tongue. Then the people go home, gather round the fire, and talk of the departed. The housewife covers the kitchen table with a white cloth, sets out cider, curds, and hot pancakes on it, and retires with the family to rest. The fire on the hearth is kept up by a huge log known as "the log of the dead" (*kef ann Anaon*). Soon doleful voices outside in the darkness break the stillness of night. It is the "singers of death" who go about the streets waking the sleepers by a wild and melancholy song, in which they remind the living in their comfortable beds to pray for the poor souls in pain. All that night the dead warm themselves at the hearth and feast on the viands prepared for them. Sometimes the awe-struck listeners hear the stools creaking in the kitchen, or the dead leaves outside rustling under the ghostly footsteps.[137] In the Vosges Mountains on All Souls' Eve the solemn sound of the church bells invites good Christians to pray for the repose of the dead. While the bells are ringing, it is customary in some families to uncover the beds and open the windows, doubtless in order to let the poor souls enter and rest. No one that evening would dare to remain deaf to the appeal of the bells. The prayers are prolonged to a late hour of the night. When the last *De profundis* has been uttered, the head of the family gently covers up the beds, sprinkles them with holy water, and shuts the windows. In some villages fire is kept up on the hearth and a basket of nuts is placed beside it for the use of the ghosts.[138] Again, in some parts of Saintonge and Aunis a Candlemas candle used to be lit before the domestic [pg 070] crucifix on All Souls' Day at the very hour when the last member of the family departed this life; and some people, just as in Tonquin, refrained from sweeping the house that day lest they should thereby disturb the ghostly visitors.[139]

Souls in Belgium.

In Bruges, Dinant, and other towns of Belgium holy candles burn all night in the houses on the Eve of All Souls, and the bells toll till midnight, or even till morning. People, too, often set lighted candles on the graves. At Scherpenheuvel the houses are illuminated, and the people walk in procession carrying lighted candles in their hands. A very common custom in Belgium is to eat "soul-cakes" or "soul-bread" on the eve or the day of All Souls. The eating of them is believed to benefit the dead in some way. Perhaps originally, as among the Esquimaux of Alaska to this day,[140] the ghosts were thought to enter into the bodies of their relatives and so to share the victuals which the survivors consumed. Similarly at festivals in honour of the dead in Northern India it is customary to feed Brahmans, and the food which these holy men partake of is believed to pass to the deceased and to refresh their languid spirits.[141] The same idea of eating and drinking by proxy may perhaps partly explain many other funeral feasts. Be that as it may, at Dixmude and elsewhere in Belgium they say that you deliver a soul from Purgatory for every cake you eat. At Antwerp they give a local colour to the soul-cakes by baking them with plenty of saffron, the deep yellow tinge being suggestive of the flames of Purgatory. People in Antwerp at the same season are careful not to slam doors or windows for fear of hurting the ghosts.[142]

Souls in Lechrain.

In Lechrain, a district of Southern Bavaria which extends along the valley of the Lech from its source to near the point where the river flows into the Danube, the two festivals of All Saints and All Souls, on the first [pg 071] and second of November, have significantly fused in popular usage into a single festival of the dead. In fact, the people pay little or no heed to the saints and give all their thoughts to the souls of their departed kinsfolk. The Feast of All Souls begins immediately after vespers on All Saints' Day. Even on the eve of All Saints' Day, that is, on the thirty-first of October, which we call Hallowe'en, the graveyard is cleaned and every grave adorned. The decoration consists in weeding the mounds, sprinkling a layer of charcoal on the bare earth, and marking out patterns on it in red service-berries. The marigold, too, is still in bloom at that season in cottage gardens, and garlands of its orange blooms, mingled with other late flowers left by the departing summer, are twined about the grey mossgrown tombstones. The basin of holy water is filled with fresh water and a branch of box-wood put into it; for box-wood in the popular mind is associated with death and the dead. On the eve of All Souls' Day the people begin to visit the graves and to offer the soul-cakes to the hungry souls. Next morning, before eight o'clock, commence the vigil, the requiem, and the solemn visitation of the graves. On that day every household offers a plate of meal, oats, and spelt on a side-altar in the church; while in the middle of the sacred edifice a bier is set, covered with a pall, and surrounded by lighted tapers and vessels of holy water. The tapers burnt on that day and indeed generally in services for the departed are red. In the evening people go, whenever they can do so, to their native village, where their dear ones lie in the churchyard; and there at the graves they pray for the poor souls, and leave an offering of soul-cakes also on a side-altar in the church. The soul-cakes are baked of dough in the shape of a coil of hair and are made of all sizes up to three feet long. They form a perquisite of the sexton.[143]

nd All Souls' Day in Southern Germany.

The custom of baking soul-cakes, sometimes called simply "souls," on All Souls' Day is widespread in Southern Germany and Austria;[144] everywhere, we may assume, the cakes were originally intended for the benefit of the hungry dead, though [pg 072] they are often eaten by the living. In the Upper Palatinate people throw food into the fire on All Souls' Day for the poor souls, set lights on the table for them, and pray on bended knees for their repose. On the graves, too, lights are kindled, vessels of holy water placed, and food deposited for the refreshment of the souls. All over the Upper Palatinate on All Souls' Day it is also customary to bake special cakes of fine bread and distribute them to the poor,[145] who eat them perhaps as the deputies of the dead.

Souls in Bohemia.

The Germans of Bohemia observe All Souls' Day with much solemnity. Each family celebrates the memory of its dead. On the eve of the day it is customary to eat cakes and to drink cold milk for the purpose of cooling the poor souls who are roasting in purgatory; from which it appears that spirits feel the soothing effect of victuals consumed vicariously by their friends on earth. The ringing of the church bells to prayer on that evening is believed to be the signal at which the ghosts, released from the infernal gaol, come trooping to the old familiar fire-side, there to rest from their pangs for a single night. So in many places people fill a lamp with butter, light it, and set it on the hearth, that with the butter the poor ghosts may anoint the burns they have received from the sulphureous and tormenting flames of purgatory. Next morning the chime of the church bells, ringing to early mass, is the knell that bids the souls return to their place of pain; but such as have completed their penance take flight to heaven. So on the eve of All Saints' Day each family gathers in the parlour or the kitchen, speaks softly of those they have lost, recalls what they said and did in life, and prays for the repose of their souls. While the prayer is being said, the children kindle little wax lights which have been specially bought for the purpose that day. Next morning the families go to church, where mass is celebrated for the dead; then they wend their way to the [pg 073] churchyard, where they deck the graves of their kinsfolk with flowers and wreaths and set little lights upon them. This custom of illumining the graves and decking them with flowers on the Eve or Day of All Souls is common all over Bohemia; it is observed in Prague as well as in the country, by Czechs as well as by Germans. In some Czech villages four-cornered cakes of a special sort, baked of white wheaten meal with milk, are eaten on All Souls' Day or given to beggars that they may pray for the dead.[146] Among the Germans of Western Bohemia poor children go from house to house on All Souls' Day, begging for soul-cakes, and when they receive them they pray God to bless all poor souls. In the southern districts every farmer used to grind a great quantity of corn against the day and to bake it into five or six hundred little black soul-cakes which he gave away to the poor who came begging for them.[147]

Souls in Moravia.

All Souls' Day is celebrated with similar rites by the Germans of Moravia. "The festival of the farewell to summer," says a German writer on this subject, "was held by our heathen forefathers in the beginning of November, and with the memory of the departed summer they united the memory of the departed souls, and this last has survived in the Feast of All Souls, which is everywhere observed with great piety. On the evening of All Souls the relations of the departed assemble in the churchyards and adorn the graves of their dear ones with flowers and lights, while the children kindle little wax tapers, which have been bought for them, to light the 'poor souls.' According to the popular belief, the dead go in procession to the church about midnight, and any stout-hearted young man can there see all the living men who will die within the year."[148]

Souls in the Tyrol and Baden.

In the Tyrol the beliefs and customs are similar. There, too, "soul-lights," that is, lamps filled with lard or butter are lighted and placed on the hearth on All Souls' Eve in order that poor souls, escaped from the fires of purgatory, may smear the melted grease on their burns and so alleviate their pangs. [pg 074] Some people also leave milk and dough-nuts for them on the table all night. The graves also are illuminated with wax candles and decked with such a profusion of flowers that you might think it was springtime.[149] In the Italian Tyrol it is customary to give bread or money to the poor on All Souls' Day; in the Val di Ledro children threaten to dirty the doors of houses if they do not get the usual dole. Some rich people treat the poor to bean-soup on that day. Others put pitchers full of water in the kitchen on All Souls' night that the poor souls may slake their thirst.[150] In Baden it is still customary to deck the graves with flowers and lights on All Saints' Day and All Souls' Day. The lights are sometimes kindled in hollow turnips, on the sides of which inscriptions are carved and shine out in the darkness. If any child steals a turnip-lantern or anything else from a grave, the indignant ghost who has been robbed appears to the thief the same night and reclaims his stolen property. A relic of the old custom of feeding the dead survives in the practice of giving soul-cakes to godchildren.[151]

vals of the dead among the Letts and Samagitians.

The Letts used to entertain and feed the souls of the dead for four weeks from Michaelmas (September 29) to the day of St. Simon and St. Jude (October 28). They called the season *Wellalaick* or *Semlicka*, and regarded it as so holy that while it lasted they would not willingly thresh the corn, alleging that grain threshed at that time would be useless for sowing, since the souls of the dead would not allow it to sprout. But we may suspect that the original motive of the abstinence was a fear lest the blows of the flails should fall upon the poor ghosts swarming in the air. At this season the people were wont to prepare food of all sorts for the spirits and set it on the floor of a room, which had been well heated and swept for the purpose. Late in the evening the master of the house went into the room, tended the fire, and called upon his dead kinsfolk by their names to come and eat and drink. If he saw the ghosts, he would die within the year; but if [pg 075] he did not see them he would outlive it. When he thought the souls had eaten and drunk enough, he took the staff which served as a poker and laying it on the threshold cut it in two with an axe. At the same time he bade the spirits go their way, charging them to keep to the roads and paths and not to tread upon the rye. If the crops turned out ill next year, the people laid the failure at the door of the ghosts, who fancied themselves scurvily treated and had taken their revenge by trampling down the corn.[152] The Samagitians annually invited the dead to come from their graves and enjoy a bath and a feast. For their entertainment they prepared a special hut, in which they set out food and drink, together with a seat and a napkin for every soul who had been invited. They left the souls to revel by themselves for three days in the hut; then they deposited the remains of the banquet on the graves and bade the ghosts farewell. The good things, however, were usually consumed by charcoal burners in the forest. This feast of the dead fell early in November.[153] The Esthonians prepare a meal for their dead on All Souls' Day, the second of November, and invite them by their names to come and partake of it. The ghosts arrive in the early morning at the first cock-crow, and depart at the second, being ceremoniously lighted out of the house by the head of the family, who waves a white cloth after them and bids them come again next year.[154]

he dead in Russia.

In some parts of the Russian Government of Olonets the inhabitants of a village sometimes celebrate a joint festival in honour of all their dead. Having chosen a house for the purpose, they spread three tables, one outside the front door, one in the passage, and one in the room which is heated by a stove. Then they go out to meet their [pg 076] unseen guests and usher them into the house with these words, "Ye are tired, our own ones; take something to eat." The ghosts accordingly refresh themselves at each table in succession. Then the master of the house bids them warm themselves at the stove, remarking that they must have grown cold in the damp earth. After that the living guests sit down to eat at the tables. Towards the end of the meal the host opens the window and lets the ghosts gently out of it by means of the shroud in which they were lowered into the grave. As they slide down it from the warm room into the outer air, the people tell them, "Now it is time for you to go home, and your feet must be tired; the way is not a little one for you to travel. Here it is softer for you. Now, in God's name, farewell!"[155]

vals of the dead among the Votiaks of Russia.

Among the Votiaks of Russia every family sacrifices to its dead once a year in the week before Palm Sunday. The sacrifice is offered in the house about midnight. Flesh, bread, or cakes and beer are set on the table, and on the floor beside the table stands a trough of bark with a lighted wax candle stuck on the rim. The master of the house, having covered his head with his hat, takes a piece of meat in his hand and says, "Ye spirits of the long departed, guard and preserve us well. Make none of us cripples. Send no plagues upon us. Cause the corn, the wine, and the food to prosper with us."[156] The Votiaks of the Governments of Wjatka and Kasan celebrate two memorial festivals of the dead every year, one in autumn and the other in spring. On a certain day koumiss is distilled, beer brewed, and potato scones baked in every house. All the members of a clan, who trace their descent through women from one mythical ancestress, assemble in a single house, generally in one which lies at the boundary of the clan land. Here an old man moulds wax candles; and when the requisite number is made he sticks them on the shelf of the stove, and begins to mention the dead relations of the master of the house by name.

For each of them he crumbles a piece of bread, [pg 077] gives each of them a piece of pancake, pours koumiss and beer, and puts a spoonful of soup into a trough made for the purpose. All persons present whose parents are dead follow his example. The dogs are then allowed to eat out of the trough. If they eat quietly, it is a sign that the dead live at peace; if they do not eat quietly, it argues the contrary. Then the company sit down to table and partake of the meal. Next morning both the dead and the living refresh themselves with a drink, and a fowl is boiled. The proceedings are the same as on the evening before. But now they treat the souls for the last time as a preparation for their journey, saying: "Eat, drink, and go home to your companions. Live at peace, be gracious to us, keep our children, guard our corn, our beasts and birds." Then the people banquet and indulge in all sorts of improprieties. The women refrain from feasting until the dead have taken their departure; but when the souls are gone, there is no longer any motive for abstinence, the koumiss circulates freely among the women, and they grow wanton. Yet at this, as at every other festival, the men and women eat in different parts of the room.[157]

Souls in the Abruzzi.

On All Saints' Day, the first of November, shops and streets in the Abruzzi are filled with candles, which people buy in order to kindle them in the evening on the graves of their relations. For all the dead come to visit their homes that night, the Eve of All Souls, and they need lights to show them the way. For their use, too, lights are kept burning in the houses all night. Before people go to sleep they place on the table a lighted lamp or candle and a frugal meal of bread and water. The dead issue from their graves and stalk in procession through every street of the village. You can see them if you stand at a cross-road with your chin resting on a forked stick. First pass the souls of the good, and then the souls of the murdered and the damned. Once, they say, a man was thus peeping at the ghastly procession. The good souls told him he had [pg 078] better go home. He did not, and when he saw the tail of the procession he died of fright.[158]

n All-Souls' Day in England. "Souling Day" in Shropshire.

In our own country the old belief in the annual return of the dead long lingered in the custom of baking "soul-cakes" and eating them or distributing them to the poor on All Souls' Day. Peasant girls used to go from farmhouse to farmhouse on that day, singing,

> "Soul, soul, for a soul cake,
>
> Pray you, good mistress, a soul cake."[159]

In Shropshire down to the seventeenth century it was customary on All Souls' Day to set on the table a high heap of soul-cakes, and most visitors to the house took one of them. The antiquary John Aubrey, who records the custom, mentions also the appropriate verses:

"A soul-cake, a soul-cake,

Have mercy on all Christen soules for a soule-cake."[160]

Indeed the custom of soul-cakes survived in Shropshire down to the latter part of the nineteenth century and may not be extinct even now. "With us, All Saints' Day is known as 'Souling Day,' and up to the present time in many places, poor children, and sometimes men, go out 'souling': which means that they go round to the houses of all the more well-to-do people within reach, reciting a ditty peculiar to the day, and looking for a dole of cakes, broken victuals, ale, apples, or money. The two latter are now the usual rewards, but there are few old North Salopians who cannot remember when 'soul-cakes' were made at all the farms and 'bettermost' houses in readiness for the day, and were given to all who came for them. We are told of [pg 079] liberal housewives who would provide as many as a clothes-basket full."[161] The same custom of going out "a-souling" on All Saints' Day or All Souls' Day used to be observed in the neighbouring counties of Staffordshire, Cheshire, Lancashire, Herefordshire, and Monmouthshire. In Herefordshire the soul-cakes were made of oatmeal, and he or she who received one of them was bound to say to the giver:

"God have your saul,

Beens and all."[162]

Thus the practice of "souling" appears to have prevailed especially in the English counties which border on Wales. In many parts of Wales itself down to the first half of the nineteenth century poor peasants used to go about begging for bread on All Souls' Day. The bread bestowed on them was called *bara ran* or dole-bread. "This custom was a survival of the Middle Ages, when the poor begged bread for the souls of their departed relatives and friends."[163] However, the custom was not confined to the west of England, for at Whitby in Yorkshire down to the early part of the nineteenth century it was usual to make "soul mass loaves" on or about All Souls' Day. They were small round loaves, sold by bakers at a farthing apiece, chiefly for presents to children. In former times people used to keep one or two of them for good luck.[164] In Aberdeenshire, also, "on All Souls' Day, baked cakes of a particular sort are given away to those who may chance to visit the house, where they are [pg 080] made. The cakes are called 'dirge-loaf.' "[165] Even in the remote island of St. Kilda it was customary on All Saints' Day to bake a large cake in the form of a triangle, furrowed round; the cake must be all eaten that night.[166]

Souls among the Indians of Ecuador.

The same mode of celebrating All Souls' Day has been transported by Catholicism to the New World and imparted to the aborigines of that continent. Thus in Carchi, a province of Ecuador, the Indians prepare foods of various sorts against All Souls' Day, and when the day has come they take some of the provisions to the church and there deposit them on tables set out for the purpose. These good things are the perquisite of the priest, who celebrates mass for the dead. After the service the Indians repair to the cemetery, where with burning candles and pots of holy water they prostrate themselves before the tombs of their relations, while the priest or the sacristan recites prayers for the souls of the departed. In the evening the Indians return to their houses. A table with four lights on it is spread with food and drink, especially with such things as the dead loved in their life. The door is left open all night, no doubt to let the spirits of the dead enter, and the family sits up, keeping the invisible guests company through the long hours of darkness. From seven o'clock and onwards troops of children traverse the village and its neighbourhood. They go from house to house ringing a bell and crying, "We are angels, we descend from the sky, we ask for bread." The people go to their doors and beg the children to recite a *Pater Noster* or an *Ave Maria* for the dead whom they name. When the prayer has been duly said, they give the children a little of the food from the table. All night long this goes on, band succeeding band of children. At five o'clock in the morning the family consumes the remainder of the food of the souls.[167] Here the children going from door to door during the night of All Souls appear to personate the souls of the dead who are also abroad at that time; hence to give bread to the children is the same thing as to [pg 081] give bread to the poor hungry souls. Probably the same explanation applies to the giving of soul-cakes to children and the poor on All Souls' Day in Europe.

ly Christian feast of All Souls on Nov. 2 appears to be an old Celtic festival of the dead adopted by the 8 A.D. Institution of the Feast of All Souls by the Abbot of Clugny.

A comparison of these European customs with the similar heathen rites can leave no room for doubt that the nominally Christian feast of All Souls is nothing but an old pagan festival of the dead which the Church, unable or unwilling to suppress, resolved from motives of policy to connive at. But whence did it borrow the practice of solemnizing the festival on that particular day, the second of November? In order to answer this question we should observe, first, that celebrations of this sort are often held at the beginning of a New Year,[168] and, second, that the peoples of North-Western Europe, the Celts and the Teutons, appear to have dated the beginning of their year from the beginning of winter, the Celts reckoning it from the first of November[169] and the Teutons from the first of October.[170] The difference of reckoning may be due to a difference of climate, the home of the Teutons in

Central and Northern Europe being a region where winter sets in earlier than on the more temperate and humid coasts of the Atlantic, the home of the Celts. These considerations suggest that the festival of All Souls on the second of November originated with the Celts, and spread from them to the rest of the European peoples, who, while they preserved their old feasts of the dead practically unchanged, may have transferred them to the second of November. This conjecture is supported by what we know of the ecclesiastical institution, or rather recognition, of the festival. For [pg 082] that recognition was first accorded at the end of the tenth century in France, a Celtic country, from which the Church festival gradually spread over Europe. It was Odilo, abbot of the great Benedictine monastery of Clugny, who initiated the change in 998 A.D. by ordering that in all the monasteries over which he ruled, a solemn mass should be celebrated on the second of November for all the dead who sleep in Christ. The example thus set was followed by other religious houses, and the bishops, one after another, introduced the new celebration into their dioceses. Thus the festival of All Souls gradually established itself throughout Christendom, though in fact the Church has never formally sanctioned it by a general edict nor attached much weight to its observance. Indeed, when objections were raised to the festival at the Reformation, the ecclesiastical authorities seemed ready to abandon it.[171] These facts are explained very simply by the theory that an old Celtic commemoration of the dead lingered in France down to the end of the tenth century, and was then, as a measure of policy and a concession to ineradicable paganism, at last incorporated in the Catholic ritual. The consciousness of the heathen origin of the practice would naturally prevent the supreme authorities from insisting strongly on its observance. They appear rightly to have regarded it as an outpost which they could surrender to the forces of rationalism without endangering the citadel of the faith.

All Saints on Nov. 1 seems also to have displaced a heathen festival of the dead.

Perhaps we may go a step further and explain in like manner the origin of the feast of All Saints on the first of November. For the analogy of similar customs elsewhere would lead us to suppose that the old Celtic festival of the dead was held on the Celtic New Year's Day, that is, on the first, not the second, of November. May not then the institution of the feast of All Saints on that day have been the first attempt of the Church to give a colour of Christianity to the ancient heathen rite by substituting the saints for the souls of the dead as the true object of worship? [pg 083] The facts of history seem to countenance this hypothesis. For the feast of All Saints was instituted in France and Germany by order of the Emperor Lewis the Pious in 835 A.D., that is, about a hundred and sixty years before the introduction of the feast of All Souls. The innovation was made by the advice of the pope, Gregory IV., whose motive may well have been that of suppressing an old pagan custom which was still notoriously practised in France and Germany. The idea, however, was not a novel one, for the testimony of Bede proves that in Britain, another Celtic country, the feast of All Saints on the first of November was already celebrated in the eighth century.[172] We may conjecture that this attempt to divert the devotion of the faithful from the souls of the dead to the saints proved a failure, and that finally the Church reluctantly decided to sanction the popular superstition by frankly admitting a feast of All Souls into the calendar. But it could not assign the new, or rather the old, festival to the old day, the first of November, since that was already occupied by the feast of All Saints. Accordingly it placed the mass for the dead on the next day, the second of November. On this theory the feasts of All Saints and of All Souls mark two successive efforts of the Catholic Church to eradicate an old heathen festival of the dead. Both efforts failed. "In all Catholic countries the day of All Souls has preserved the serious character of a festival of the dead which no worldly gaieties are allowed to disturb. It is then the sacred duty of the survivors to visit the graves of their loved ones in the churchyard, to deck them with flowers and lights, and to utter a devout prayer —a pious custom with which in cities like Paris and Vienna even the gay and frivolous comply for the sake of appearance, if not to satisfy an impulse of the heart."[173]

[pg 084]

§ 3. The Festival in the Month of Athyr.

he death and resurrection of Osiris in the month of Athyr. The finding of Osiris.

The foregoing evidence lends some support to the conjecture—for it is only a conjecture—that the great festival of Osiris at Sais, with its accompanying illumination of the houses, was a night of All Souls, when the ghosts of the dead swarmed in the streets and revisited their old homes, which were lit up to welcome them back again. Herodotus, who briefly describes the festival, omits to mention its date, but we can determine it with some probability from other sources. Thus Plutarch tells us that Osiris was murdered on the seventeenth of the month Athyr, and that the Egyptians accordingly observed mournful rites for four days from the seventeenth of Athyr.[174] Now in the Alexandrian calendar, which Plutarch used, these four days corresponded to the thirteenth, fourteenth, fifteenth, and sixteenth of November, and this date answers exactly to the other indications given by Plutarch, who says that at the time of the festival the Nile was sinking, the north winds dying away, the nights lengthening, and the leaves falling from the trees. During these four days a gilt cow swathed in a black pall was exhibited as an image of Isis. [pg 085] This, no doubt, was the image mentioned by Herodotus in his account of the festival.[175] On the nineteenth day of the month the people went down to the sea, the priests carrying a shrine which contained a golden casket. Into this casket they poured fresh water, and thereupon the spectators raised a shout that Osiris was found. After that they took some vegetable mould, moistened it with water, mixed it with precious spices and incense, and moulded the paste into a small moon-shaped image, which was then robed and ornamented.[176] Thus it appears that the purpose of the ceremonies described by Plutarch was to represent dramatically, first, the search for the dead body of Osiris, and, second, its joyful discovery, followed by the resurrection of the dead god who came to life again in the new image of vegetable mould and spices. Lactantius tells us how on these occasions the priests, with their shaven bodies, beat their breasts and lamented, imitating the sorrowful search of Isis for her lost son Osiris, and how afterwards their sorrow was turned to joy when the jackal-headed god Anubis, or rather a mummer in his stead, produced a small boy, the living representative of the god who was lost and was found.[177] Thus Lactantius regarded Osiris as the son instead of the husband of Isis, and he makes no mention of the image of vegetable mould. It is probable that the boy who figured in the sacred drama played the part, not of Osiris, but of his son Horus;[178] but as the death and resurrection of the god were celebrated in many cities of Egypt, it is also possible that in some places the part of the god come to life was played by a living actor instead of by [pg

57

086] an image. Another Christian writer describes how the Egyptians, with shorn heads, annually lamented over a buried idol of Osiris, smiting their breasts, slashing their shoulders, ripping open their old wounds, until, after several days of mourning, they professed to find the mangled remains of the god, at which they rejoiced.[179] However the details of the ceremony may have varied in different places, the pretence of finding the god's body, and probably of restoring it to life, was a great event in the festal year of the Egyptians. The shouts of joy which greeted it are described or alluded to by many ancient writers.[180]

§ 4. The Festival in the Month of Khoiak.

irian inscription at Denderah.

The funeral rites of Osiris, as they were observed at his great festival in the sixteen provinces of Egypt, are described in a long inscription of the Ptolemaic period, which is engraved on the walls of the god's temple at Denderah, the Tentyra of the Greeks, a town of Upper Egypt situated on the western bank of the Nile about forty miles north of Thebes.[181] Unfortunately, while the information thus furnished is remarkably full and minute on many points, the arrangement adopted in the inscription is so confused and the expression often so obscure that a clear and consistent account of the ceremonies as a whole can hardly be extracted from it. Moreover, we learn from the document that the ceremonies varied somewhat in the several cities, the ritual of Abydos, for example, differing from that of Busiris. Without attempting to trace all the particularities of local usage I shall briefly indicate what seem to have been the leading features of the festival, so far as these can be ascertained with tolerable certainty.[182]

[pg 087]

Osiris in the month of Khoiak represented the god as dead, dismembered, and then reconstituted by the scattered limbs.

The rites lasted eighteen days, from the twelfth to the thirtieth of the month Khoiak, and set forth the nature of Osiris in his triple aspect as dead, dismembered, and finally reconstituted by the union of his scattered limbs. In the first of these aspects he was called Chent-Ament (Khenti-Amenti), in the second Osiris-Sep, and in the third Sokari (Seker).[183] Small images of the god were moulded of sand or vegetable earth and corn, to which incense was sometimes added;[184] his face was painted yellow and his cheek-bones green.[185] These images were cast in a mould of pure gold, which represented the god in the form of a mummy, with the white crown of Egypt on his head.[186] The festival opened on the twelfth day of Khoiak with a ceremony of ploughing and sowing. Two black cows were yoked to the plough, which was made of tamarisk wood, while the share was of black copper. A boy scattered the seed. One end of the field was sown with barley, the other with spelt, and the middle with flax. During the operation the chief celebrant recited the ritual chapter of "the sowing of the fields."[187] At Busiris on the twentieth of Khoiak sand and barley were put in the god's [pg 088] "garden," which appears to have been a sort of large flower-pot. This was done in the presence of the cow-goddess Shenty, represented seemingly by the image of a cow made of gilt sycamore wood with a headless human image in its inside. "Then fresh inundation water was poured out of a golden vase over both the goddess and the 'garden' and the barley was allowed to grow as the emblem of the resurrection of the god after his burial in the earth, 'for the growth of the garden is the growth of the divine substance.' "[188] On the twenty-second of Khoiak, at the eighth hour, the images of Osiris, attended by thirty-four images of deities, performed a mysterious voyage in thirty-four tiny boats made of papyrus, which were illuminated by three hundred and sixty-five lights.[189] On the twenty-fourth of Khoiak, after sunset, the effigy of Osiris in a coffin of mulberry wood was laid in the grave, and at the ninth hour of the night the effigy which had been made and deposited the year before was removed and placed upon boughs of sycamore.[190] Lastly, on the thirtieth day of Khoiak they repaired to the holy sepulchre, a subterranean chamber over which appears to have grown a clump of Persea-trees. Entering the vault by the western door, they laid the coffined effigy of the dead god reverently on a bed of sand in the chamber. So they left him to his rest, and departed from the sepulchre by the eastern door. Thus ended the ceremonies in the month of Khoiak.[191]

[pg 089]

§ 5. The Resurrection of Osiris.

In the foregoing account of the festival, drawn from the great inscription of Denderah, the burial of Osiris figures prominently, while his resurrection is implied rather than expressed. This defect of the document, however, is amply compensated by a remarkable series of bas-reliefs which accompany and illustrate the inscription. These exhibit in a series of scenes the dead god lying swathed as a mummy on his bier, then gradually raising himself up higher and higher, until at last he has entirely quitted the bier and is seen erect between the guardian wings of the faithful Isis, who stands behind him, while a male figure holds up before his eyes the *crux ansata*, the Egyptian symbol of life.[192] The resurrection of the god could hardly be portrayed more graphically. Even more instructive, however, is another representation of the same event in a chamber dedicated to Osiris in the great temple of Isis at Philae. Here we see the dead body of Osiris with stalks of corn springing from it, while a priest waters the stalks from a pitcher which he holds in his hand. The accompanying inscription sets forth that "this is the form of him whom one may not name, Osiris of the mysteries, who springs from the returning waters."[193] Taken together, the picture and the words seem to leave no doubt that Osiris was here conceived and represented as a personification of the corn which springs from [pg 090] the fields after they have been fertilized by the inundation. This, according to the inscription, was the kernel of the mysteries, the innermost secret revealed to the initiated. So in the rites of Demeter at Eleusis a reaped ear of corn was exhibited to the worshippers as the central mystery of their religion.[194] We can now fully understand why at the great festival of sowing in the month of Khoiak the priests used to bury effigies of Osiris made of earth and corn. When these effigies were taken up again at the end of a year or of a shorter interval, the corn would be found to have sprouted from the body of Osiris, and this sprouting of the grain would be hailed as an omen, or rather as the cause, of the growth of the crops.[195] The corn-god produced the corn from himself: he gave his own body to feed the people: he died that they might live.

And from the death and resurrection of their great god the Egyptians drew not only their support and sustenance in this life, but also their hope of a life eternal beyond the grave. This hope is indicated in the clearest manner by the very remarkable effigies of Osiris which have come to light in Egyptian cemeteries. Thus in the Valley of the Kings at Thebes there was found the tomb of a royal fan-bearer who lived about 1500 B.C. Among the rich contents of the tomb there was a bier on which rested a mattress of reeds covered with three layers of linen. On the upper side of the linen was painted a life-size figure of Osiris; and the interior of the figure, which was waterproof, contained a mixture of vegetable mould, barley, and a sticky fluid. The barley had sprouted and sent out shoots two or three inches long.[196] Again, in the cemetery at Cynopolis "were numerous burials of Osiris figures. These were made of grain wrapped up in cloth and roughly shaped like an Osiris, and placed inside a bricked-up recess at the side of the tomb, sometimes [pg 091] in small pottery coffins, sometimes in wooden coffins in the form of a hawk-mummy, sometimes without any coffins at all."[197] These corn-stuffed figures were bandaged like mummies with patches of gilding here and there, as if in imitation of the golden mould in which the similar figures of Osiris were cast at the festival of sowing.[198] Again, effigies of Osiris, with faces of green wax and their interior full of grain, were found buried near the necropolis of Thebes.[199] Finally, we are told by Professor Erman that between the legs of mummies "there sometimes lies a figure of Osiris made of slime; it is filled with grains of corn, the sprouting of which is intended to signify the resurrection of the god."[200] We cannot doubt that, just as the burial of corn-stuffed images of Osiris in the earth at the festival of sowing was designed to quicken the seed, so the burial of similar images in the grave was meant to quicken the dead, in other words, to ensure their spiritual immortality.

§ 6. Readjustment of Egyptian Festivals.

of Osiris in the months of Athyr and Khoiak seem to have been substantially the same.

The festival of Osiris which Plutarch assigns to the month of Athyr would seem to be identical in substance with the one which the inscription of Denderah assigns to the following month, namely, to Khoiak. Apparently the essence of both festivals was a dramatic representation of the death and resurrection of the god; in both of them Isis was figured by a gilt cow, and Osiris by an image moulded of moist vegetable earth. But if the festivals were the same, why were they held in different months? It is easy to suggest that different towns in Egypt celebrated the festival at different dates. But when we remember that according to the great inscription of Denderah, the authority of which is indisputable, the festival fell in the month of Khoiak in [pg 092] every province of Egypt, we shall be reluctant to suppose that at some one place, or even at a few places, it was exceptionally held in the preceding month of Athyr, and that the usually well-informed Plutarch described the exception as if it had been the rule, of which on this supposition he must have been wholly ignorant. More probably the discrepancy is to be explained by the great change which came over the Egyptian calendar between the date of the inscription and the lifetime of Plutarch. For when the inscription was drawn up in the Ptolemaic age the festivals were dated by the old vague or movable year, and therefore rotated gradually through the whole circle of the seasons; whereas at the time when Plutarch wrote, about the end of the first century, they were seemingly dated by the fixed Alexandrian year, and accordingly had ceased to rotate.[201]

ival of Khoiak may have been transferred to Athyr when the Egyptians adopted the fixed Alexandrian c.

But even if we grant that in Plutarch's day the festivals had become stationary, still this would not explain why the old festival of Khoiak had been transferred to Athyr. In order to understand that transference it seems necessary to suppose that when the Egyptians gave to their months fixed places in the solar year by accepting the Alexandrian system of intercalation, they at the same time transferred the festivals from what may be called their artificial to their natural dates. Under the old system a summer festival was sometimes held in winter and a winter festival in summer; a harvest celebration sometimes fell at the season of sowing, and a sowing celebration at the season of harvest. People might reconcile themselves to such anomalies so long as they knew that they were only temporary, and that in the course of time the festivals would necessarily return to their proper seasons. But it must have been otherwise when they adopted a fixed instead of a movable year, and so arrested the rotation of the festivals for ever. For they could not but be aware that every festival would thenceforth continue to occupy for all time that particular place in the solar year which it chanced to occupy in the year 30 B.C., when the calendar became fixed. If in that particular year it happened, as it might have happened, that the summer [pg 093] festivals were held in winter and the winter festivals in summer, they would always be so held in future; the absurdity and anomaly would never again be rectified as it had been before. This consideration, which could not have escaped intelligent men, must have suggested the advisability of transferring the festivals from the dates at which they chanced to be celebrated in 30 B.C. to the dates at which they ought properly to be celebrated in the course of nature.

ence would be intelligible if we suppose that in 30 B.C. the dates of all the Egyptian festivals were ward by about a month in order to restore them to their natural places in the calendar.

Now what in the year 30 B.C. was the actual amount of discrepancy between the accidental and the natural dates of the festivals? It was a little more than a month. In that year Thoth, the first month of the Egyptian calendar, happened to begin on the twenty-ninth of August,[202] whereas according to theory it should have begun with the heliacal rising of Sirius on the twentieth of July, that is, forty days or, roughly speaking, a month earlier. From this it follows that in the year 30 B.C. all the Egyptian festivals fell about a month later than their natural dates, and they must have continued to fall a month late for ever if they were allowed to retain those places in the calendar which they chanced to occupy in that particular year. In these circumstances it would be a natural and sensible thing to restore the festivals to their proper places in the solar year by celebrating them one calendar month earlier than before.[203] If this measure were adopted the [pg 094] festivals which had hitherto been held, for example, in the third month Athyr would henceforth be held in the second month Phaophi; the festivals which had hitherto fallen in the fourth month Khoiak would thenceforth fall in the third month Athyr; and so on. Thus the festal calendar would be reduced to harmony with the seasons instead of being in more or less flagrant discord with them, as it had generally been before, and must always have been afterwards if the change which I have indicated had not been introduced. It is only to credit the native astronomers and the Roman rulers of Egypt with common sense to suppose that they actually adopted the measure. On that supposition we can perfectly understand why the festival of sowing, which had formerly belonged to the month of Khoiak, was transferred to Athyr. For in the Alexandrian calendar Khoiak corresponds very nearly to December, and Athyr to November. But in Egypt the month of November, not the month of December, is the season of sowing. There was therefore every reason why the great sowing festival of the corn-god Osiris should be held in Athyr and not Khoiak, in November and not in December. In like manner we may suppose that all the Egyptian festivals were restored to their true places in the solar year, and that when Plutarch dates a festival both by its calendar month and by its relation to [pg 095] the cycle of the seasons, he is perfectly right in doing so, and we may accept his evidence with confidence instead of having to accuse him of ignorantly confounding the movable Egyptian with the fixed Alexandrian year. Accusations of ignorance levelled at the best writers of antiquity are apt to recoil on those who make them.[204]

Chapter V. The Nature of Osiris.
§ 1. Osiris a Corn-God.

e of his aspects a personification of the corn. Osiris a child of Sky and Earth. The legend of the
ent of Osiris points to the dismemberment of human beings, perhaps of the kings, in the character of the

The foregoing survey of the myth and ritual of Osiris may suffice to prove
that in one of his aspects the god was a personification of the corn, which may
be said to die and come to life again every year. Through all the pomp and
glamour with which in later times the priests had invested his worship, the
conception of him as the corn-god comes clearly out in the festival of his
death and resurrection, which was celebrated in the month of Khoiak and at a
later period in the month of Athyr. That festival appears to have been
essentially a festival of sowing, which properly fell at the time when the
husbandman actually committed the seed to the earth. On that occasion an
effigy of the corn-god, moulded of earth and corn, was buried with funeral
rites in the ground in order that, dying there, he might come to life again with
the new crops. The ceremony was, in fact, a charm to ensure the growth of the
corn by sympathetic magic, and we may conjecture that as such it was
practised in a simple form by every Egyptian farmer on his fields long before
it was adopted and transfigured by the priests in the stately ritual of the
temple. In the modern, but doubtless ancient, Arab custom of burying "the
Old Man," namely, a sheaf of wheat, in the harvest-field and praying that he
may return from the dead,[205] we see the germ out of which the worship of the
corn-god Osiris was probably developed. [pg 097] Earth.[206] What more
appropriate parentage could be invented for the corn which springs from the
ground that has been fertilized by the water of heaven? It is true that the land
of Egypt owed its fertility directly to the Nile and not to showers; but the
inhabitants must have known or guessed that the great river in its turn was fed
by the rains which fell in the far interior. Again, the legend that Osiris was the
first to teach men the use of corn[207] would be most naturally told of the corn-
god himself. Further, the story that his mangled remains were scattered up and
down the land and buried in different places may be a mythical way of
expressing either the sowing or the winnowing of the grain. The latter
interpretation is supported by the tale that Isis placed the severed limbs of
Osiris on a corn-sieve.[208] Or more probably the legend may be a reminiscence
of a custom of slaying a human victim, perhaps a representative of the corn-
spirit, and distributing his flesh or scattering his ashes over the fields to
fertilize them. In modern Europe the figure of Death is sometimes torn in
pieces, and the fragments are then buried in the ground to make the crops

grow well,[209] and in other parts of the world human victims are treated in the same way.[210] With regard to the ancient Egyptians we have it on the authority of Manetho that they used to burn red-haired men and scatter their ashes with winnowing fans,[211] and it is highly significant that this barbarous sacrifice was offered by the kings at the grave of Osiris.[212] We may conjecture that the victims represented Osiris himself, who was annually slain, dismembered, and buried in their persons that he might quicken the seed in the earth.

Greek traditions of the dismemberment of kings. Modern Thracian pretence of killing a man, who is alled a king, for the good of the crops.

Possibly in prehistoric times the kings themselves [pg 098] played the part of the god and were slain and dismembered in that character. Set as well as Osiris is said to have been torn in pieces after a reign of eighteen days, which was commemorated by an annual festival of the same length.[213] According to one story Romulus, the first king of Rome, was cut in pieces by the senators, who buried the fragments of him in the ground;[214] and the traditional day of his death, the seventh of July, was celebrated with certain curious rites, which were apparently connected with the artificial fertilization of the fig.[215] Again, Greek legend told how Pentheus, king of Thebes, and Lycurgus, king of the Thracian Edonians, opposed the vine-god Dionysus, and how the impious monarchs were rent in pieces, the one by the frenzied Bacchanals, the other by horses.[216] These Greek traditions may well be distorted reminiscences of a custom of sacrificing human beings, and especially divine kings, in the character of Dionysus, a god who resembled Osiris in many points and was said like him to have been torn limb from limb.[217] We are told that in Chios men were rent in pieces [pg 099] as a sacrifice to Dionysus;[218] and since they died the same death as their god, it is reasonable to suppose that they personated him. The story that the Thracian Orpheus was similarly torn limb from limb by the Bacchanals seems to indicate that he too perished in the character of the god whose death he died.[219] It is significant that the Thracian Lycurgus, king of the Edonians, is said to have been put to death in order that the ground, which had ceased to be fruitful, might regain its fertility.[220] In some Thracian villages at Carnival time a custom is still annually observed, which may well be a mitigation of an ancient practice of putting a man, perhaps a king, to death in the character of Dionysus for the sake of the crops. A man disguised in goatskins and fawnskins, the livery of Dionysus, is shot at and falls down as dead. A pretence is made of flaying his body and of mourning over him, but afterwards he comes to life again. Further, a plough is dragged about the village and seed is scattered, while prayers are said that the wheat, rye, and barley may be plentiful. One town (Viza), where these customs are observed, was the capital of the old Thracian kings. In another town (Kosti, near the Black Sea) the principal masker is called the king. He wears goatskins or sheepskins, and is attended by a boy who dispenses wine to the people. The king himself carries seed, which he casts on the ground before the church, after being invited to throw it on two [pg 100] bands of married and unmarried men respectively. Finally, he is stripped of the skins and thrown into the river.[221]

radition of the dismemberment of a king, Halfdan the Black. Frey, the Scandinavian god of fertility, sala.

Further, we read of a Norwegian king, Halfdan the Black, whose body was cut up and buried in different parts of his kingdom for the sake of ensuring the fruitfulness of the earth. He is said to have been drowned at the age of forty through the breaking of the ice in spring. What followed his death is thus related by the old Norse historian Snorri Sturluson: "He had been the most prosperous (literally, blessed with abundance) of all kings. So greatly did men value him that when the news came that he was dead and his body removed to Hringariki and intended for burial there, the chief men from Raumariki and Westfold and Heithmörk came and all requested that they might take his body with them and bury it in their various provinces; they thought that it would bring abundance to those who obtained it. Eventually it was settled that the body was distributed in four places. The head was laid in a barrow at Steinn in Hringariki, and each party took away their own share and buried it. All these barrows are called Halfdan's barrows."[222] It should be remembered that this Halfdan belonged to the family of the Ynglings, who traced their descent from Frey, the great Scandinavian god of fertility.[223] Frey himself is said to have reigned as king of Sweden at Upsala. The years of his reign were plenteous, and the people laid the plenty to his account. So when he [pg 101] died, they would not burn him, as it had been customary to do with the dead before his time; but they resolved to preserve his body, believing that, so long as it remained in Sweden, the land would have abundance and peace. Therefore they reared a great mound, and put him in it, and sacrificed to him for plenty and peace ever afterwards. And for three years after his death they poured the tribute to him into the mound, as if he were alive; the gold they poured in by one window, the silver by a second, and the copper by a third.[224]

gician of Kiwai, said to have been cut up after death and the pieces buried in gardens to fertilize them.

The natives of Kiwai, an island lying off the mouth of the Fly River in British New Guinea, tell of a certain magician named Segera, who had sago for his totem. When his son died, the death was set down to the magic of an enemy, and the bereaved father was so angry that by his spells he caused the whole crop of sago in the country to fail; only in his own garden the sago grew as luxuriantly as ever. When many had died of famine, the people went to him and begged him to remove the spells which he had cast on the sago palms, so that they might eat food and live. The magician, touched with remorse and pity, went round planting a sago shoot in every garden, and the shoots flourished, sago was plentiful once more, and the famine came to an end. When Segera was old and ill, he told the people that he would soon die, but that, nevertheless, he would cause their gardens to thrive. Accordingly, he instructed them that when he was dead they should cut him up and place pieces of his flesh in their gardens, but his head was to be buried in his own garden. Of him it is said that he outlived the ordinary age, and that no man knew his father, but that he made the sago good and no one was hungry any more. Old men who were alive a few years ago affirmed that they had known Segera in their youth, and the general opinion of the Kiwai people seems to be that Segera died not more than two generations ago.[225]

widespread custom of dismembering a king or magician and burying the pieces in different parts of the

Taken all together, these legends point to a widespread practice of dismembering the body of a king or magician [pg 102] and burying the pieces in different parts of the country in order to ensure the fertility of the ground and probably also the fecundity of man and beast. Whether regarded as the descendant of a god, as himself divine, or simply as a mighty enchanter, the king was believed to radiate magical virtue for the good of his subjects, quickening the seed in the earth and in the womb. This radiation of reproductive energy did not cease with his life; hence the people deemed it essential to preserve his body as a pledge of the continued prosperity of the country. It would be natural to imagine that the spot where the dead king was buried would enjoy a more than ordinary share of his blessed influence, and accordingly disputes would almost inevitably arise between different districts for the exclusive possession of so powerful a talisman. These disputes could be settled and local jealousies appeased by dividing the precious body between the rival claimants, in order that all should benefit in equal measure by its life-giving properties. This was certainly done in Norway with the body of Halfdan the Black, the descendant of the harvest-god Frey; it appears to have been done with the body of Segera, the sago-magician of Kiwai; and we may conjecture that in prehistoric times it was done with the bodies of Egyptian kings, who personated Osiris, the god of fertility in general and of the corn in particular. At least such a practice would account for the legend of the mangling of the god's body and the distribution of the pieces throughout Egypt.

mberment a special virtue seems to have been ascribed to the genital organs.

In this connexion the story that the genital member of Osiris was missing when Isis pieced together his mutilated body,[226] may not be without significance. When a Zulu medicine-man wishes to make the crops grow well, he will take the body of a man who has died in full vigour and cut minute portions of tissue from the foot, the leg, the arm, the face, and the nail of a

69

single finger in order to compound a fertilizing medicine out of them. But the most important part of the medicine consists of the dead man's generative organs, which are removed entire. All these pieces of the corpse are fried with herbs [pg 103] on a slow fire, then ground to powder, and sown over the fields.[227] We have seen that similarly the Egyptians scattered the ashes of human victims by means of winnowing-fans;[228] and if my explanation of the practice is correct, it may well have been that they, like the Zulus, attributed a special power of reproduction to the genital organs, and therefore carefully excised them from the body of the victim in order to impart their virtue to the fields. I have conjectured that a similar use was made of the severed portions of the priests of Attis.[229]

n kings probably opposed the custom and succeeded in abolishing it. Precautions taken to preserve the gs from mutilation.

To an ancient Egyptian, with his firm belief in a personal immortality dependent on the integrity of the body, the prospect of mutilation after death must have been very repugnant; and we may suppose that the kings offered a strenuous resistance to the custom and finally succeeded in abolishing it. They may have represented to the people that they would attain their object better by keeping the royal corpse intact than by frittering it away in small pieces. Their subjects apparently acquiesced in the argument, or at all events in the conclusion; yet the mountains of masonry beneath which the old Egyptian kings lay buried may have been intended to guard them from the superstitious devotion of their friends quite as much as from the hostile designs of their enemies, since both alike must have been under a strong temptation to violate the sanctity of the grave in order to possess themselves of bodies which were believed to be endowed with magical virtue of the most tremendous potency. In antiquity the safety of the state was often believed to depend on the possession of a talisman, which sometimes consisted of the bones of a king or hero. Hence the graves of such persons were sometimes kept secret.[230] The violation of royal tombs by a conqueror was not a mere insult: it was a deadly blow struck at the prosperity of the kingdom. Hence Ashurbanipal carried off to Assyria the bones of the kings of Elam, believing that thus he gave their shades no repose and deprived them of food and [pg 104] drink.[231] The Moabites burned the bones of the king of Edom into lime.[232] Lysimachus is said to have opened the graves of the kings of Epirus and scattered the bones of the dead.[233]

ings and chiefs in Africa kept secret. Burial-place of chiefs in Fiji kept secret. Graves of Melanesian ept secret.

With savage and barbarous tribes in like manner it is not unusual to violate the sanctity of the tomb either for the purpose of wreaking vengeance on the dead or more commonly perhaps for the sake of gaining possession of the bones and converting them to magical uses. Hence the Mpongwe kings of the Gaboon region in West Africa are buried secretly lest their heads should fall into the hands of men of another tribe, who would make a powerful fetish out of the brains.[234] Again, in Togoland, West Africa, the kings of the Ho tribe are buried with great secrecy in the forest, and a false grave is made ostentatiously in the king's house. None but his personal retainers and a single daughter know where the king's real grave is. The intention of this secret burial is to prevent enemies from digging up the corpse and cutting off the head.[235] "The heads of important chiefs in the Calabar districts are usually cut off from the body on burial and kept secretly for fear the head, and thereby the spirit, of the dead chief, should be stolen from the town. If it were stolen it would be not only a great advantage to its new possessor, but a great danger to the chief's old town, because he would know all the peculiar ju-ju relating to it. For each town has a peculiar one, kept exceedingly secret, in addition to the general ju-jus, and this secret one would then be in the hands of the new owners of the spirit."[236] The graves of Basuto chiefs are kept secret lest certain more or less imaginary witches and wizards called *Baloi*, who haunt tombs, should get possession of the bones and work evil magic with them.[237] In the Thonga tribe of South Africa, [pg 105] when a chief dies, he is buried secretly by night in a sacred wood, and few people know the place of the grave. With some clans of the tribe it is customary to level the mound over the grave so that no sign whatever remains to show where the body has been buried. This is said to be done lest enemies should exhume the corpse and cut off the ears, the diaphragm, and other parts in order to make powerful war-charms out of them.[238] By many tribes in Fiji "the burial-place of their chief is kept a profound secret, lest those whom he injured during his lifetime should revenge themselves by digging up and insulting or even eating his body. In some places the dead chief is buried in his own house, and armed warriors of his mother's kin keep watch night and day over his grave. After a time his bones are taken up and carried by night to some far-away inaccessible cave in the mountains, whose position is known only to a few trustworthy men. Ladders are constructed to enable them to reach the cave, and are taken down when the bones have been deposited there. Many frightful stories are told in connection with this custom, and it is certain that not even decomposition itself avails to baulk the last revenge of cannibals if they can find the grave. The very bones of the dead chief are not secure from the revenge of those whose friends he killed during his lifetime, or whom he otherwise so exasperated by the tyrannous exercise of his power as to fill their hearts with a deadly hate. In one instance within my own knowledge, when the hiding-place was discovered, the bones were taken away, scraped, and stewed down into a horrible hell-broth."[239] When a Melanesian dies who enjoyed a reputation for magical powers in his lifetime, his friends will sometimes hold a sham burial and keep the real grave secret for fear that men might come and dig up the skull and bones to make charms with them.[240]

[pg 106]

Koniags of Alaska the bodies of dead whalers were cut up and used as talismans.

Beliefs and practices of this sort are by no means confined to agricultural peoples. Among the Koniags of Alaska "in ancient times the pursuit of the whale was accompanied by numerous superstitious observances kept a secret by the hunters. Lieutenant Davidof states that the whalers preserved the bodies of brave or distinguished men in secluded caves, and before proceeding upon a whale-hunt would carry these dead bodies into a stream and then drink of the water thus tainted. One famous whaler of Kadiak who desired to flatter Baranof, the first chief manager of the Russian colonies, said to him, 'When you die I shall try to steal your body,' intending thus to express his great respect for Baranof. On the occasion of the death of a whaler his fellows would cut the body into pieces, each man taking one of them for the purpose of rubbing his spear-heads therewith. These pieces were dried or otherwise preserved, and were frequently taken into the canoes as talismans."[241]

of human victims to the corn.

To return to the human victims whose ashes the Egyptians scattered with winnowing-fans,[242] the red hair of these unfortunates was probably significant. If I am right, the custom of sacrificing such persons was not a mere way of wreaking a national spite on fair-haired foreigners, whom the black-haired Egyptians of old, like the black-haired Chinese of modern times, may have regarded as red-haired devils. For in Egypt the oxen which were sacrificed had also to be red; a single black or white hair found on the beast would have disqualified it for the sacrifice.[243] If, as I conjecture, these human sacrifices were intended to promote the growth of the crops—and the winnowing of their ashes seems to support this view—red-haired victims were perhaps selected as best fitted to personate the spirit of the ruddy grain. For when a god is represented by a living person, it is natural that the human representative should be chosen on the ground of his supposed resemblance to the divine original. [pg 107] Hence the ancient Mexicans, conceiving the maize as a personal being who went through the whole course of life between seed-time and harvest, sacrificed new-born babes when the maize was sown, older children when it had sprouted, and so on till it was fully ripe, when they sacrificed old men.[244] A name for Osiris was the "crop" or "harvest";[245] and the ancients sometimes explained him as a personification of the corn.[246]

§ 2. Osiris a Tree-Spirit.

But Osiris was more than a spirit of the corn; he was also a tree-spirit, and this may perhaps have been his primitive character, since the worship of trees is naturally older in the history of religion than the worship of the cereals. However that may have been, to an agricultural people like the Egyptians, who depended almost wholly on their crops, the corn-god was naturally a far more important [pg 108] personage than the tree-god, and attracted a larger share of their devotion. The character of Osiris as a tree-spirit was represented very graphically in a ceremony described by Firmicus Maternus.[247] A pine-tree having been cut down, the centre was hollowed out, and with the wood thus excavated an image of Osiris was made, which was then buried like a corpse in the hollow of the tree. It is hard to imagine how the conception of a tree as tenanted by a personal being could be more plainly expressed. The image of Osiris thus made was kept for a year and then burned, exactly as was done with the image of Attis which was attached to the pine-tree.[248] The ceremony of cutting the tree, as described by Firmicus Maternus, appears to be alluded to by Plutarch.[249] It was probably the ritual counterpart of the mythical discovery of the body of Osiris enclosed in the *erica*-tree.[250]

Now we know from the monuments that at Busiris, Memphis, and elsewhere the great festival of Osiris closed on the thirtieth of Khoiak with the setting up of a remarkable pillar known as the *tatu, tat, tet, dad,* or *ded.* This was a column with four or five cross-bars, like superposed capitals, at the top. The whole roughly resembled a telegraph-post with the cross-pieces which support the wires. Sometimes on the monuments a human form is given to the pillar by carving a grotesque face on it, robing the lower part, crowning the top with the symbols of Osiris, and adding two arms which hold two other characteristic emblems of the god, the crook and the scourge or flail. On a Theban tomb the king himself, assisted by his relations and a priest, is represented hauling at the ropes by which the pillar is being raised, while the queen looks on and her sixteen daughters accompany the ceremony with the music of rattles and sistrums. Again, in the hall of the Osirian mysteries at Abydos the King Sety I. and the goddess Isis are depicted raising the column between them. In Egyptian theology the pillar was interpreted as the backbone of Osiris, and whatever its meaning [pg 109] may have been, it was one of the holiest symbols of the national religion. It might very well be a conventional way of representing a tree stripped of its leaves; and if Osiris was a tree-spirit, the bare trunk and branches might naturally be described as his backbone. The setting up of the column would thus, as several modern scholars believe, shadow forth the resurrection of the god, and the importance of the occasion would explain and justify the prominent part which the king appears to have taken in the ceremony.[251] It is to be noted that in the myth of Osiris the *erica*-tree which shot up and enclosed his dead body, was cut down by a king and turned by him into a pillar of his house.[252] We can hardly doubt, therefore, that this incident of the legend was supposed to be dramatically set forth in the erection of the *ded* column by the king. Like the similar custom of cutting a pine-tree and fastening an image to it in the rites of Attis, the ceremony may have belonged to that class of customs of which the bringing in of the May-pole is among the most familiar. The association of the king and queen of Egypt with the *ded* pillar reminds us of the association of a King and Queen of May with the May-pole.[253] The resemblance may be more than superficial.

[pg 110]

ated with the pine, the sycamore, the tamarisk, and the acacia.

In the hall of Osiris at Denderah the coffin containing the hawk-headed mummy of the god is clearly depicted as enclosed within a tree, apparently a conifer, the trunk and branches of which are seen above and below the coffin.[254] The scene thus corresponds closely both to the myth and to the ceremony described by Firmicus Maternus. In another scene at Denderah a tree of the same sort is represented growing between the dead and the reviving Osiris, as if on purpose to indicate that the tree was the symbol of the divine resurrection.[255] A pine-cone often appears on the monuments as an offering presented to Osiris, and a manuscript of the Louvre speaks of the cedar as sprung from him.[256] The sycamore and the tamarisk were also his trees. In inscriptions he is spoken of as residing in them;[257] and in tombs his mother Nut is often portrayed standing in the midst of a sycamore-tree and pouring a libation for the benefit of the dead.[258] In one of the Pyramid Texts we read, "Hail to thee, Sycamore, which enclosest the god";[259] and in certain temples the statue of Osiris used to be placed for seven days upon branches of sycamores. The explanation appended in the sacred texts declares that the placing of the image on the tree was intended to recall the seven months passed by Osiris in the womb of his mother Nut, the goddess of the sycamore.[260] The rite recalls the story that Adonis was born after ten months' gestation from a myrrh-tree.[261] Further, in a sepulchre at How (Diospolis Parva) a tamarisk is depicted overshadowing the tomb of Osiris, while a bird is perched among the branches with the significant legend "the soul of Osiris,"[262] [pg 111] showing that the spirit of the dead god was believed to

74

haunt his sacred tree.[263] Again, in the series of sculptures which illustrate the mystic history of Osiris in the great temple of Isis at Philae, a tamarisk is figured with two men pouring water on it. The accompanying inscription leaves no doubt, says Brugsch, that the verdure of the earth was believed to be connected with the verdure of the tree, and that the sculpture refers to the grave of Osiris at Philae, of which Plutarch tells us that it was overshadowed by a *methide* plant, taller than any olive-tree. This sculpture, it may be observed, occurs in the same chamber in which the god is represented as a corpse with ears of corn springing from him.[264] In inscriptions he is referred to as "the one in the tree," "the solitary one in the acacia," and so forth.[265] On the monuments he sometimes appears as a mummy covered with a tree or with plants;[266] and trees are represented growing from his grave.[267]

tion to fruit-trees, wells, the vine, and ivy.

It accords with the character of Osiris as a tree-spirit that his worshippers were forbidden to injure fruit-trees, and with his character as a god of vegetation in general that they were not allowed to stop up wells of water, which are so important for the irrigation of hot southern lands.[268] [pg 112] According to one legend, he taught men to train the vine to poles, to prune its superfluous foliage, and to extract the juice of the grape.[269] In the papyrus of Nebseni, written about 1550 B.C., Osiris is depicted sitting in a shrine, from the roof of which hang clusters of grapes;[270] and in the papyrus of the royal scribe Nekht we see the god enthroned in front of a pool, from the banks of which a luxuriant vine, with many bunches of grapes, grows towards the green face of the seated deity.[271] The ivy was sacred to him, and was called his plant because it is always green.[272]

§ 3. Osiris a God of Fertility.

As a god of vegetation Osiris was naturally conceived as a god of creative energy in general, since men at a certain stage of evolution fail to distinguish between the reproductive powers of animals and of plants. Hence a striking feature in his worship was the coarse but expressive symbolism by which this aspect of his nature was presented to the eye not merely of the initiated but of the multitude. At his festival women used to go about the villages singing songs in his praise and carrying obscene images of him which they set in motion by means of strings.[273] The custom was probably a charm to ensure the growth of the crops. A similar image of him, decked with all the fruits of the earth, is said to have stood in a temple before a figure of Isis,[274] and in the chambers dedicated to him at Philae the dead god is portrayed lying on his bier in an attitude which indicates in the plainest way that even in death his generative virtue was not extinct but only suspended, ready to prove a source of life and fertility to the world when the opportunity should offer.[275] Hymns [pg 113] addressed to Osiris contain allusions to this important side of his nature. In one of them it is said that the world waxes green in triumph through him; and another declares, "Thou art the father and mother of mankind, they live on thy breath, they subsist on the flesh of thy body."[276] We may conjecture that in this paternal aspect he was supposed, like other gods of fertility, to bless men and women with offspring, and that the processions at his festival were intended to promote this object as well as to quicken the seed in the ground. It would be to misjudge ancient religion to denounce as lewd and profligate the emblems and the ceremonies which the Egyptians employed for the purpose of giving effect to this conception of the divine power. The ends which they proposed to themselves in these rites were natural and laudable; only the means they adopted to compass them were mistaken. A similar fallacy induced the Greeks to adopt a like symbolism in their Dionysiac festivals, and the superficial but striking resemblance thus produced between the two religions has perhaps more than anything else misled inquirers, both ancient and modern, into identifying worships which, though certainly akin in nature, are perfectly distinct and independent in origin.[277]

§ 4. Osiris a God of the Dead.

We have seen that in one of his aspects Osiris was the ruler and judge of the dead.[278] To a people like the Egyptians, who not only believed in a life beyond the grave but actually spent much of their time, labour, and money in preparing for it, this office of the god must have appeared hardly, if at all, less important than his function of making the earth to bring forth its fruits in due season. We may assume that in the faith of his worshippers the two provinces of the [pg 114] god were intimately connected. In laying their dead in the grave they committed them to his keeping who could raise them from the dust to life eternal, even as he caused the seed to spring from the ground. Of that faith the corn-stuffed effigies of Osiris found in Egyptian tombs furnish an eloquent and unequivocal testimony.[279] They were at once an emblem and an instrument of resurrection. Thus from the sprouting of the grain the ancient Egyptians drew an augury of human immortality. They are not the only people who have built the same far-reaching hopes on the same slender foundation. "Thou fool, that which thou sowest, thou sowest not that body that shall be, but bare grain, it may chance of wheat, or of some other grain: but God giveth it a body as it hath pleased him, and to every seed his own body. So also is the resurrection of the dead. It is sown in corruption; it is raised in incorruption: it is sown in weakness; it is raised in power: it is sown a natural body; it is raised a spiritual body."[280]

A god who thus fed his people with his own broken body in this life, and who held out to them a promise of a blissful eternity in a better world hereafter, naturally reigned supreme in their affections. We need not wonder, therefore, that in Egypt the worship of the other gods was overshadowed by that of Osiris, and that while they were revered each in his own district, he and his divine partner Isis were adored in all.[281]

[pg 115]

Chapter VI. Isis.

attributes of Isis.

The original meaning of the goddess Isis is still more difficult to determine than that of her brother and husband Osiris. Her attributes and epithets were so numerous that in the hieroglyphics she is called "the many-named," "the thousand-named," and in Greek inscriptions "the myriad-named."[282] The late eminent Dutch scholar C. P. Tiele confessed candidly that "it is now impossible to tell precisely to what natural phenomena the character of Isis at first referred." Yet he adds, "Originally she was a goddess of fecundity."[283] Similarly Dr. Budge writes that "Isis was the great and beneficent goddess and mother, whose influence and love pervaded all heaven and earth and the abode of the dead, and she was the personification of the great feminine, creative power which conceived, and brought forth every living creature and thing, from the gods in heaven to man on the earth, and to the insect on the ground; what she brought forth she protected, and cared for, and fed, and nourished, and she employed her life in using her power graciously and successfully, not only in creating new beings but in restoring those that were dead. She was, besides these things, the highest type of a faithful and loving wife [pg 116] and mother, and it was in this capacity that the Egyptians honoured and worshipped her most."[284]

embled yet differed from the Mother Goddesses of Asia. Isis perhaps originally a goddess of the corn.

Thus in her character of a goddess of fecundity Isis answered to the great mother goddesses of Asia, though she differed from them in the chastity and fidelity of her conjugal life; for while they were unmarried and dissolute, she had a husband and was a true wife to him as well as an affectionate mother to their son. Hence her beautiful Madonna-like figure reflects a more refined state of society and of morals than the coarse, sensual, cruel figures of Astarte, Anaitis, Cybele, and the rest of that crew. A clear trace, indeed, of an ethical standard very different from our own lingers in her double relation of sister and wife to Osiris; but in most other respects she is rather late than primitive, the full-blown flower rather than the seed of a long religious development. The attributes ascribed to her were too various to be all her own. They were graces borrowed from many lesser deities, sweets rifled from a thousand humbler plants to feed the honey of her superb efflorescence. Yet in her complex nature it is perhaps still possible to detect the original nucleus round which by a slow process of accretion the other elements gathered. For if her brother and husband Osiris was in one of his aspects the corn-god, as we have seen reason to believe, she must surely have been the corn-goddess. There are at least some grounds for thinking so. For if we may trust Diodorus Siculus, whose authority appears to have been the Egyptian historian Manetho, the discovery of wheat and barley was attributed to Isis, and at her festivals stalks of these grains were carried in procession to commemorate the boon she had conferred on men.[285] A further detail is added by Augustine. He says that Isis made the discovery of barley at the moment when she was sacrificing to the common ancestors of her husband and herself, all of whom had been kings, and that she showed the newly discovered ears of barley to Osiris and his councillor Thoth or Mercury, as Roman writers called him. That is why, [pg 117] adds Augustine, they identify Isis with Ceres.[286] Further, at harvest-time, when the Egyptian reapers had cut the first stalks, they laid them down and beat their breasts, wailing and calling upon Isis.[287] The custom has been already explained as a lament for the corn-spirit slain under the sickle.[288] Amongst the epithets by which Isis is designated in the inscriptions are "Creatress of green things," "Green goddess, whose green colour is like unto the greenness of the earth," "Lady of Bread," "Lady of Beer," "Lady of Abundance."[289] According to Brugsch she is "not only the creatress of the fresh verdure of vegetation which covers the earth, but is actually the green corn-field itself, which is personified as a goddess."[290] This is confirmed by her epithet *Sochit* or *Sochet*, meaning "a corn-field," a sense which the word still retains in Coptic.[291] The Greeks conceived of Isis as a corn-goddess, for they identified her with Demeter.[292] In a Greek epigram she is described as "she who has given birth to the fruits of the earth," and "the mother of the ears of corn";[293] and in a hymn composed in her honour she speaks of herself as "queen of the wheat-field," and is described as "charged with the care of the fruitful furrow's wheat-rich path."[294] Accordingly, Greek or Roman artists often represented her with ears of corn on her head or in her hand.[295]

and spiritualization of Isis in later times: the popularity of her worship in the Roman empire.
e of Isis to the Madonna.

Such, we may suppose, was Isis in the olden time, a rustic Corn-Mother adored with uncouth rites by Egyptian swains. But the homely features of the clownish goddess could hardly be traced in the refined, the saintly form which, spiritualized by ages of religious evolution, she presented to her worshippers of after days as the true wife, the tender [pg 118] mother, the beneficent queen of nature, encircled with the nimbus of moral purity, of immemorial and mysterious sanctity. Thus chastened and transfigured she won many hearts far beyond the boundaries of her native land. In that welter of religions which accompanied the decline of national life in antiquity her worship was one of the most popular at Rome and throughout the empire. Some of the Roman emperors themselves were openly addicted to it.[296] And however the religion of Isis may, like any other, have been often worn as a cloak by men and women of loose life, her rites appear on the whole to have been honourably distinguished by a dignity and composure, a solemnity and decorum well fitted to soothe the troubled mind, to ease the burdened heart. They appealed therefore to gentle spirits, and above all to women, whom the bloody and licentious rites of other Oriental goddesses only shocked and repelled. We need not wonder, then, that in a period of decadence, when traditional faiths were shaken, when systems clashed, when men's minds were disquieted, when the fabric of empire itself, once deemed eternal, began to show ominous rents and fissures, the serene figure of Isis with her spiritual calm, her gracious promise of immortality, should have appeared to many like a star in a stormy sky, and should have roused in their breasts a rapture of devotion not unlike that which was paid in the Middle Ages to the Virgin Mary. Indeed her stately ritual, with its shaven and tonsured priests, its matins and vespers, its tinkling music, its baptism and aspersions of holy water, its solemn processions, its jewelled images of the Mother of God, presented many points of similarity to the pomps and ceremonies of Catholicism.[297] The resemblance need not be purely accidental. [pg 119] Ancient Egypt may have contributed its share to the gorgeous symbolism of the Catholic Church as well as to the pale abstractions of her theology.[298] Certainly in art the figure of Isis suckling the infant Horus is so like that of the Madonna and child that it has sometimes received the adoration of ignorant Christians.[299] And to Isis in her later character of patroness of mariners the Virgin Mary perhaps owes her beautiful epithet of *Stella Maris*, "Star of the Sea," under which she is adored by tempest-tossed sailors.[300] The attributes of a marine deity may have been bestowed on Isis by the sea-faring Greeks of Alexandria. They are quite foreign to her original character and to the habits of the Egyptians, who had no love of the sea.[301] On this hypothesis Sirius, the bright star of Isis, which on July mornings rises from the glassy waves of the eastern Mediterranean, a harbinger of halcyon weather to mariners, was the true *Stella Maris*, "the Star of the Sea."

[pg 120]

Chapter VII. Osiris and the Sun.

Osiris has been sometimes interpreted as the sun-god; and in modern times this view has been held by so many distinguished writers that it deserves a brief examination. If we inquire on what evidence Osiris has been identified with the sun or the sun-god, it will be found on analysis to be minute in quantity and dubious, where it is not absolutely worthless, in quality. The diligent Jablonski, the first modern scholar to collect and sift the testimony of classical writers on Egyptian religion, says that it can be shown in many ways that Osiris is the sun, and that he could produce a cloud of witnesses to prove it, but that it is needless to do so, since no learned man is ignorant of the fact.[302] Of the writers whom he condescends to quote, the only two who expressly identify Osiris with the sun are Diodorus and Macrobius. The passage in Diodorus runs thus:[303] "It is said that the aboriginal inhabitants of Egypt, looking up to the sky, and smitten with awe and wonder at the nature of the universe, supposed that there were two gods, eternal and primaeval, the sun and the moon, of whom they named the sun Osiris and the moon Isis." Even if Diodorus's authority for this statement is Manetho, as there is some ground for believing,[304] little or no weight can be attached to it. For it is plainly a philosophical, and therefore a late, explanation of the first beginnings of Egyptian religion, reminding us of Kant's familiar saying about the starry heavens and the moral law rather than of the [pg 121] rude traditions of a primitive people. Jablonski's second authority, Macrobius, is no better, but rather worse. For Macrobius was the father of that large family of mythologists who resolve all or most gods into the sun. According to him Mercury was the sun, Mars was the sun, Janus was the sun, Saturn was the sun, so was Jupiter, also Nemesis, likewise Pan, and so on through a great part of the pantheon.[305] It was natural, therefore, that he should identify Osiris with the sun,[306] but his reasons for doing so are exceedingly slight. He refers to the ceremonies of alternate lamentation and joy as if they reflected the vicissitudes of the great luminary in his course through the sky. Further, he argues that Osiris must be the sun because an eye was one of his symbols. It is true that an eye was a symbol of Osiris,[307] and it is also true that the sun was often called "the eye of Horus";[308] yet the coincidence hardly suffices to establish the identity of the two deities. The opinion that Osiris was the sun is also mentioned, but not accepted, by Plutarch,[309] and it is referred to by Firmicus Maternus.[310]

81

Amongst modern scholars, Lepsius, in identifying Osiris with the sun, appears to rely mainly on the passage of Diodorus already quoted. But the monuments, he adds, also show "that down to a late time Osiris was sometimes conceived as *Ra*. In this quality he is named *Osiris-Ra* [pg 122] even in the 'Book of the Dead,' and Isis is often called 'the royal consort of Ra.' "[311] That Ra was both the physical sun and the sun-god is undisputed; but with every deference for the authority of so great a scholar as Lepsius, we may doubt whether the identification of Osiris with Ra can be accepted as proof that Osiris was originally the sun. For the religion of ancient Egypt[312] may be described as a confederacy of local cults which, while maintaining against each other a certain measure of jealous and even hostile independence, were yet constantly subjected to the fusing and amalgamating influence of political centralization and philosophic thought. The history of the religion appears to have largely consisted of a struggle between these opposite forces or tendencies. On the one side there was the conservative tendency to preserve the local cults with all their distinctive features, fresh, sharp, and crisp as they had been handed down from an immemorial past. On the other side there was the progressive tendency, favoured by the gradual fusion of the people under a powerful central government, first to dull the edge of these provincial distinctions, and finally to break them down completely and merge them in a single national religion. The conservative party probably mustered in its ranks the great bulk of the people, their prejudices and affections being warmly enlisted in favour of the local deity, with whose temple and rites they had been familiar from childhood; and the popular dislike of change, based on the endearing effect of old association, must have been strongly reinforced by the less disinterested opposition of the local clergy, whose material interests would necessarily suffer with any decay of their shrines. On the other hand the kings, whose power and glory rose with the political and ecclesiastical consolidation of the realm, were the natural champions of religious unity; and their efforts would be seconded by the refined and [pg 123] thoughtful minority, who could hardly fail to be shocked by the many barbarous and revolting elements in the local rites. As usually happens in such cases, the process of religious unification appears to have been largely effected by discovering points of similarity, real or imaginary, between the provincial deities, which were thereupon declared to be only different names or manifestations of the same god.

an gods were at some time identified with the sun. Attempt of Amenophis IV. to abolish all gods except Failure of the attempt.

Of the deities who thus acted as centres of attraction, absorbing in themselves a multitude of minor divinities, by far the most important was the sun-god Ra.

There appear to have been few gods in Egypt who were not at one time or other identified with him. Ammon of Thebes, Horus of the East, Horus of Edfu, Chnum of Elephantine, Tum of Heliopolis, all were regarded as one god, the sun. Even the water-god Sobk, in spite of his crocodile shape, did not escape the same fate. Indeed one king, Amenophis IV., undertook to sweep away all the old gods at a stroke and replace them by a single god, the "great living disc of the sun."[313] In the hymns composed in his honour, this deity is referred to as "the living disc of the sun, besides whom there is none other." He is said to have made "the far heaven" and "men, beasts, and birds; he strengtheneth the eyes with his beams, and when he showeth himself, all flowers [pg 124] live and grow, the meadows flourish at his upgoing and are drunken at his sight, all cattle skip on their feet, and the birds that are in the marsh flutter for joy." It is he "who bringeth the years, createth the months, maketh the days, calculateth the hours, the lord of time, by whom men reckon." In his zeal for the unity of god, the king commanded to erase the names of all other gods from the monuments, and to destroy their images. His rage was particularly directed against the god Ammon, whose name and likeness were effaced wherever they were found; even the sanctity of the tomb was violated in order to destroy the memorials of the hated deity. In some of the halls of the great temples at Carnac, Luxor, and other places, all the names of the gods, with a few chance exceptions, were scratched out. The monarch even changed his own name, Amenophis, because it was compounded of Ammon, and took instead the name of Chu-en-aten, "gleam of the sun's disc." Thebes itself, the ancient capital of his glorious ancestors, full of the monuments of their piety and idolatry, was no longer a fit home for the puritan king. He deserted it, and built for himself a new capital in Middle Egypt at the place now known as Tell-el-Amarna. Here in a few years a city of palaces and gardens rose like an exhalation at his command, and here the king, his dearly loved wife and children, and his complaisant courtiers led a merry life. The grave and sombre ritual of Thebes was discarded. The sun-god was worshipped with songs and hymns, with the music of harps and flutes, with offerings of cakes and fruits and flowers. Blood seldom stained his kindly altars. The king himself celebrated the offices of religion. He preached with unction, and we may be sure that his courtiers listened with at least an outward semblance of devotion. From the too-faithful portraits of himself which he has bequeathed to us we can still picture to ourselves the heretic king in the pulpit, with his tall, lanky figure, his bandy legs, his pot-belly, his long, lean, haggard face aglow with the fever of religious fanaticism. Yet "the doctrine," as he loved to call it, which he proclaimed to his hearers was apparently no stern message of renunciation in this world, of terrors in the world to [pg 125] come. The thoughts of death, of judgment, and of a life beyond the grave, which weighed like a nightmare on the minds of the Egyptians, seem to have been banished for a time. Even the name of Osiris, the awful judge of the dead, is not once mentioned in the graves at Tell-el-Amarna. All this lasted only during the life of the reformer. His death was followed by a violent reaction. The old gods were reinstated in their rank and privileges: their names and images were restored, and new temples were built. But all the shrines and palaces reared by the late king were thrown down: even the sculptures that referred to him and to his god in rock-tombs and on the sides of hills were erased or filled up with stucco: his name appears on no later monument, and was carefully omitted from all official lists. The new capital was abandoned, never to be inhabited again. Its plan can still be traced in the sands of the desert.

n with the sun is no evidence of the original character of an Egyptian god.

This attempt of King Amenophis IV. is only an extreme example of a tendency which appears to have affected the religion of Egypt as far back as we can trace it. Therefore, to come back to our point, in attempting to discover the original character of any Egyptian god, no weight can be given to the identification of him with other gods, least of all with the sun-god Ra. Far from helping to follow up the trail, these identifications only cross and confuse it. The best evidence for the original character of the Egyptian gods is to be found in their ritual and myths, so far as these are known, and in the manner in which they are portrayed on the monuments. It is mainly on evidence drawn from these sources that I rest my interpretation of Osiris.

ory of Osiris does not explain his death and resurrection.

The ground upon which some modern writers seem chiefly to rely for the identification of Osiris with the sun is that the story of his death fits better with the solar phenomena than with any other in nature. It may readily be admitted that the daily appearance and disappearance of the sun might very naturally be expressed by a myth of his death and resurrection; and writers who regard Osiris as the sun are careful to indicate that it is the diurnal, and not the annual, course of the sun to which they understand the [pg 126] myth to apply. Thus Renouf, who identified Osiris with the sun, admitted that the Egyptian sun could not with any show of reason be described as dead in winter.[314] But if his daily death was the theme of the legend, why was it celebrated by an annual ceremony? This fact alone seems fatal to the interpretation of the myth as descriptive of sunset and sunrise. Again, though the sun may be said to die daily, in what sense can he be said to be torn in pieces?[315]

d resurrection of Osiris are more naturally explained by the annual decay and growth of vegetation.

In the course of our inquiry it has, I trust, been made clear that there is another natural phenomenon to which the conception of death and resurrection is as applicable as to sunset and sunrise, and which, as a matter of fact, has been so conceived and represented in folk-custom. That phenomenon is the annual growth and decay of vegetation. A strong reason for interpreting the death of Osiris as the decay of vegetation rather than as the sunset is to be found in the general, though not unanimous, voice of antiquity, which classed together the worship and myths of Osiris, Adonis, Attis, Dionysus, and Demeter, as religions of essentially the same type.[316] The consensus of ancient [pg 127] opinion on this subject seems too great to be rejected as a mere fancy. So closely did the rites of Osiris resemble those of Adonis at Byblus that some of the people of Byblus themselves maintained that it was Osiris and not Adonis whose death was mourned by them.[317] Such a view could certainly not have been held if the rituals of the two gods had not been so alike as to be almost indistinguishable. Herodotus found the similarity between the rites of Osiris and Dionysus so great, that he thought it impossible the latter could have arisen independently; they must, he supposed, have been recently borrowed, with slight alterations, by the Greeks from the Egyptians.[318] Again, Plutarch, a very keen student of comparative religion, insists upon the detailed resemblance of the rites of Osiris to those of Dionysus.[319] We cannot reject the evidence of such intelligent and trustworthy witnesses on plain matters of fact which fell under their own cognizance. Their explanations of the worships it is indeed possible to reject, for the meaning of religious cults is often open to question; but resemblances of ritual are matters of observation. Therefore, those who explain Osiris as the sun are driven to the alternative of either dismissing as mistaken the testimony of antiquity to the similarity of the rites of Osiris, Adonis, Attis, Dionysus, and Demeter, or of interpreting all these rites as sun-worship. No modern scholar has fairly faced and accepted either side of this alternative. To accept the former would be to affirm [pg 128] that we know the rites of these deities better than the men who practised, or at least who witnessed them. To accept the latter would involve a wrenching, clipping, mangling, and distorting of myth and ritual from which even Macrobius shrank.[320] On the other hand, the view that the essence of all these rites was the mimic death and revival of vegetation, explains them separately and collectively in an easy and natural way, and harmonizes with the general testimony borne by the ancients to their substantial similarity.

[pg 129]

Chapter VIII. Osiris and the Moon.

ometimes interpreted by the ancients as the moon.

Before we conclude this study of Osiris it will be worth while to consider an ancient view of his nature, which deserves more attention than it has received in modern times. We are told by Plutarch that among the philosophers who saw in the gods of Egypt personifications of natural objects and forces, there were some who interpreted Osiris as the moon and his enemy Typhon as the sun, "because the moon, with her humid and generative light, is favourable to the propagation of animals and the growth of plants; while the sun with his fierce fire scorches and burns up all growing things, renders the greater part of the earth uninhabitable by reason of his blaze, and often overpowers the moon herself."[321] Whatever may be thought of the physical qualities here attributed to the moon, the arguments adduced by the ancients to prove the identity of Osiris with that luminary carry with them a weight which has at least not been lightened by the results of modern research. An examination of them and of other evidence pointing in the same direction will, perhaps, help to set the original character of the Egyptian deity in a clearer light.[322]

1. Osiris was said to have lived or reigned twenty-eight years. This might fairly be taken as a mythical expression for a lunar month.[323]

2. His body was reported to have been rent into fourteen pieces.[324] This might be interpreted of the waning moon, [pg 130] which appears to lose a portion of itself on each of the fourteen days that make up the second half of a lunar month. It is expressly said that his enemy Typhon found the body of Osiris at the full moon;[325] thus the dismemberment of the god would begin with the waning of the moon. To primitive man it seems manifest that the waning moon is actually dwindling, and he naturally enough explains its diminution by supposing that the planet is being rent or broken in pieces or eaten away. The Klamath Indians of Oregon speak of the moon as "the one broken to pieces" with reference to its changing aspect; they never apply such a term to the sun,[326] whose apparent change of bulk at different seasons of the year is far too insignificant to attract the attention of the savage, or at least to be described by him in such forcible language. The Dacotas believe that when the moon is full, a great many little mice begin to nibble at one side of it and do not cease till they have eaten it all up, after which a new moon is born and grows to maturity, only to share the fate of its countless predecessors.[327] A similar belief is held by the Huzuls of the Carpathians, except that they ascribe the destruction of the old moon to wolves instead of to mice.[328]

3. At the new moon of the month Phamenoth, which was the beginning of spring, the Egyptians celebrated what they called "the entry of Osiris into the moon."[329]

4. At the ceremony called "the burial of Osiris" the Egyptians made a crescent-shaped chest "because the moon, when it approaches the sun, assumes the form of a crescent and vanishes."[330]

5. The bull Apis, held to be an image of the soul of Osiris,[331] was born of a cow which was believed to have been [pg 131] impregnated, not in the vulgar way by a bull, but by a divine influence emanating from the moon.[332]

6. Once a year, at the full moon, pigs were sacrificed simultaneously to the moon and Osiris.[333]

7. In a hymn supposed to be addressed by Isis to Osiris, it is said that Thoth—

> "*Placeth thy soul in the bark Ma-at,*
>
> *In that name which is thine, of GOD MOON.*"

And again:—

> "*Thou who comest to us as a child each month,*
>
> *We do not cease to contemplate thee.*
>
> *Thine emanation heightens the brilliancy*
>
> *Of the stars of Orion in the firmament.*"[334]

Here then Osiris is identified with the moon in set terms. If in the same hymn he is said to "illuminate us like Ra" (the sun), that is obviously no reason for identifying him with the sun, but quite the contrary. For though the moon may reasonably be compared to the sun, neither the sun nor anything else can reasonably be compared to itself.

8. In art Osiris is sometimes represented as a human-headed mummy grasping in his hands his characteristic emblems and wearing on his head, instead of the usual crown, a full moon within a crescent.[335]

ation of Osiris with the moon appears to be based on a comparatively late theory that all things grow ith the waxing and waning of the moon.

Now if in one of his aspects Osiris was originally a deity of vegetation, we can easily enough understand why in a later and more philosophic age he should come to be thus identified or confounded with the moon.[336] For as soon as he begins to meditate upon the causes of [pg 132] things, the early philosopher is led by certain obvious, though fallacious, appearances to regard the moon as the ultimate cause of the growth of plants. In the first place he associates its apparent growth and decay with the growth and decay of sublunary things, and imagines that in virtue of a secret sympathy the celestial phenomena really produce those terrestrial changes which in point of fact they merely resemble. Thus Pliny says that the moon may fairly be considered the planet of breath, "because it saturates the earth and by its approach fills bodies, while by its departure it empties them. Hence it is," he goes on, "that shell-fish increase with the increase of the moon and that bloodless creatures especially feel breath at that time; even the blood of men grows and diminishes with the light of the moon, and leaves and herbage also feel the same influence, since the lunar energy penetrates all things."[337] "There is no doubt," writes Macrobius, "that the moon is the author and framer of mortal bodies, so much so that some things expand or shrink as it waxes or wanes."[338] Again, Aulus Gellius puts in the mouth of a friend the remark that "the same things which grow with the waxing, do dwindle with the waning moon," and he quotes from a commentary of Plutarch's on Hesiod a statement that the onion is the only vegetable which violates this great law of nature by sprouting in the wane and withering in the increase of the moon.[339] Scottish Highlanders allege that in the increase of the moon everything has a tendency to grow or stick together;[340] and they call the second moon of autumn "the ripening moon" (*Gealach an abachaidh*), because they imagine that crops ripen as much by its light as by day.[341]

es founded on this lunar theory. Supposed influence of the phases of the moon on the operations of

From this supposed influence of the moon on the life of plants and animals, men in ancient and modern times have deduced a whole code of rules for the guidance of the husbandman, the shepherd, and others in the conduct of [pg 133] their affairs. Thus an ancient writer on agriculture lays it down as a maxim, that whatever is to be sown should be sown while the moon is waxing, and that whatever is to be cut or gathered should be cut or gathered while it is waning.[342] A modern treatise on superstition describes how the superstitious man regulates all his conduct by the moon: "Whatever he would have to grow, he sets about it when she is in her increase; but for what he would have made less he chooses her wane."[343] In Germany the phases of the moon are observed by superstitious people at all the more or even less important actions of life, such as tilling the fields, building or changing houses, marriages, hair-cutting, bleeding, cupping, and so forth. The particular rules vary in different places, but the principle generally followed is that whatever is done to increase anything should be done while the moon is waxing; whatever is done to diminish anything should be done while the moon is waning. For example, sowing, planting, and grafting should be done in the first half of the moon, but the felling of timber and mowing should be done in the second half.[344] In various parts of Europe it is believed that plants, nails, hair, and corns, cut while the moon is on the increase, will grow again fast, but that if cut while it is on the decrease they will grow slowly or waste [pg 134] away.[345] Hence persons who wish their hair to grow thick and long should cut it in the first half of the moon.[346] On the same principle sheep are shorn when the moon is waxing, because it is supposed that the wool will then be longest and most enduring.[347] Some negroes of the Gaboon think that taro and other vegetables never thrive if they are planted after full moon, but that they grow fast and strong if they are planted in the first quarter.[348] The Highlanders of Scotland used to expect better crops of grain by sowing their seed in the moon's increase.[349] On the other hand they thought that garden vegetables, such as onions and kail, run to seed if they are sown in the increase, but that they grow to pot-herbs if they are sown in the wane.[350] So Thomas Tusser advised the peasant to sow peas and beans in the wane of the moon "that they with the planet may rest and arise."[351] The Zulus welcome [pg 135] the first appearance of the new moon with beating of drums and other demonstrations of joy; but next day they abstain from all labour, "thinking that if anything is sown on those days they can never reap the benefit thereof."[352] But in this matter of sowing and planting a refined distinction is sometimes drawn by French, German, and Esthonian peasants; plants which bear fruit above ground are sown by them when the moon is waxing, but plants which are cultivated for the sake of their roots, such as potatoes and turnips, are sown when the moon is waning.[353] The reason for this distinction seems to be a vague idea that the waxing moon is coming up and the waning moon going down, and that accordingly fruits which grow upwards should be sown in the former period, and fruits which grow downwards in the latter. Before beginning to plant their cacao the Pipiles of Central America exposed the finest seeds for four nights to the moonlight,[354] but whether they did so at the waxing or waning of the moon is not said. Even pots, it would seem, are not exempt from this great law of nature. In Uganda "potters waited for the new moon to appear before baking their pots; when it was some days old, they prepared their fires and baked the vessels. No potter would bake pots when the moon was past the full, for he believed that they would be a failure, and would be sure to crack or break in the burning, if he did so, and that his labour accordingly would go for nothing."[355]

f the moon in relation to the felling of timber.

Again, the waning of the moon has been commonly recommended both in ancient and modern times as the proper time for felling trees,[356] apparently because it was [pg 136] thought fit and natural that the operation of cutting down should be performed on earth at the time when the lunar orb was, so to say, being cut down in the sky. In France before the Revolution the forestry laws enjoined that trees should only be felled after the moon had passed the full; and in French bills announcing the sale of timber you may still read a notice that the wood was cut in the waning of the moon.[357] So among the Shans of Burma, when a house is to be built, it is a rule that "a lucky day should be chosen to commence the cutting of the bamboos. The day must not only be a fortunate one for the builder, but it must also be in the second half of the month, when the moon is waning. Shans believe that if bamboos are cut during the first half of the month, when the moon is waxing, they do not last well, as boring insects attack them and they will soon become rotten. This belief is prevalent all over the East."[358] A like belief obtains in various parts of Mexico. No Mexican will cut timber while the moon is increasing; they say it must be cut while the moon is waning or the wood will certainly rot.[359] In Colombia, South America, people think that corn should only be sown and timber felled when the moon is on the wane. They say that the waxing moon draws the sap up through the trunk and branches, whereas the sap flows down and leaves the wood dry during the wane of the moon.[360] But sometimes the opposite rule is [pg 137] adopted, and equally forcible arguments are urged in its defence. Thus, when the Wabondei of Eastern Africa are about to build a house, they take care to cut the posts for it when the moon is on the increase; for they say that posts cut when the moon is wasting away would soon rot, whereas posts cut while the moon is waxing are very durable.[361] The same rule is observed for the same reason in some parts of Germany.[362]

garded as the source of moisture.

But the partisans of the ordinarily received opinion have sometimes supported it by another reason, which introduces us to the second of those fallacious appearances by which men have been led to regard the moon as the cause of growth in plants. From observing rightly that dew falls most thickly on cloudless nights, they inferred wrongly that it was caused by the moon, a theory which the poet Alcman expressed in mythical form by saying that dew was a daughter of Zeus and the moon.[363] Hence the ancients concluded that the moon is the great source of moisture, as the sun is the great source of heat.[364] And as the humid power of the moon was assumed to be greater when the planet was waxing than when it was waning, they thought that timber cut during the increase of the luminary would be saturated with moisture, whereas timber cut in the wane would be comparatively dry. Hence we are told that in antiquity carpenters would reject timber felled when the moon was growing or full, because they believed that such timber teemed with sap;[365] and in the Vosges at the present day people allege that wood cut at the new moon does not dry.[366] We have seen that the same reason is assigned for the same practice in Colombia.[367] In the Hebrides peasants [pg 138] give the same reason for cutting their peats when the moon is on the wane; "for they observe that if they are cut in the increase, they continue still moist and never burn clear, nor are they without smoke, but the contrary is daily observed of peats cut in the decrease."[368]

eing viewed as the cause of vegetable growth, is naturally worshipped by agricultural peoples.

Thus misled by a double fallacy primitive philosophy comes to view the moon as the great cause of vegetable growth, first, because the planet seems itself to grow, and second, because it is supposed to be the source of dew and moisture. It is no wonder, therefore, that agricultural peoples should adore the planet which they believe to influence so profoundly the crops on which they depend for subsistence. Accordingly we find that in the hotter regions of America, where maize is cultivated and manioc is the staple food, the moon was recognized as the principal object of worship, and plantations of manioc were assigned to it as a return for the service it rendered in the production of the crops. The worship of the moon in preference to the sun was general among the Caribs, and, perhaps, also among most of the other Indian tribes who cultivated maize in the tropical forests to the east of the Andes; and the same thing has been observed, under the same physical conditions, among the aborigines of the hottest region of Peru, the northern valleys of Yuncapata. Here the Indians of Pacasmayu and the neighbouring valleys revered the moon as their principal divinity. The "house of the moon" at Pacasmayu was the chief temple of the district; and the same sacrifices of maize-flour, of wine, and of children which were offered by the mountaineers of the Andes to the Sun-god, were offered by the lowlanders to the Moon-god in order that he might cause their crops to thrive.[369] In ancient [pg 139] Babylonia, where the population was essentially agricultural, the moon-god took precedence of the sun-god and was indeed reckoned his father.[370]

the old corn-god, was afterwards identified with the moon.

Hence it would be no matter for surprise if, after worshipping the crops which furnished them with the means of subsistence, the ancient Egyptians should in later times have identified the spirit of the corn with the moon, which a false philosophy had taught them to regard as the ultimate cause of the growth of vegetation. In this way we can understand why in their most recent forms the myth and ritual of Osiris, the old god of trees and corn, should bear many traces of efforts made to bring them into a superficial conformity with the new doctrine of his lunar affinity.

[pg 140]

Chapter IX. The Doctrine of Lunar Sympathy.

In the preceding chapter some evidence was adduced of the sympathetic influence which the waxing or waning moon is popularly supposed to exert on growth, especially on the growth of vegetation. But the doctrine of lunar sympathy does not stop there; it is applied also to the affairs of man, and various customs and rules have been deduced from it which aim at the amelioration and even the indefinite extension of human life. To illustrate this application of the popular theory at length would be out of place here, but a few cases may be mentioned by way of specimen.

all things wax or wane with the moon. The ceremonies observed at new moon are often magical rather s, being intended to renew sympathetically the life of man.

The natural fact on which all the customs in question seem to rest is the apparent monthly increase and decrease of the moon. From this observation men have inferred that all things simultaneously wax or wane in sympathy with it.[371] Thus the Mentras or Mantras of the Malay Peninsula have a tradition that in the beginning men did not die but grew thin with the waning of the moon, and waxed fat as she neared the full.[372] Of the Scottish Highlanders we are told that "the moon in her increase, full growth, and in her wane are with them the emblems of a rising, flourishing, and declining fortune. At the last period of her revolution they carefully avoid to engage in any business of importance; but the first and middle they seize with avidity, presaging the most auspicious issue to their undertakings."[373] Similarly [pg 141] in some parts of Germany it is commonly believed that whatever is undertaken when the moon is on the increase succeeds well, and that the full moon brings everything to perfection; whereas business undertaken in the wane of the moon is doomed to failure.[374] This German belief has come down, as we might have anticipated, from barbaric times; for Tacitus tells us that the Germans considered the new or the full moon the most auspicious time for business;[375] and Caesar informs us that the Germans despaired of victory if they joined battle before the new moon.[376] The Spartans seem to have been of the same opinion, for it was a rule with them never to march out to war except when the moon was full. The rule prevented them from sending troops in time to fight the Persians at Marathon,[377] and but for Athenian valour this paltry superstition might have turned the scale of battle and decided the destiny of Greece, if not of Europe, for centuries. The Athenians themselves paid dear for a similar scruple: an eclipse of the moon cost them the loss of a gallant fleet and army before Syracuse, and practically sealed the fate of Athens, for she never recovered from the blow.[378] So heavy is the sacrifice which superstition demands of its votaries. In this respect the Greeks were on a level with the negroes of the Sudan, among whom, if a march has been decided upon during the last quarter of the moon, the departure is always deferred until the first day of the new moon. No chief would dare to undertake an expedition and lead out his warriors before the appearance of the crescent. Merchants and private persons observe the same rule on their journeys.[379] In like manner the Mandingoes of Senegambia pay great attention to the changes of the moon, and think it very unlucky to begin a journey or any other work of consequence in the last quarter.[380]

It is especially the appearance of the new moon, with [pg 142] its promise of growth and increase, which is greeted with ceremonies intended to renew and invigorate, by means of sympathetic magic, the life of man. Observers, ignorant of savage superstition, have commonly misinterpreted such customs as worship or adoration paid to the moon. In point of fact the ceremonies of new moon are probably in many cases rather magical than religious. The Indians of the Ucayali River in Peru hail the appearance of the new moon with great joy. They make long speeches to her, accompanied with vehement gesticulations, imploring her protection and begging that she will be so good as to invigorate their bodies.[381] On the day when the new moon first appeared, it was a custom with the Indians of San Juan Capistrano, in California, to call together all the young men for the purpose of its celebration. "*Correr la luna!*" shouted one of the old men, "Come, my boys, the moon! the moon!" Immediately the young men began to run about in a disorderly fashion as if they were distracted, while the old men danced in a circle, saying, "As the moon dieth, and cometh to life again, so we also having to die will again live."[382] An old traveller tells us that at the appearance of every new moon the negroes of the Congo clapped their hands and cried out, sometimes falling on their knees, "So may I renew my life as thou art renewed." But if the sky happened to be clouded, they did nothing, alleging that the planet had lost its virtue.[383] A somewhat similar custom prevails among the Ovambo of South-Western Africa. On the first moonlight night of the new moon, young and old, their bodies smeared with white earth, perhaps in imitation of the planet's silvery light, dance to the moon and address to it wishes which they feel sure will be granted.[384] We may conjecture that among these wishes is a prayer for a renewal of life. When a Masai sees the new moon he throws a twig or stone at it with his left hand, and says, "Give me [pg 143] long life," or "Give me strength"; and when a pregnant woman sees the new moon she milks some milk into a small gourd, which she covers with green grass. Then she pours the milk away in the direction of the moon and says, "Moon, give me my child safely."[385] Among the Wagogo of German East Africa, at sight of the new moon some people break a stick in pieces, spit on the pieces, and throw them towards the moon, saying, "Let all illness go to the west, where the sun sets."[386] Among the Boloki of the Upper Congo there is much shouting and gesticulation on the appearance of a new moon. Those who have enjoyed good health pray that it may be continued, and those who have been sick ascribe their illness to the coming of the luminary and beg her to take away bad health and give them good health instead.[387] The Esthonians think that all the misfortunes which might befall a man in the course of a month may be forestalled and shifted to the moon, if a man will only say to the new moon, "Good morrow, new moon. I must grow young, you must grow old. My eyes must grow bright, yours must grow dark. I must grow light as a bird, you must grow heavy as iron."[388] On the fifteenth day of the moon, that is, at the time when the luminary has begun to wane, the Coreans take round pieces of paper, either red or white, which represent the moon, and having fixed them perpendicularly on split sticks they place them on the tops of the houses. Then persons who have been forewarned by fortune-tellers of impending evil pray to the moon to remove it from them.[389]

[pg 144]

eat or drink the moonlight.

In India people attempt to absorb the vital influence of the moon by drinking water in which the luminary is reflected. Thus the Mohammedans of Oude fill a silver basin with water and hold it so that the orb of the full moon is mirrored in it. The person to be benefited must look steadfastly at the moon in the basin, then shut his eyes and drink the water at one gulp. Doctors recommend the draught as a remedy for nervous disorders and palpitation of the heart. Somewhat similar customs prevail among the Hindoos of Northern India. At the full moon of the month of Kuar (September-October) people lay out food on the house-tops, and when it has absorbed the rays of the moon they distribute it among their relations, who are supposed to lengthen their life by eating of the food which has thus been saturated with moonshine. Patients are often made to look at the moon reflected in melted butter, oil, or milk as a cure for leprosy and the like diseases.[390]

d influence of moonlight on children: presentation of infants to the new moon.

Naturally enough the genial influence of moonshine is often supposed to be particularly beneficial to children; for will not the waxing moon help them to wax in strength and stature? Hence in the island of Kiriwina, one of the

Trobriands Group to the east of New Guinea, a mother always lifts up or presents her child to the first full moon after its birth in order that it may grow fast and talk soon.[391] So among the Baganda of Central Africa it was customary for each mother to take her child out at the first new moon after its birth, and to point out the moon to the infant; this was thought to make the child grow healthy and strong.[392] Among the Thonga of South Africa the presentation of the baby to the moon does not take place until the mother has resumed her monthly periods, which usually happens in the third month after the birth. When the new moon appears, the mother takes a torch or a burning brand from the fire and goes to the ash-heap behind the hut. She is followed by the grandmother carrying the child. At the ash-heap the mother throws the burning stick towards the moon, while the grandmother tosses the [pg 145] baby into the air, saying, "This is your moon!" The child squalls and rolls over on the ash-heap. Then the mother snatches up the infant and nurses it; so they go home.[393]

nted to the moon by the Guarayos Indians of Bolivia and the Apinagos Indians of Brazil.

The Guarayos Indians, who inhabit the gloomy tropical forests of Eastern Bolivia, lift up their children in the air at new moon in order that they may grow.[394] Among the Apinagos Indians, on the Tocantins River in Brazil, the French traveller Castelnau witnessed a remarkable dance by moonlight. The Indians danced in two long ranks which faced each other, the women on one side, the men on the other. Between the two ranks of dancers blazed a great fire. The men were painted in brilliant colours, and for the most part wore white or red skull-caps made of maize-flour and resin. Their dancing was very monotonous and consisted of a jerky movement of the body, while the dancer advanced first one leg and then the other. This dance they accompanied with a melancholy song, striking the ground with their weapons. Opposite them the women, naked and unpainted, stood in a single rank, their bodies bent slightly forward, their knees pressed together, their arms swinging in measured time, now forward, now backward, so as to join hands. A remarkable figure in the dance was a personage painted scarlet all over, who held in his hand a rattle composed of a gourd full of pebbles. From time to time he leaped across the great fire which burned between the men and the women. Then he would run rapidly in front of the women, stopping now and then before one or other and performing a series of strange gambols, while he shook his rattle violently. Sometimes he would sink with one knee to the ground, and then suddenly throw himself backward. Altogether the agility and endurance which he displayed were remarkable. This dance lasted for hours. When a woman was tired out she withdrew, and her place was taken by another; but the same men danced the monotonous dance all night. Towards midnight the moon attained the zenith and flooded the scene with her bright rays. A change [pg 146] now took place in the dance. A long line of men and women advanced to the fire between the ranks of the dancers. Each of them held one end of a hammock in which lay a new-born infant, whose squalls could be heard. These babes were now to be presented by their parents to the moon. On reaching the end of the line each couple swung the hammock, accompanying the movement by a chant, which all the Indians sang in chorus. The song seemed to consist of three words, repeated over and over again. Soon a shrill voice was heard, and a hideous old hag, like a skeleton, appeared with her arms raised above her head. She went round and round the assembly several times, then disappeared in silence. While she was present, the scarlet dancer with the rattle bounded about more furiously than ever, stopping only for a moment while he passed in front of the line of women. His body was contracted and bent towards them, and described an undulatory movement like that of a worm writhing. He shook his rattle violently, as if he would fain kindle in the women the fire which burned in himself. Then rising abruptly he would resume his wild career. During this time the loud voice of an orator was heard from the village repeating a curious name without cessation. Then the speaker approached slowly, carrying on his back some gorgeous bunches of brilliant feathers and under his arm a stone axe. Behind him walked a young woman bearing an infant in a loose girdle at her waist; the child was wrapped in a mat, which protected it against the chill night air. The couple paced slowly for a minute or two, and then vanished without speaking a word. At the same moment the curious name which the orator had shouted was taken up by the whole assembly and repeated by them again and again. This scene in its turn lasted a long time, but ceased suddenly with the setting of the moon. The French traveller who witnessed it fell asleep, and when he awoke all was calm once more: there was nothing to recall the infernal dances of the night.[395]

tion of infants to the moon is probably intended to make them grow.

In explanation of these dances Castelnau merely observes [pg 147] that the Apinagos, like many other South American Indians, pay a superstitious respect to the moon. We may suppose that the ceremonious presentation of the infants to the moon was intended to ensure their life and growth. The names solemnly chanted by the whole assembly were probably those which the parents publicly bestowed on their children. As to the scarlet dancer who leaped across the fire, we may conjecture that he personated the moon, and that his strange antics in front of the women were designed to impart to them the fertilizing virtue of the luminary, and perhaps to facilitate their delivery.

emonies at new moon.

Among the Baganda of Central Africa there is general rejoicing when the new moon appears, and no work is done for seven days. When the crescent is first visible at evening, mothers take out their babies and hold them at arms' length, saying, "I want my child to keep in health till the moon wanes." At the same time a ceremony is performed which may be intended to ensure the king's life and health throughout the ensuing month. It is a custom with the Baganda to preserve the king's navel-string with great care during his life. The precious object is called the "Twin" of the king, as if it were his double; and the ghost of the royal afterbirth is believed to be attached to it. Enclosed in a pot, which is wrapt in bark cloths, the navel-string is kept in a temple specially built for it near the king's enclosure, and a great minister of state acts as its guardian and priest. Every new moon, at evening, he carries it in state, wrapped in bark cloths, to the king, who takes it into his hands, examines it, and returns it to the minister. The keeper of the navel-string then goes back with it to the house and sets it in the doorway, where it remains all night. Next morning it is taken from its wrappings and again placed in the doorway until the evening, when it is once more swathed in bark cloths and restored to its usual place.[396] Apparently the navel-string is conceived as a vital portion, a sort of external soul, of the [pg 148] king; and the attentions bestowed on it at the new moon may be supposed to refresh and invigorate it, thereby refreshing and invigorating the king's life.

ence supposed to be exercised by the moon on children.

The Armenians appear to think that the moon exercises a baleful influence on little children. To avert that influence a mother will show the moon to her child and say, "Thine uncle, thine uncle." For the same purpose the father and mother will mount to the roof of the house at new moon on a Wednesday or Friday. The father then puts the child on a shovel and gives it to the mother, saying, "If it is thine, take it to thee. But if it is mine, rear it and give it to me back." The mother then takes the child and the shovel, and returns them to the father in like manner.[397] A similar opinion as to the noxious influence of moonshine on children was apparently held by the ancient Greeks; for Greek nurses took great care never to show their infants to the moon.[398] Some Brazilian Indians in like manner guard babies against the moon, believing that it would make them ill. Immediately after delivery mothers will hide themselves and their infants in the thickest parts of the forest in order that the moonlight may not fall on them.[399] It would be easy to understand why the waning moon should be deemed injurious to children; they might be supposed to peak and pine with its dwindling light. Thus in Angus it is thought that if a child be weaned during the waning of the moon, it will decay all the time that the moon continues to wane.[400] But it is less easy to see why the same deleterious influence on children should be ascribed to moonlight in general.

oon to increase money or decrease sickness.

There are many other ways in which people have sought to turn lunar sympathy to practical account. Clearly the increase of the moon is the time to increase your goods, and the decrease of the moon is the time to diminish your ills. Acting on this imaginary law of nature many persons in Europe show their money to the new moon or turn it in [pg 149] their pockets at that season, in the belief that the money will grow with the growth of the planet; sometimes, by way of additional precaution, they spit on the coin at the same time.[401] "Both Christians and Moslems in Syria turn their silver money in their pockets at the new moon for luck; and two persons meeting under the new moon will each take out a silver coin and embrace, saying, 'May you begin and end; and may it be a good month to us.'"[402] Conversely the waning of the moon is the most natural time to get rid of bodily ailments. In Brittany they think that warts vary with the phases of the moon, growing as it waxes and vanishing away as it wanes.[403] Accordingly, they say in Germany that if you would rid yourself of warts you should treat them when the moon is on the decrease.[404] And a German cure for toothache, earache, headache, and so forth, is to look towards the waning moon and say, "As the moon decreases, so may my pains decrease also."[405] However, some Germans reverse the rule. They say, for example, that if you are afflicted with a wen, you should face the waxing moon, lay your finger on the wen, and say thrice, "What I see waxes; what I touch, let it vanish away." After each of these two sentences you should cross yourself thrice. Then go home without speaking to any one, and repeat three paternosters behind the kitchen door.[406] The Huzuls of the Carpathians recommend a somewhat similar, and no doubt equally efficacious, cure for waterbrash. They say that at new moon the patient should run thrice round the house and then say to the moon, "Moon, moon, where wast thou?" "Behind the mountain." "What hast thou eaten there?" "Horse flesh." "Why hast thou brought me nothing?" "Because I forgot." "May the waterbrash [pg 150] forget to burn me!"[407] Thus a curative virtue appears to be attributed by some people to the waning and by others to the waxing moon. There is perhaps just as much, or as little, to be said for the one attribution as for the other.

[pg 151]

Chapter X. The King As Osiris.

nated by the king of Egypt.

In the foregoing discussion we found reason to believe that the Semitic Adonis and the Phrygian Attis were at one time personated in the flesh by kings, princes, or priests who played the part of the god for a time and then either died a violent death in the divine character or had to redeem their life in one way or another, whether by performing a make-believe sacrifice at some expense of pain and danger to themselves, or by delegating the duty to a substitute.[408] Further, we conjectured that in Egypt the part of Osiris may have been played by the king himself.[409] It remains to adduce some positive evidence of this personation.

ival celebrated in Egypt at intervals of thirty years.

A great festival called the Sed was celebrated by the Egyptians with much solemnity at intervals of thirty years. Various portions of the ritual are represented on the ancient monuments of Hieraconpolis and Abydos and in the oldest decorated temple of Egypt known to us, that of Usirniri at Busiris, which dates from the fifth dynasty. It appears that the ceremonies were as old as the Egyptian civilization, and that they continued to be observed till the end of the Roman period.[410] The reason for holding them at intervals of thirty [pg 152] years is uncertain, but we can hardly doubt that the period was determined by astronomical considerations. According to one view, it was based on the observation of Saturn's period of revolution round the sun, which is, roughly speaking, thirty years, or, more exactly, twenty-nine years and one hundred and seventy-four days.[411] According to another view, the thirty years' period had reference to Sirius, the star of Isis. We have seen that on account of the vague character of the old Egyptian year the heliacal rising of Sirius shifted its place gradually through every month of the calendar.[412] In one hundred and twenty years the star thus passed through one whole month of thirty days. To speak more precisely, it rose on the first of the month during the first four years of the period: it rose on the second of the month in the second four years, on the third of the month in the third four years; and so on successively, till in the last four years of the hundred and twenty years it rose on the last day of the month. As the Egyptians watched the annual summer rising of the star with attention and associated it with the most popular of their goddesses, it would be natural that its passage from one month to another, at intervals of one hundred and twenty years, should be the occasion of a great festival, and that the long period of one hundred and twenty years should be

99

divided into four minor periods of thirty years respectively, each celebrated by a minor festival.[413] If this theory of the Sed festivals is correct, we should expect to find that every fourth celebration was distinguished from the rest by a higher degree of solemnity, since it marked the completion of a twelfth part of the star's journey through the twelve [pg 153] months. Now it appears that in point of fact every fourth Sed festival was marked off from its fellows by the adjective *tep* or "chief," and that these "chief" celebrations fell as a rule in the years when Sirius rose on the first of the month.[414] These facts confirm the view that the Sed festival was closely connected with the star Sirius, and through it with Isis.

the Sed festival to renew the king's life.

However, we are here concerned rather with the meaning and the rites of the festival than with the reasons for holding it once every thirty years. The intention of the festival seems to have been to procure for the king a new lease of life, a renovation of his divine energies, a rejuvenescence. In the inscriptions of Abydos we read, after an account of the rites, the following address to the king: "Thou dost recommence thy renewal, thou art granted to flourish again like the infant god Moon, thou dost grow young again, and that from season to season, like Nun at the beginning of time, thou art born again in renewing the Sed festivals. All life comes to thy nostril, and thou art king of the whole earth for ever."[415] In short, on these occasions it appears to have been supposed that the king was in a manner born again.

ntified with the dead Osiris at the Sed festival.

But how was the new birth effected? Apparently the essence of the rites consisted in identifying the king with Osiris; for just as Osiris had died and risen again from the dead, so the king might be thought to die and to live again with the god whom he personated. The ceremony would thus be for the king a death as well as a rebirth. Accordingly in pictures of the Sed festival on the monuments we see the king posing as the dead Osiris. He sits in a shrine like a god, holding in his hands the crook and flail of Osiris: he is wrapped in tight bandages like the mummified Osiris; indeed, there is nothing but his name to prove that he is not Osiris himself. This enthronement of the king in the attitude of the dead god seems to have been the principal event of the festival.[416] Further, the queen and the king's daughters figured prominently in the ceremonies.[417] A [pg 154] discharge of arrows formed part of the rites;[418] and in some sculptures at Carnac the queen is portrayed shooting arrows towards the four quarters of the world, while the king does the same with rings.[419] The oldest illustration of the festival is on the mace of Narmer, which is believed to date from 5500 B.C. Here we see the king seated as Osiris in a shrine at the top of nine steps. Beside the shrine stand fan-bearers, and in front of it is a figure in a palanquin, which, according to an inscription in another representation of the scene, appears to be the royal child. An enclosure of curtains hung on poles surrounds the dancing-ground, where three men are performing a sacred dance. A procession of standards is depicted beside the enclosure; it is headed by the standard of the jackal-god Up-uat, the "opener of ways" for the dead.[420] Similarly on a seal of King Zer, or rather Khent, one of the early kings of the first dynasty, the monarch appears as Osiris with the standard of the jackal-god before him. In front of him, too, is the ostrich feather on which "the dead king was supposed to ascend into heaven. Here, then, the king, identified with Osiris, king of the dead, has before him the jackal-god, who leads the dead, and the ostrich feather, which symbolizes his reception into the sky."[421] There are even grounds for thinking that in order to complete the mimic death of the king at the Sed festival an effigy of him, clad in the costume of Osiris, was solemnly buried in a cenotaph.[422]

nders Petrie's explanation of the Sed festival.

According to Professor Flinders Petrie, "the conclusion may be drawn thus. In the savage age of prehistoric times, the Egyptians, like many other African and Indian peoples, killed their priest-king at stated intervals, in order that the ruler should, with unimpaired life and health, be enabled to maintain the kingdom in its highest condition. The royal daughters were present in order that they might be married to his successor. The jackal-god went before [pg 155] him, to open the way to the unseen world; and the ostrich feather received and bore away the king's soul in the breeze that blew it out of sight. This was the celebration of the 'end,' the *sed* feast. The king thus became the dead king, patron of all those who had died in his reign, who were his subjects here and hereafter. He was thus one with Osiris, the king of the dead. This fierce custom became changed, as in other lands, by appointing a deputy king to die in his stead; which idea survived in the Coptic Abu Nerūs, with his tall crown of Upper Egypt, false beard, and sceptre. After the death of the deputy, the real king renewed his life and reign. Henceforward this became the greatest of the royal festivals, the apotheosis of the king during his life, after which he became Osiris upon earth and the patron of the dead in the underworld."[423]

oret's theory that at the Sed festivals the king was supposed to die and to be born again.

A similar theory of the Sed festival is maintained by another eminent Egyptologist, M. Alexandre Moret. He says: "In most of the temples of Egypt, of all periods, pictures set forth for us the principal scenes of a solemn festival called 'festival of the tail,' the Sed festival. It consisted essentially in a representation of the ritual death of the king followed by his rebirth. In this case the king is identified with Osiris, the god who in historical times is the hero of the sacred drama of humanity, he who guides us through the three stages of life, death, and rebirth in the other world. Hence, clad in the funeral costume of Osiris, with the tight-fitting garment clinging to him like a shroud, Pharaoh is conducted to the tomb; and from it he returns rejuvenated and reborn like Osiris emerging from the dead. How was this fiction carried out? how was this miracle performed? By the sacrifice of human or animal victims. On behalf of the king a priest lay down in the skin of the animal victim: he assumed the posture characteristic of an embryo in its mother's womb: when he came forth from the skin he was deemed to be reborn; and Pharaoh, for whom this rite was celebrated, was himself reborn, or to adopt the Egyptian expression, [pg 156] 'he renewed his births.' And in testimony of the due performance of the rites the king girt his loins with the tail, a compendious representative of the skin of the sacrificed beast, whence the name of 'the festival of the tail.'

"How are we to explain the rule that at a certain point of his reign every Pharaoh must undergo this ritual death followed by fictitious rebirth? Is it simply a renewal of the initiation into the Osirian mysteries? or does the festival present some more special features? The ill-defined part played by the royal children in these rites seems to me to indicate that the Sed festival represents other episodes which refer to the transmission of the regal office. At the dawn of civilization in Egypt the people were perhaps familiar with the alternative either of putting their king to death in his full vigour in order that his power should be transmitted intact to his successor, or of attempting to rejuvenate him and to 'renew his life.' The latter measure was an invention of the Pharaohs. How could it be carried out more effectively than by identifying themselves with Osiris, by applying to themselves the process of resurrection, the funeral rites by which Isis, according to the priests, had magically saved her husband from death? Perhaps the fictitious death of the king may be regarded as a mitigation of the primitive murder of the divine king, a transition from a barbarous reality to symbolism."[424]

[pg 157]

nated by the king of Egypt.

Whether this interpretation of the Sed festival be accepted in all its details or not, one thing seems quite certain: on these solemn occasions the god Osiris was personated by the king of Egypt himself. That is the point with which we are here chiefly concerned.

[pg 158]

Chapter XI. The Origin of Osiris.

conception of Osiris as a god of vegetation and of the dead originate?

Thus far we have discussed the character of Osiris as he is presented to us in the art and literature of Egypt and in the testimonies of Greek writers; and we have found that judged by these indications he was in the main a god of vegetation and of the dead. But we have still to ask, how did the conception of such a composite deity originate? Did it arise simply through observation of the great annual fluctuations of the seasons and a desire to explain them? Was it a result of brooding over the mystery of external nature? Was it the attempt of a rude philosophy to lift the veil and explore the hidden springs that set the vast machine in motion? That man at a very early stage of his long history meditated on these things and evolved certain crude theories which partially satisfied his craving after knowledge is certain; from such meditations of Babylonian and Phrygian sages appear to have sprung the pathetic figures of Adonis and Attis; and from such meditations of Egyptian sages may have sprung the tragic figure of Osiris.

is and Attis were subordinate figures in their respective pantheons, Osiris was the greatest and most of Egypt.

Yet a broad distinction seems to sever the myth and worship of Osiris from the kindred myths and worships of Adonis and Attis. For while Adonis and Attis were minor divinities in the religion of Western Asia, completely overshadowed by the greater deities of their respective pantheons, the solemn figure of Osiris towered in solitary grandeur over all the welter of Egyptian gods, like a pyramid of his native land lit up by the last rays of the setting sun when all below it is in shadow. And whereas legend generally represented Adonis and Attis as simple swains, mere herdsmen [pg 159] or hunters whom the fatal love of a goddess had elevated above their homely sphere into a brief and melancholy pre-eminence, Osiris uniformly appears in tradition as a great and beneficent king. In life, he ruled over his people, beloved and revered for the benefits he conferred on them and on the world; in death he reigned in their hearts and memories as lord of the dead, the awful judge at whose bar every man must one day stand to give an account of the deeds done in the body and to receive the final award. In the faith of the Egyptians the cruel death and blessed resurrection of Osiris occupied the same place as the death and resurrection of Christ hold in the faith of Christians. As Osiris died and rose again from the dead, so they hoped through him and in his dear name to wake triumphant from the sleep of death to a blissful eternity. That was their sheet-anchor in life's stormy sea; that was the hope which supported and consoled millions of Egyptian men and women for a period of time far longer than that during which Christianity has now existed on earth. In the long history of religion no two divine figures resemble each other more closely in the fervour of personal devotion which they have kindled and in the high hopes which they have inspired than Osiris and Christ. The sad figure of Buddha indeed has been as deeply loved and revered by countless millions; but he had no glad tidings of immortality for men, nothing but the promise of a final release from the burden of mortality.

1 devotion of the Egyptians to Osiris suggests that he may have been a real man; for all the permanent semi-religious systems of the world have been founded by individual great men.

And if Osiris and Christ have been the centres of the like enthusiastic devotion, may not the secret of their influence have been similar? If Christ lived the life and died the death of a man on earth, may not Osiris have done so likewise? The immense and enduring popularity of his worship speaks in favour of the supposition; for all the other great religious or semi-religious systems which have won for themselves a permanent place in the affections of mankind, have been founded by individual great men, who by their personal life and example exerted a power of attraction such as no cold abstractions, no pale products of the collective wisdom or folly could ever exert on the minds and hearts of humanity. Thus it was with Buddhism, with [pg 160] Confucianism, with Christianity, and with Mohammedanism; and thus it may well have been with the religion of Osiris. Certainly we shall do less violence to the evidence if we accept the unanimous tradition of ancient Egypt on this point than if we resolve the figure of Osiris into a myth pure and simple. And when we consider that from the earliest to the latest times Egyptian kings were worshipped as gods both in life and in death, there appears to be nothing extravagant or improbable in the view that one of them by his personal qualities excited a larger measure of devotion than usual during his life and was remembered with fonder affection and deeper reverence after his death; till in time his beloved memory, dimmed, transfigured, and encircled with a halo of glory by the mists of time, grew into the dominant religion of his people. At least this theory is reasonable enough to deserve a serious consideration. If we accept it, we may suppose that the mythical elements, which legend undoubtedly ascribed to Osiris, were later accretions which gathered about his memory like ivy about a ruin. There is no improbability in such a supposition; on the contrary, all analogy is in its favour, for nothing is more certain than that myths grow like weeds round the great historical figures of the past.

al reality of Osiris as an old king of Egypt can be supported by modern African analogies.

In recent years the historical reality of Osiris as a king who once lived and reigned in Egypt has been maintained by more than one learned scholar;[425] and without venturing to pronounce a decided opinion on so obscure and difficult a question, I think it worth while, following the example of Dr. Wallis Budge, to indicate certain modern African analogies which tend to confirm the view that beneath the mythical wrappings of Osiris there lay the mummy of a dead man. At all events the analogies which I shall cite suffice to prove that the custom of worshipping dead kings has not been confined to Egypt, but has been apparently widespread throughout Africa, though the evidence now at our disposal only enables us to detect the observance of the [pg 161] custom at a few points of the great continent. But even if the resemblance in this respect between ancient Egypt and modern Africa should be regarded as established, it would not justify us in inferring an ethnical affinity between the fair or ruddy Egyptians and the black aboriginal races who occupy almost the whole of Africa except a comparatively narrow fringe on the northern sea-board. Scholars are still divided on the question of the original home and racial relationship of the ancient Egyptians. It has been held on the one hand that they belong to an indigenous white race which has been always in possession of the Mediterranean coasts of Africa; and on the other hand it has been supposed that they are akin to the Semites in blood as well as in language, and that they entered Africa from the East, whether by gradual infiltration or on a sudden wave of conquest like the Arabs in the decline of the Roman empire.[426] On either view a great gulf divided them from the swarthy natives of the Sudan, with whom they were always in contact on their southern border; and though a certain admixture may have taken place through marriage between the two races, it seems unsafe to assume that the religious and political resemblances which can be traced between them are based on any closer relationship than the general similarity in structure and functions of the human mind.

f dead kings worshipped by the Shilluks of the White Nile. Sacrifices to the dead kings.

In a former part of this work we saw that the Shilluks, a pastoral and partially agricultural people of the White Nile, worship the spirits of their dead kings.[427] The graves of the deceased monarchs form indeed the national or tribal [pg 162] temples; and as each king is interred at the village where he was born and where his afterbirth is buried, these grave-shrines are scattered over the country. Each of them usually comprises a small group of round huts, resembling the common houses of the people, the whole being enclosed by a fence; one of the huts is built over the grave, the others are occupied by the guardians of the shrine, who at first are generally the widows or old menservants of the deceased king. When these women or retainers die, they are succeeded in office by their descendants, for the tombs are maintained in perpetuity, so that the number of temples and of gods is always on the increase. Cattle are dedicated to these royal shrines and animals sacrificed at them. For example, when the millet crop threatens to fail or a murrain breaks out among the beasts, one of the dead kings will appear to somebody in a dream and demand a sacrifice. The dream is reported to the king, and he immediately orders a bullock and a cow to be sent to the grave of the dead king who appeared in a vision of the night to the sleeper. This is done; the bullock is killed and the cow added to the sacred herd of the shrine. It is customary, also, though not necessary, at harvest to offer some of the new millet at the temple-tombs of the kings; and sick people send animals to be sacrificed there on their behalf. Special regard is paid to trees that grow near the graves of the kings; and the spirits of the departed monarchs are believed to appear from time to time in the form of certain animals. One of them, for example, always takes the shape of a certain insect, which seems to be the larva of the *Mantidae*. When a Shilluk finds one of these insects, he will take it up in his hands and deposit it reverently at the shrine. Other kings manifest themselves as a certain species of white birds; others assume the form of giraffes. When one of these long-legged and long-necked creatures comes stalking up fearlessly to a village where there is a king's grave, the people know that the king's soul is in the animal, and the attendants at the royal tomb testify their joy at the appearance of their master by sacrificing a sheep or even a bullock.

Nyakang, the first of the Shilluk kings.

But of all the dead kings none is revered so deeply or [pg 163] occupies so large a place in the minds of the people as Nyakang, the traditional founder of the dynasty and the ancestor of all the kings who have reigned after him to the present day. Of these kings the Shilluks have preserved the memory and the genealogy; twenty-six seem to have sat on the throne since Nyakang, but the period of time covered by their reigns is much shorter than it would have been under conditions such as now prevail in Europe; for down to the time when their country came under British rule it was the regular custom of the Shilluks to put their kings to death as soon as they showed serious symptoms of bodily or mental decay. The custom was based on "the conviction that the king must not be allowed to become ill or senile, lest with his diminishing vigour the cattle should sicken and fail to bear their increase, the crops should rot in the fields, and man, stricken with disease, should die in ever-increasing numbers."[428] It is said that Nyakang, like Romulus, disappeared in a great storm, which scattered all the people about him; in their absence the king took a cloth, tied it tightly round his neck, and strangled himself. According to one account, that is the death which all his successors on the throne have died;[429] but while tradition appears to be unanimous as to the custom of regicide, it varies as to the precise mode in which the kings were relieved of their office and of life. But still the people are convinced that Nyakang did not really die but only vanished mysteriously away like the wind. When a missionary asked the Shilluks as to the manner of Nyakang's death, they were filled with amazement at his ignorance and stoutly maintained that he never died, for were he to die all the Shilluks would die also.[430] The graves of this deified king are shown in various parts of the country.

Nyakang supposed to manifest itself in certain animals.

From time to time the spirit of Nyakang manifests itself to his people in the form of an animal. Any creature of regal port or surpassing beauty may serve as his temporary incarnation. Such among wild animals are lions, crocodiles, little yellow snakes that crawl about men's houses, the finest sorts of antelopes, flamingoes with their rose-pink and scarlet [pg 164] plumage, and butterflies of all sorts with their brilliant and varied hues. An unusually fine head of cattle is also recognized as the abode of the great king's soul; for example he once appeared in the shape of a white bull, whereupon the living king commanded special sacrifices to be offered in honour of his deified predecessor. When a bird in which the royal spirit is known to be lodged lights on a tree, that tree becomes sacred to Nyakang; beads and cloths are hung on its boughs, sacrifices and prayers are offered below it. Once when the Turks unknowingly felled such a tree, fear and horror fell on the Shilluks who beheld the sacrilege. They filled the air with lamentations and killed an ox to appease their insulted ancestor.[431] Particular regard is also paid to trees that grow near the graves of Nyakang, though they are not regularly worshipped.[432] In one place two gigantic baobab trees are pointed out as marking the spot where Nyakang once stood, and sacrifices are now offered under their spreading shade.[433]

Nyakang seems to have been a real man. Relation of Nyakang to the creator Juok.

There seems to be no doubt that in spite of the mythical elements which have gathered round his memory, Nyakang was a real man, who led the Shilluks to their present home on the Nile either from the west or from the south; for on this point tradition varies. "The first and most important ancestor, who is everywhere revered, is Nyakang, the first Shilluk king. He always receives the honourable titles of Father (*uò*), Ancestor (*qua*), King (*red*) or Kings (*ror*), Ancestors, and Great Man Above (*čal duongmal*) to distinguish him from the other great men on earth. Nyakang, as we know, was an historical personage; he led the Shilluks to the land which they now occupy; he helped them to victory, made them great and warlike, regulated marriage and law, distributed the country among them, divided it into districts, and in order to increase the dependence of the people on him and to show them his power, became their greatest benefactor by giving himself out as the bestower of rain."[434] Yet Nyakang is now universally revered by the people as a demi-god; indeed for all practical purposes [pg 165] his worship quite eclipses that of the supreme god Juok, the creator, who, having ordered the world, committed it to the care of ancestral spirits and demons, and now, dwelling aloft, concerns himself no further with human affairs. Hence men pay little heed to their creator and seldom take his name into their lips except in a few conventional forms of salutation at meeting and parting like our "Good-bye." Far otherwise is it with Nyakang. He "is the ancestor of the Shilluk nation and the founder of the Shilluk dynasty. He is worshipped, sacrifices and prayers are offered to him; he may be said to be lifted to the rank of a demi-god, though they never forget that he has been a real man. He is expressly designated as 'little' in comparison with God." Yet "in the political, religious and personal life Nyakang takes a far more important place than Juok. Nyakang is the national hero, of whom each Shilluk feels proud, who is praised in innumerable popular songs and sayings; he is not only a superior being, but also a man. He is the sublime model for every true Shilluk; everything they value most in their national and private life has its origin in him: their kingdom and their fighting as well as cattle-breeding and farming. While Nyakang is their good father, who only does them good, Juok is the great, uncontrollable power, which is to be propitiated, in order to avoid his inflictions of evil."[435] Indeed "the whole working religion of the Shilluk is a cult of Nyakang, the semi-divine ancestor of their kings, in each of whom his spirit is immanent."[436] The transmission of the divine or semi-divine spirit of Nyakang to the reigning monarch appears to take place at the king's installation and to be effected by means of a rude wooden effigy of Nyakang, in which the spirit of that deified man is perhaps supposed to be immanent. But however the spiritual transmission may be carried out, "the fundamental idea of the cult of the Shilluk divine kings is the immanence in each of the spirit of Nyakang."[437] Thus the Shilluk kings are encircled with a [pg 166] certain halo of divinity because they are thought to be animated by the divine spirit of their ancestor, the founder of the dynasty.

the former humanity of Nyakang is confirmed by the analogy of his worship to that of the dead Shilluk

The universal belief of the Shilluks in the former humanity of Nyakang is strongly confirmed by the exact parallelism which prevails between his worship and that of the dead kings his successors. Like them he is worshipped at his tomb; but unlike them he has not one tomb only, but ten scattered over the country. Each of these tombs is called "the grave of Nyakang," though the people well know that nobody is buried there. Like the grave-shrines of the other kings, those of Nyakang consist of a small group of circular huts of the ordinary pattern enclosed by a fence. Only children under puberty and the few old people whose duty it is to take care of the shrines may enter these sacred enclosures. The rites performed at them resemble those observed at the shrines of the kings. Two great ceremonies are annually performed at the shrines of Nyakang: one is observed before the beginning of the rainy season in order to ensure a due supply of rain; the other is a thanksgiving at harvest, when porridge made from the new grain is poured out on the threshold of Nyakang's hut and smeared on the outer walls of the building. Even before the millet is reaped the people cut some of the ripening ears and thrust them into the thatch of the sacred hut. Thus it would seem that the Shilluks believe themselves to be dependent on the favour of Nyakang for the rain and the crops. "As the giver of rain, Nyakang is the first and greatest benefactor of the people. In that country rain is everything, without rain there is nothing. The Shilluk does not trouble his head about artificial irrigation, he waits for the rain. If the rain falls, then the millet grows, the cows thrive, man has food and can dance and marry; for that is the ideal of the Shilluks."[438] Sick people also bring or send sheep as an offering to the nearest shrine of Nyakang in order that they may be healed of their sickness. The attendants of the [pg 167] sanctuary slaughter the animal, consume its flesh, and give the sufferer the benefit of their prayers.[439]

of Nyakang with Osiris.

The example of Nyakang seems to show that under favourable circumstances the worship of a dead king may develop into the dominant religion of a people. There is, therefore, no intrinsic improbability in the view that in ancient Egypt the religion of Osiris originated in that way. Certainly some curious resemblances can be traced between the dead Nyakang and the dead Osiris. Both died violent and mysterious deaths: the graves of both were pointed out in many parts of the country: both were deemed the great sources of fertility for the whole land: and both were associated with certain sacred trees and animals, particularly with bulls. And just as Egyptian kings identified themselves both in life and in death with their deified predecessor Osiris, so Shilluk kings are still believed to be animated by the spirit of their deified predecessor Nyakang and to share his divinity.

f dead kings worshipped by the Baganda of Central Africa.

Another African people who regularly worship, or rather used to worship, the spirits of their dead kings are the Baganda. Their country Uganda lies at the very source of the Nile, where the great river issues from Lake Victoria Nyanza. Among them the ghosts of dead kings were placed on an equality with the gods and received the same honour and worship; they foretold events which concerned the State, and they advised the living king, warning him when war was likely to break out. The king consulted them periodically, visiting first one and then another of the temples in which the mortal remains of his predecessors were preserved with religious care. But the temple (*malolo*) of a king contained only his lower jawbone and his navel-string (*mulongo*); his body was buried elsewhere.[440] For curiously enough the Baganda believed that the part of the body to which the ghost of a dead man adheres above all others is the lower jawbone; wherever that portion of his person may be carried, the ghost, in the opinion of these people, will follow it, even to the ends of the earth, and will be perfectly content to remain with it so long as the jawbone is [pg 168] honoured.[441] Hence the jawbones of all the kings of Uganda from the earliest times to the present day have been preserved with the utmost care, each of them being deposited, along with the stump of the monarch's navel-string, in a temple specially dedicated to the worship of the king's ghost; for it is believed that the ghosts of the deceased monarchs would quarrel if they shared the same temple, the question of precedence being one which it would be very difficult for them to adjust to their mutual satisfaction.[442] All the temples of the dead kings stand in the district called Busiro, which means the place of the graves, because the tombs as well as the temples of the departed potentates are situated within its boundaries. The supervision of the temples and of the estates attached to them was a duty incumbent on the *Mugema* or earl of Busiro, one of the few hereditary chiefs in the country. His principal office was that of Prime Minister (*Katikiro*) to the dead kings.[443]

e dead kings of Uganda.

When a king dies, his body is sent to Busiro and there embalmed. Then it is laid to rest in a large round house, which has been built for its reception on the top of a hill. This is the king's tomb. It is a conical structure supported by a central post, with a thatched roof reaching down to the ground. Round the hut a high strong fence of reeds is erected, and an outer fence encircles the whole at some distance lower down the hill. Here the body is placed on a bedstead; the sepulchral chamber is filled with bark cloths till it can hold no more, the mainpost is cut down, and the door of the tomb closed, so that no one can enter it again. When that was done, the wives of the late king used to be brought, with their arms pinioned, and placed at intervals round the outer wall of the tomb, where they were clubbed to death. Hundreds of men were also killed in the space between the two fences, that their ghosts might wait on the ghost of the dead king in the other world. None of their bodies were buried; they were left to rot where they fell. Then the gates in the fences were closed; and three chiefs [pg 169] with their men guarded the dead bodies from the wild beasts and the vultures. But the hut in which the king's body reposed was never repaired; it was allowed to moulder and fall into decay.[444]

Five months later the jawbone of the royal corpse was removed in order to be fashioned into an effigy or representative of the dead king. For this purpose three chiefs entered the tomb, not through the door, but by cutting a hole through the wall, and having severed the head from the body they brought it out, carefully filling up the hole in the wall behind them, replacing the thatch, and securing the gates in the fence. When the jawbone had been removed by a chief of the Civet clan, the skull was sent back to Busiro and buried with honour near the mouldering tomb. In contrast to the neglect of the tomb where the royal body lay, the place where the skull was buried was kept in good repair and guarded by some of the old princesses and widows. As for the jawbone, it was put in an ant-hill and left there till the ants had eaten away all the flesh. Then, after it had been washed in beer and milk, it was decorated with cowry-shells and placed in a wooden vessel; this vessel was next wrapt in bark cloths till it assumed a conical shape, about two and a half feet high by a foot and a half broad at the base. This conical packet, decorated on the outside with beads, was treated as an image of the deceased king or rather as if it were the king himself in life, for it was called simply "The King." Beside it was placed the stump of the king's navel-string, similarly wrapt in bark cloths and decorated, though not made up into a conical shape.[445] The reason for preserving both the jawbone and the navel-string was that the ghost of the king was supposed to attach itself to his jawbone, and the ghost of his double to his navel-string. For in the belief of the Baganda every person has a double, namely, the afterbirth or placenta, which is born immediately after him and is regarded by the [pg 170] people as a second child. Now that double has a ghost of its own, which adheres to the navel-string; and if the person is to remain healthy, it is essential that the ghost of his double should be carefully preserved. Hence every Baganda man and woman keeps his or her navel-string wrapt up in bark cloth as a treasure of great price on which his health and prosperity are dependent; the precious little bundle is called his Twin (*mulongo*), because it contains the ghost of his double, the afterbirth. If that is deemed necessary for everybody, much more is it deemed essential for the welfare of the king; hence during his life the stump of his navel-string is kept, as we saw,[446] by one of the principal ministers of state and is inspected by the king himself every month. And when his majesty has departed this life, the unity of his spirit imperatively demands that his own ghost and the ghost of his double should be kept together in the same place; that is why the jawbone and the navel-string of every dead king are carefully preserved in the same temple, because the two ghosts adhere respectively to these two parts of his person, and it would be unreasonable and indeed cruel to divide them.[447]

The two ghosts having been thus safely lodged in the two precious parcels, the next thing was to install them in the temple, where they were to enter on their career of beneficent activity. A site having been chosen, the whole country supplied the labour necessary for building the temple; and ministers were appointed to wait upon the dead king. The officers of state who had held important posts during his life retained their titles and continued to discharge their duties towards their old master in death. Accordingly houses were built for them near the temple. The dowager queen also took up her residence at the entrance to the temple enclosure, and became its principal guardian. Many also of the king's widows of lower rank were drafted off to live inside the enclosure and keep watch over it. When the queen or any of these widows died, her place was supplied by another princess or a [pg 171] woman of the same clan; for the temple was maintained in perpetuity. However, when the reigning king died, the temple of his predecessor lost much of its importance, though it was still kept up in a less magnificent style; indeed no temple of a dead king was allowed to disappear altogether.[448] Of all the attendants at the temple the most important probably was the prophet or medium (*mandwa*), whose business it was from time to time to be inspired by the ghost of the deceased monarch and to give oracles in his name. To this holy office he dedicated himself by drinking a draught of beer and a draught of milk out of the dead king's skull.[449]

n by the dead kings of Uganda by the mouth of an inspired prophet.

The temple consecrated to the worship of a king regularly stood on a hill. The site was generally chosen by the king in his life, but sometimes his choice was set aside by his successor, who gave orders to build the temple in another place.[450] The structure was a large conical or bee-hive-shaped hut of the ordinary pattern, divided internally into two chambers, an outer and an inner. Any person might enter the outer chamber, but the inner was sacred and no profane person might set foot in it; for there the holy relics of the dead king, his jawbone and his navel-string, were kept for safety in a cell dug in the floor, and there, in close attendance on them, the king's ghost was believed to dwell. In front of the partition which screened this Holy of Holies from the gaze of the multitude there stood a throne, covered with lion and leopard skins and fenced off from the rest of the sacred edifice by a glittering rail of brass spears, shields, and knives. A forest of poles, supporting the roof, formed a series of aisles in perfect line, and at the end of the central nave appeared, like the altar of a Christian church, the throne in all its glory. When the king's ghost held a reception, the holy relics, the jawbone and the navel-string, each in its decorated wrappings, were brought forth and set on the throne; and every person who entered the temple bowed to the ground [pg 172] and greeted the jawbone in an awestruck voice, for he regarded it as the king in person. Solemn music played during the reception, the drums rolling and the women chanting, while they clapped their hands to the rhythm of the songs. Sometimes the dead king spoke to the congregation by the voice of his prophet. That was a great event. When the oracle was about to be given to the expectant throng, the prophet stepped up to the throne, and addressing the spirit informed him of the business in hand. Then he smoked one or two pipes, and the fumes bringing on the prophetic fit, he began to rave and to speak in the very voice and with the characteristic turns of speech of the departed monarch, for the king's spirit was now in him. This message from the world beyond the grave was naturally received with rapt attention. Gradually the fit of inspiration passed: the voice of the prophet resumed its natural tones: the spirit had departed from him and returned to its abode in the inner room. Such a solemn audience used to be announced beforehand by the beating of the drums in the early morning, and the worshippers brought with them to the temple offerings of food for the dead king, as if he were still alive.[451]

y the living king to the temple of his dead father. Human victims sacrificed in order that their ghosts the ghost of the dead king.

But the greatest day of all was when the reigning king visited the temple of his father. This he did as a rule only once during his reign. Nor did the people approve of the visits being repeated, for each visit was the signal for the death of many. Yet, attracted by a painful curiosity, crowds assembled, followed the monarch to the temple, and thronged to see the great ceremony of the meeting between the king and the ghost of his royal father. The sacred relics were displayed: an old man explained them to the monarch and placed them in his hands: the prophet, inspired by the dead king's spirit, revealed to the living king his destiny. The interview over, the king was carried back to his house. It was on the return journey that he always gave, suddenly and without warning, the signal of death. Obedient to his [pg 173] orders the guards rushed upon the crowd, captured hundreds of spectators, pinioned them, marched them back to the temple, and slaughtered them within the precincts, that their ghosts might wait on the ghost of the dead king.[452] But though the king rarely visited his father's ghost at the temple, he had a private chapel for the ghost within the vast enclosure of the royal residence; and here he often paid his devotions to the august spirit, of whom he stood greatly in awe. He took his wives with him to sing the departed monarch's praise, and he constantly made offerings at the shrine. Thither, too, would come the prophet to suck words of wisdom from the venerable ghost and to impart them to the king, who thus walked in the counsel of his glorified father.[453]

dead kings worshipped in Kiziba.

In Kiziba, a district of Central Africa on the western side of Lake Victoria

113

Nyanza, the souls of dead kings become ruling spirits; temples are built in their honour and priests appointed to serve them. The people are composed of two different races, the Bairu, who are aboriginals, and the Bahima, who are immigrants from the north. The royal family belongs to the Bahima stock. In his lifetime the king's person is sacred; and all his actions, property, and so forth are described by special terms appropriated to that purpose. The people are divided into totemic clans: the totems (*muziro*) are mostly animals or parts of animals: no man may kill or eat his totem animal, nor marry a woman who has the same totem as himself. The royal family seems to have serpents for their totem; after death the king's soul lives in a serpent, while his body is buried in the hut where he died. The people revere a supreme god named Rugaba, who is believed to have created man and cattle; but they know little about him, and though they [pg 174] occasionally pray to him, particularly in the case of a difficult birth, he has no priests and receives no sacrifices. The business of the priests is to act as intermediaries, not between God and man, but between men and the spirits. The spirits are believed to have been formerly kings of the world. The highest of them is a certain Wamara, who rules over the souls of the dead, and who would seem to have been a great king in his life. Temples are built for him; they are like the houses of men, but only half as large. A perpetual holy fire is kept up in each temple, and the priest passes the night in it. He receives white sheep or goats as victims, and generally acts also as a diviner or physician. When a man is very ill, he thinks that Wamara, the lord of the spirits of the dead, is summoning him to the far country; so he sends a sacrifice to Wamara's priest, who prays to the spirit to let the sick man live yet a while.[454] This great spirit of an ancient king, who now rules over the dead, resembles the Egyptian Osiris.

114

The Bantu tribes who inhabit the great tableland of Northern Rhodesia revere a supreme being whom they call Leza, but their ideas about him are hazy. Thunder, lightning, earthquakes, rain, and other natural phenomena are grouped together under his name as manifestations of his power. Among the more progressive tribes, such as the Awemba and the Wabisa, the great god is thought to take some interest in human affairs; and though they do not pray to him, they nevertheless invoke him by his names of praise, which set forth his attributes as the protector and judge of mankind. It is he, too, who receives the souls of the departed. "Yet, as far as the dominant Wemba tribe is concerned, the cult of Leza is outside their ordinary religion. There is no direct access to him by prayer or by sacrifices, which are made to Mulenga and the other great [pg 175] tribal and ancestral spirits instead. For upon such animism is founded the whole fabric of Wemba religion."[455] The ancestral spirits whom the Awemba and all other tribes of this region worship may be divided into two main classes. First come the spirits of departed chiefs, who are publicly worshipped by the whole tribe; and second come the spirits of near relations who are worshipped privately by each head of a family.[456] "Among the Awemba there is no special shrine for these purely family spirits, who are worshipped inside the hut, and to whom family sacrifice of a sheep, a goat, or a fowl is made, the spirit receiving the blood spilt on the ground, while all the members of the family partake of the flesh together. For a religious Wemba man the cult of the spirit of his nearest relations (of his grandparents, or of his deceased father, mother, elder brother, or maternal uncle) is considered quite sufficient. Out of these spirit relatives a man will worship one whom he considers as his special familiar, for various reasons. For instance, the diviner may have told him that his last illness was caused because he had not respected the spirit of his uncle; accordingly he will be careful in future to adopt his uncle as his tutelary spirit. As a mark of such respect he may devote a cow or a goat to one of the spirits of his ancestors. Holding the fowl, for instance, in his hands, he will dedicate it, asking the spirit to come and abide in it, upon which the fowl is let go, and is afterwards called by the name of the spirit. If the necessities, however, of the larder demand that it should be killed, another animal is taken, and the spirit is asked to accept it as a substitute! Before beginning any special task, such as hoeing a new garden, or going on a journey, Wemba men invoke their tutelary spirits to be with them and to assist their efforts, in short ejaculatory prayers usually couched in a set formula. Among many of the tribes in the North Luangwa district longer formal prayers are still made to all the deceased ancestors of the clan at the time of harvest, asking them to protect the crops and to drive away illnesses and evil spirits from [pg 176] the family, which honours them with libations of beer and offerings of the first-fruits."[457]

of ancestral spirits is apparently the main practical religion of all the Bantu tribes.

Thus among these tribes, who all belong to the great Bantu family, the public worship which a whole tribe pays to the souls of its dead chiefs is probably nothing but an extension of the private worship which every family pays privately to the souls of its dead members. And just as the members of his family whom a man worships privately are not mythical beings conjured up by imagination out of a distant past, but were once real men like himself whom he knew in life, it may be his father, or uncle, or elder brother, so we may be sure that in like manner the dead chiefs revered by the whole tribe are not creations of the mythical fancy, but were once real men of flesh and blood, who ruled over the tribe, and whose memory has been more or less faithfully preserved by tradition. In this respect the tribes of Northern Rhodesia are typical of all the tribes of that great Bantu family which occupies nearly the whole southern half of Africa, from the great equatorial lakes to the Cape of Good Hope. The main practical religion of all these numerous and widespread peoples appears to be the worship of their ancestors.

of ancestral spirits among the Bantu tribes of South Africa.

To adduce in full the evidence which points to this conclusion would lead us too far from our present subject; it must suffice to cite a few typical statements of competent authorities which refer to different tribes of the Bantu stock. Speaking with special reference to the tribes of South-Eastern Africa, the Rev. James Macdonald tells us that "the religion of the Bantu, which they not only profess but really regulate their conduct by, is based on the belief that the spirits of their ancestors interfere constantly in their affairs. Every man worships his own ancestors and offers sacrifices to avert their wrath. The clan worships the spirits of the ancestors of its chiefs, and the tribe worships the spirits of the ancestors of the paramount chief."[458] "The religion of the Bantu was based upon the supposition of the [pg 177] existence of spirits that could interfere with the affairs of this world. These spirits were those of their ancestors and their deceased chiefs, the greatest of whom had control over lightning. When the spirits became offended or hungry they sent a plague or disaster until sacrifices were offered and their wrath or hunger was appeased. The head of a family of commoners on such an occasion killed an animal, and all ate of the meat, as the hungry ghost was supposed to be satisfied with the smell."[459] For example, in the year 1891 the son of a chief of the Pondomisi tribe was arrested for an assault and sent for trial before a colonial court. It chanced to be a season of intense heat and severe drought, and the Pondomisi tribe attributed these calamities to the wrath of a dead chief named Gwanya, very famous in his lifetime, whose body, fastened to a

116

log, had been buried under a heap of stones in a deep pool of the Lina river. This redoubtable chieftain was the seventh ancestor in the direct line of the man who had committed the assault; and he warmly resented the indignity which the whites had done to a noble scion of his house by consigning him to durance vile. To appease the natural indignation of the ghost, the tribesmen killed cattle on the banks of the pool which contained his grave, and threw the flesh into the water along with new dishes full of beer. The prisoner, however, was convicted of the assault and sentenced by the ruthless magistrate, who was no respecter of ghosts, to pay a fine. But the tribe clubbed together and paid the fine for him; and a few days later rain fell in plenty. The mollified ghost had opened the celestial sluices.[460]

the dead among the Bantu tribes of South Africa.

Another writer, describing the religion of the South [pg 178] African Bantus, tells us that "the ancestral spirits love the very things they loved before they passed through the flesh; they cherish the same desires and have the same antipathies. The living cannot add to the number of the wives of ancestral spirits; but they can kill cattle in their honour and keep their praise and memory alive on earth. Above all things, they can give them beef and beer. And if the living do not give them sufficient of these things the spirits are supposed to give the people a bad time: they send drought, and sickness, and famine, until people kill cattle in their honour. When men are alive they love to be praised and flattered, fed and attended to; after death they want the very same things, for death does not change personality.... In time of drought, or sickness, or great trouble, there would be great searchings of heart as to which ancestor had been neglected, for the trouble would be supposed to be caused by the neglected ancestor. Most of the people would get the subject on their nerves (at least, as far as a Kafir could get anything on the leather strings which do duty for nerves), and some one would be sure to have a vivid dream in which an ancestor would complain that the people had not praised him half enough of late. So an ox would be killed, either by the head-man of the kraal or by a diviner. Then the man would say over the ox as it was being killed, 'Cry out, ox of So-and-So; listen to us, So-and-So; this is your ox; we praise you by all your laud-giving names, and tell of all your deeds; do not be angry with us any more; do you not see that this is your ox? Do not accuse us of neglecting you; when, forsooth, have we ceased to praise you and offer you meat and beer? Take note, then, that here is another ox we are offering to you.' When the ox is dead some of the meat is mixed with herbs and medicines and placed in a hut with a bowlful of blood. This meat is placed in the part of the hut where the man loved to sit while he was alive, and some one is told off to guard the sacrifice. The meat is left for a night, or longer, and the spirits are supposed to come and enjoy the smell, or drink the serum which oozes from the meat, and to inhale the smell of the beer. The priest or diviner will then sprinkle the people and the huts with medicine made from the contents of the [pg 179] stomach of the ox. He places a little on a sherd; when this is dry he burns it and calls on the spirits to smell the incense. After the meat has been left for a certain time it is taken out and cooked, and eaten by the men near the cattle kraal in public.... If the trouble does not vanish after this ceremony the people get angry and say to the spirits, 'When have we ceased to kill cattle for you, and when have we ever refused to praise you by your praise-names? Why, then, do you treat us so shabbily? If you do not behave better we shall utterly forget your names, and then what will you do when there is no one to praise you? You will have to go and live on grasshoppers. If you do not mend your ways we shall forget you. What use is it that we kill oxen for you and praise you? You do not give us rain or crops, or cause our cattle to bear well; you show no gratitude in return for all we do for you. We shall utterly disown you. We shall tell the people that, as for us, we have no ancestral spirits, and this will be to your shame. We are disgusted with you.' "[461] Thus the sweet savour of beef and beer does not suffice to content Caffre ghosts; they share the love of praise and flattery with many gods of higher rank.

he dead among the Basutos.

Among the Basutos, an important Bantu people of South Africa, "each family is supposed to be under the direct influence and protection of its ancestors; but the tribe, taken as a whole, acknowledges for its national gods the ancestors of the reigning sovereign. Thus, the Basutos address their prayers to Monaheng and Motlumi, from whom their chiefs are descended. The Baharutsis and the Barolongs invoke Tobege and his wife Mampa. Mampa makes known the will of her husband, announcing each of her revelations by these words, '*O re! O re!*' 'He has said! he has said!' They make a distinction between the ancient and modern divinities. The latter are considered inferior in power, but more accessible; hence this formula, which is often used: 'New gods! entreat the ancient gods for us!' In all countries spirits are more the objects of fear than of love. A deep feeling of terror generally accompanies the idea that the dead dispose of the lot of the living. [pg 180] The ancients spoke much of incensed shades. If they sacrificed to the manes, it was generally in order to appease them. These ideas perfectly correspond to those of the Basutos. They conjure rather than pray; although they seek to gain favours, they think more of averting chastisement. Their predominating idea as to their ancestors is, that they are continually endeavouring to draw them to themselves. Every disease is attributed to them; thus medicine among these people is almost entirely a religious affair. The first thing is to discover, by means of the *litaola* (divining bones), under the influence of what *molimo* the patient is supposed to be. Is it an ancestor on the father's side or the mother's? According as fate decides, the paternal or maternal uncle will offer the purifying sacrifice, but rarely the father or brother. This sacrifice alone can render efficacious the medicines prescribed by the *ngaka* (doctor).... As soon as a person is dead he takes his place among the family gods. His remains are deposited in the cattle-pen. An ox is immolated over his grave: this is the first oblation made to the new divinity, and at the same time an act of intercession in his favour, serving to ensure his happy reception in the subterranean regions. All those present aid in sprinkling the grave, and repeat the following prayer: 'Repose in peace with the gods; give us tranquil nights.'"[462]

he dead among the Thonga.

Similarly among the Thonga, another Bantu tribe of South Africa, "any man, who has departed this earthly life, becomes a *shikwembu*, a god";[463] "when an old decrepit man or woman dies, he at once becomes a god: he has entered the domain of infinity."[464] In this tribe "the spirits of the ancestors are the main objects of religious worship. They form the principal category of spirits."[465] "On the one hand, the ancestor-gods are truly gods, endowed with the attributes of divinity; whilst, on the other, they seem to be nothing but mere human beings, exactly on the same level as their worshippers."[466] There are two great classes [pg 181] of these ancestor-gods, to wit, "those of the family, and those of the country, the latter being those of the reigning family. They do not differ as regards their nature. In national calamities those of the country are invoked, whilst, for purely family matters, those of the family are called upon. Moreover, each family has two sets of gods, those on the father's side and those on the mother's, those of *kweru* and those of *bakokwana*. They are equal in dignity. Both can be invoked, and the divinatory bones are always asked to which the offering must be made. It seems, however, as if the gods on the mother's side were more tender-hearted and more popular than those on the father's. The reason for this is, perhaps, that relations are easier with the family of the mother than with that of the father. It is also just possible that it is a relic of the matriarchal period, when the ancestors of the mother only were known, and consequently invoked. At any rate, the part played by *batukulu* [uterine] nephews in the offerings shows that they are the true representatives of the gods, not of those of their father, but of their mother."[467] Among the Thonga "the belief in the continuation of life after death is universal, being at the base of the ancestrolatry, which is the religion of the tribe."[468] "How real is the ancestrolatry, the religion of the Thonga, of, in fact, all the South African Bantus! How frequent and manifold are its manifestations! This is the first, and the most perceptible set of their religious intuitions, and any European, who has stayed in their villages, learnt their language, and tried to understand their customs, has had the opportunity of

119

familiarizing himself with this religion."[469]

dead chiefs among the Basutos and Bechuanas.

Among the Basutos and Bechuanas, who also belong to the great Bantu family, the sacrificial ritual is not highly developed. "Only in great misfortunes which affect the whole people or the royal family, a black ox is slaughtered; for in such cases they always think that the angry spirits of the departed are the cause of all the suffering. '*Re amogioa ki badimo,*' say the people, 'the spirits are robbing us.' The ox is led to the chiefs grave; there they [pg 182] pray, 'Lord, we are come to call upon thee, we who are thy children; make not our hearts troubled; take not, Lord, that which is ours.' The old chief is honoured and praised in songs, he is invoked by all his praise-names, the ox is killed and its flesh eaten, but the blood and the contents of the stomach are poured on the grave, and there the bones of the sacrificed animal are also deposited."[470]

he dead among the Zulus.

The Zulus, another great Bantu tribe of South Africa, believe in the existence of a being whom they call Unkulunkulu, which means "the Old-Old-one, the most ancient man." They say that "it is he who was the first man; he broke off in the beginning. We do not know his wife; and the ancients do not tell us that he had a wife."[471] This Old-Old-one or Great-Great-one "is represented as having made all things—men, cattle, water, fire, the mountains, and whatever else is seen. He is also said to have appointed their names. Creation was effected by splitting a reed, when the first man and other things issued from the cleft."[472] Further, the Zulus and other Caffre tribes of Natal "believe that, when a person dies, his *i-hloze* or *isi-tute* survives. These words are translated 'spirit,' and there seems no objection to the rendering. They refer to something manifestly distinguished from the body, and the nature of which the prophets endeavour to explain by saying that it is identical with the shadow. The residence of the *ama-hloze*, or spirits, seems to be beneath; the practice of breaking a man's assagais, before they are buried with him, shows that he is believed to return to earth through the grave; while it appears to be generally thought that, if the earth were removed from the grave, the ghost would return and frighten his descendants. When spirits have entered the future state, they are believed to possess great power; prosperity is ascribed to their favour, and misfortune to their anger; they are elevated in fact to the rank of deities, and (except where the Great-Great is worshipped concurrently with them) they are the only objects of a Kafir's adoration. Their attention [pg 183] (or providence) is limited to their own relatives—a father caring for the family, and a chief for the tribe, which they respectively left behind them. They are believed to occupy the same relative position as they did in the body, the departed spirit of a chief being sometimes invoked to compel a man's ancestors to bless him."[473]

d prayers to the dead among the Zulus.

"To these shades of the dead, especially to the ghosts of their great men, as Jama, Senzangakona, and Chaka, their former kings, they look for help, and offer sacrifices; that is, slaughter cattle to them, and offer a sort of prayer, in time of danger and distress.... When they are sick, they slaughter cattle to the shades, and say, 'Father, look on me, that this disease may cease from me. Let me have health on the earth, and live a long time.' They carry the meat into the house, and shut it up there, saying, 'Let the paternal shades eat, so shall they know that the offering was made for them, and grant us great wealth, so that both we and our children may prosper.' In the cattle-fold they talk a long time, praising the ghosts; they take the contents of the stomach, and strew it upon all the fold. Again they take it, and strew it within the houses, saying, 'Hail, friend! Thou of such a place, grant us a blessing, beholding what we have done. You see this distress; may you remove it, since we have given you our animal. We know not what more you want, whether you still require anything more or not.' They say, 'May you grant us grain, that it may be abundant, that we may eat, of course, and not be in need of anything, since now we have given you what you want.' They say, 'Yes, for a long time have you preserved me in all my going. Behold, you see, I have just come to have a kraal. This kraal was built by yourself, father; and now why do you consent to diminish your own kraal? Build on us as you have begun, let it be large, that your offspring, still here above, may increase, increasing in knowledge of you, whence cometh great power.' Sometimes they make beer for the ghosts, and leave a little in the pot, saying, 'It will be eaten by the ghosts that they may grant an abundant harvest again, that we may not have a famine.' If one is on the point of being injured by anything, he says, 'I was preserved [pg 184] by our divinity, which was still watching over me.' Perhaps he slaughters a goat in honour of the same, and puts the gall on his head; and when the goat cries out for pain of being killed, he says, 'Yes, then, there is your animal, let it cry, that ye may hear, ye our gods who have preserved me; I myself am desirous of living on thus a long time here on the earth; why then do you call me to account, since I think I am all right in respect to you? And while I live, I put my trust in you, our paternal and maternal gods.' "[474]

u account of the worship of the dead.

"Black people," say the Zulus, "do not worship all Amatongo indifferently, that is, all the dead of their tribe. Speaking generally, the head of each house is worshipped by the children of that house; for they do not know the ancients who are dead, nor their laud-giving names, nor their names. But their father whom they knew is the head by whom they begin and end in their prayer, for they know him best, and his love for his children; they remember his kindness to them whilst he was living; they compare his treatment of them whilst he was living, support themselves by it, and say, 'He will still treat us in the same way now he is dead. We do not know why he should regard others besides us; he will regard us only.' So it is then although they worship the many Amatongo of their tribe, making a great fence around them for their protection; yet their father is far before all others when they worship the Amatongo. Their father is a great treasure to them even when he is dead. And those of his children who are already grown up know him thoroughly, his gentleness, and his bravery. And if there is illness in the village, the eldest son lauds him with the laud-giving names which he gained when fighting with the enemy, and at the same time lauds all the other Amatongo; the son reproves the father, saying, 'We for our parts may just die. Who are you looking after? Let us die all of us, that we may see into whose house you will enter.[475] You will eat grasshoppers; you will no longer be [pg 185] invited to go anywhere, if you destroy your own village.' After that, because they have worshipped him, they take courage saying, 'He has heard; he will come and treat our diseases, and they will cease.' Such then is the faith which children have in the Itongo [ancestral spirit] which is their father. And if there is a chief wife of a village, who has given birth to children, and if her husband is not dead, her Itongo is much reverenced by her husband and all the children. And that chief wife becomes an Itongo which takes great care of the village. But it is the father especially that is the head of the village."[476] Thus among the Zulus it is the spirits of those who have just died, especially the spirits of fathers and mothers, who are most revered and worshipped. The spirits of the more remote dead are forgotten.

of the dead among the Herero of German South-West Africa. Ancestral spirits (*Ovakuru*) worshipped o.

When the missionaries inquired into the religious ideas of the Herero, a Bantu tribe of German South-West Africa, they heard much of a certain Mukuru, whom at first they took to be the great god of heaven and earth. Accordingly they adopted Mukuru as the native name for the Christian God, and set out on their mission to preach the glad tidings of Mukuru and his divine Son to the poor benighted heathen. But their first experiences were disconcerting. Again and again when they arrived in a village and announced their intention to the chief, they were brought up very short by that great man, who told them with an air of astonishment that he himself was Mukuru. For example, Messrs. Büttner and Irle paid a visit to an old chief named Tjenda and remonstrated with him on the impropriety of which he had been guilty in giving a baptized girl in marriage to a native gentleman whose domestic arrangements were framed on the polygamous patriarchal pattern. "Mukuru will punish you for that," said Mr. Büttner. "What?" roared the chief. "Who's Mukuru? Why, I am

Mukuru in my own tribe," and he [pg 186] bundled the two missionaries out of the village. A repetition of these painful incidents at last impressed on the minds of the missionaries the conviction that Mukuru was not God at all but merely the head of a family, an ancestor, whether alive or dead.[477] They ascertained at the same time that the Herero recognize a good god who dwells in heaven and bears the name of Ndjambi Karunga. But they do not worship him nor bring him offerings, because he is so kind that he hurts nobody, and therefore they need not fear him. "Rather they share the opinion of the other Bantu tribes that Ndjambi, the good Creator, has withdrawn to heaven and left the government on earth to the demons."[478] "It is true that the Herero are acquainted with punishment for what is bad. But that punishment they ascribe to Mukuru or their ancestors. It is their ancestors (*Ovakuru*[479]) whom they must fear; it is they who are angry and can bring danger and misfortune on a man. So it is intelligible that the whole of their worship turns, not on Ndjambi Karunga, but on their ancestors. It is in order to win and keep their favour, to avert their displeasure and wrath, in short to propitiate them, that the Herero bring their many offerings; they do so not out of gratitude, but out of fear, not out of love, but out of terror. Their religion is a worship of ancestors with here and there touches of fetishism."[480] "Thus among the Herero, as among all Bantu tribes, there exists a religious dualism: they know the highest, the true God, but they worship their ancestors."[481] And among the worshipful [pg 187] ancestors "the old dead chiefs of every tribe take the first place. The son of a great dead chief and the whole tribe worship that old father as their god. But the remote ancestors of that chief they do not worship, indeed they hardly know them by name and can no longer point to their graves."[482] Thus with the Herero, as with the Zulus, it is the recent and well-remembered dead who are chiefly or exclusively worshipped; as the souls of the departed recede [pg 188] further and further into the past their memory perishes, and the nimbus of supernatural glory which encircled it for a time fades gradually away.

of the dead among the Ovambo.

The religion of the Ovambo, another Bantu tribe of German South-West Africa, is similar. They also recognize a great being named Kalunga, who created the world and man, but they neither fear nor worship him. A far greater part is played in the religion of the Ovambo by their belief in spirits, and amongst the worshipful spirits a conspicuous place is assigned to the souls of the dead. Every man leaves behind him at death a spirit, which continues to exist on earth and can influence the living; for example, it may enter into their bodies and thereby cause all sorts of sickness. However, the souls of ordinary dead men can exert their influence only on members of their own families; the souls of dead chiefs, on the other hand, have power over the rain, which they can either give or withhold. To these powerful spirits a

123

portion of the new corn is offered at harvest as a thank-offering for their forbearance in not visiting the people with sickness, and above all for their bounty in sending down the fertilizing showers on the crops. The souls of dead magicians are particularly dreaded; and to prevent the multiplication of these dangerous spirits it is customary to dismember their bodies, severing the arms and legs from the trunk and cutting the tongue out of the mouth. If these precautions are taken immediately after death, the soul of the dead man cannot become a dangerous ghost; the mutilation of his body has practically disarmed his spirit.[483]

of the dead among the Wahehe of German East Africa.

The Wahehe, a Bantu tribe of German East Africa, believe in a great invisible spirit named Nguruhi, who created the world and rules both human destiny and the elements. He it is who makes the rain to fall, the sun to shine, the wind to blow, the thunder to roll, and the crops to grow. "This god is accordingly conceived as all-powerful, yet with the limitation that he only exercises a general power of direction over the world, especially human fate, while the *masoka*, the spirits of the dead, wield a permanent [pg 189] and very considerable influence on the course of particular events. Nguruhi is lord also of all the spirits of the dead (*masoka*), but his relation to them has not been further thought out. With this Supreme Being the people hold no intercourse by means of prayer, sacrifice, or in any other way. He stands remote from the religious life of the Wahehe and really serves only as an explanation of all those things and events which are otherwise inexplicable. All religious intercourse, all worship centres alone on the spirits of the dead. Hence if we speak of a religion of the Wahehe, it must be described as a pure worship of ancestors."[484] The human soul quits the body at death and at once becomes an ancestral spirit (*m'soka*), invisible and endowed with complete liberty of motion. Even the youngest children have souls which rank among the ancestral spirits at death. Hence the great multitude of the dead comprises spirits of all ages, from the infant one day old to the grey-haired patriarch. They are good or bad according as they were good or bad in life, and their social position also is unchanged. He who was powerful in life is powerful also in death; he who was a nobody among men is a nobody also among the spirits. Hence the ghost of a great man can do more for the living than the ghost of a common man; and the ghost of a man can do more than the ghost of a woman. Yet even the meanest ghost has power over the greatest living man, who can only defend himself by appealing for help to stronger ancestral spirits. Thus while the Supreme Being exercises a general superintendence over affairs, the real administration is in the hands of the ancestral spirits. While he, for example, regulates the weather as a whole, it is the ghosts who cause each particular shower to fall or the sun to break out in glory from the clouds. If he sends plagues on the whole people or stays the ravages of disease, it is the ghosts who make each individual sick or sound. These powerful spirits exert themselves especially to help their descendants, though they [pg 190] do not hesitate to plague their own kith and kin if they think themselves neglected. They flit freely through the air and perch on trees, mountains, and so forth, but they lodge by preference at their graves, and you are always sure of finding them there, if you wish to consult them.[485] That is why in the country of the Wahehe the only places of sacrifice are the graves; temples and altars are unknown.[486] However, it is only the bodies of considerable persons that are buried; the corpses of common folk are simply thrown away in the bush;[487] so that the number of graves and consequently of sacrificial places is strictly limited. The spirits of the dead appear to the living most commonly in dreams to give them information or warning, but oftener to chide and torment them. So the sleeper wakes in a fright and consults a diviner, who directs him what he must do in order to appease the angry ghost. Following the directions of his spiritual adviser the man sacrifices an ox, or it may be only a sheep or a fowl, at the tomb of one of his ancestors, prays to the ghost, and having scattered a few morsels of the victim's flesh on the grave, and spat a mouthful of beer upon it, retires with his family to feast on the remainder of the carcase. Such sacrifices to the dead are offered on occasion of sickness, the lack of male heirs, a threatened war, an intended journey, in short, before any important undertaking of which the issue is doubtful; and, they are accompanied by prayers for health, victory, good harvests, and so forth.[488]

of the dead among the Bahima of Ankole, in Central Africa.

Once more, the Bahima, a Bantu people of Ankole, in Central Africa, believe in a supreme god Lugaba, who dwells in the sky and created man and beast; but "this supreme being is not worshipped nor are offerings made to him; he has no sacred place. Although they talk freely about him, and acknowledge him to be their great benefactor, they accept all his gifts as a matter of course, and make him no offering in return.... One must not, therefore, conclude that the Bahima are an irreligious people; like most of the Bantu tribes their religion consists chiefly in dealing with ghosts of departed relatives, and in standing well with them; [pg 191] from the king to the humblest peasant the ghosts call for daily consideration and constant offerings, whilst the deities are only sought in case of great trials or national calamities."[489]

To return, now, to the worship of dead chiefs or kings among the Bantu tribes of Northern Rhodesia. The spirits of dead chiefs had priestesses to wait upon them, who were called the "wives of the departed." These were elderly women who led a celibate life and swept the huts dedicated to the ghosts of the chiefs. The aid of these dead potentates was invoked in time of war and in seasons of drought, and special offerings were brought to their shrines at harvest.[490] Among the Awemba, who form the aristocracy of the country,[491] when a diviner announced that a drought was caused by the spirits of dead chiefs or kings buried at Mwaruli, a bull would be sent to be sacrificed to the souls of the deceased rulers; or if the drought was severe, a human victim would be despatched, and the high priest would keep him caged in a stoutly woven fish-basket, until the preparations for the sacrifice were complete.[492] Among the Yombe no one might eat of the first-fruits of the crops until the living chief had sacrificed a bull before the tomb of his grandfather, and had deposited pots of fresh beer and porridge, made from the first-fruits, in front of the shrine. The ground about the tomb was then carefully weeded, and the blood of the sacrificial victim sprinkled on the freshly turned up soil and on the rafters of the little hut. After thanking the ghost of his grandfather for the harvest, and begging him to partake of the first-fruits, the chief and his train withdrew to feast on the carcase and the fresh porridge and beer at the village.[493] When the head chief or king of the Awemba had resolved [pg 192] to make war on a distant enemy, he and the older men of the tribe would pray daily for victory to the spirits of the dead kings, his predecessors. The day before the army was to set forth, the great war-drum boomed out and the warriors flocked together from the outlying districts under their respective captains. In the dusk of the evening the king and the elderly women, who passed for the wives of the dead kings and tended their shrines at the capital, went and prayed at these shrines that the souls of the departed monarchs would keep the war-path free from foes and lead the king in a straight course to the enemy's stockade. These solemn prayers the king led in person, and the women beat their bare breasts as they joined in the earnest appeal. Next morning the whole army was marshalled in front of the ghost-huts of the dead kings: the living king danced a war-dance before his ancestors, while his chief wife sprinkled him with holy flour; and all prostrated themselves in supplication before the shrines.[494]

e tribes the spirits of dead chiefs or kings are thought sometimes to take bodily possession of men and be incarnate in animals.

Among these tribes of Northern Rhodesia the spirits of dead chiefs or kings sometimes take possession of the bodies of live men or women and prophesy through their mouths. When the spirit of a dead chief comes over a man, he begins to roar like a lion, whereupon the women gather together and beat the drums, shouting that the chief has come to visit the village. The man thus temporarily inspired will prophesy of future wars or impending attacks by lions. While the inspiration lasts, he may eat nothing cooked by fire, but only unfermented dough. However, the spirit of a departed chief takes possession of women oftener than of men. "These women assert that they are possessed by the soul of some dead chief, and when they feel the divine afflatus, whiten their faces to attract attention, and anoint themselves with flour, which has a religious and sanctifying potency. One of their number beats a drum, and the others dance, singing at the same time a weird song, with curious intervals. Finally, when they have arrived at the requisite pitch of religious exaltation, the possessed woman falls to the ground, and bursts forth [pg 193] into a low and almost inarticulate chant, which has a most uncanny effect. All are silent at once, and the *bashing'anga* (medicine-men) gather round to interpret the voice of the spirit."[495] Sometimes the spirits of departed chiefs are reincarnated in animals, which are then revered as the abodes of the dead rulers. Thus the paramount chief of the Amambwe is incarnated after death in the form of a young lion, while Bisa and Wiwa chiefs come back in the shape of pythons. In one of the rest-houses near Fife a tame python waxed fat on the offerings of fowls and sour beer which the Winamwanga presented to it in the fond belief that it housed the spirit of one of their dead chiefs. One day unfortunately for himself the reptile deity ventured to dispute the possession of the rest-house with a German cattle-dealer who was passing by; a discharge of shot settled the dispute in favour of the cattle-dealer, and the worshippers of the deity beheld him no more.[496]

Barotse in a supreme god Niambe.

Another Bantu people who worship the spirits of their dead kings are the Barotse or Marotse of the Upper Zambesi. The Barotse believe in a supreme god, the creator of all things, whom they call Niambe. He lives in the sun, and by his marriage with the moon begat the world, the animals, and last of all men. But the cunning and ferocity of his creature man terrified the beneficent creator, so that he fled from earth and escaped up the thread of a spider's web to heaven. There he still retains a certain power to interfere in human affairs, and that is why men sometimes pray and sacrifice to him. For example, the worshipper salutes the rising sun and offers him a vessel of water, no doubt to quench the thirst of the deity on his hot journey across the sky. Again, when a long drought has prevailed, a black ox is sacrificed to Niambe "as a symbol of the clouds big with the longed-for rain." And before they sow the fields, the women pile the seeds and their digging hoes in a heap, and pray to the god that he would render their labour fruitful.[497]

[pg 194]

127

Yet while they acknowledge the divine supremacy of Niambe, the Barotse address their prayers most frequently to the inferior deities, the *ditino*, who are the deified kings of the country. The tombs of the departed monarchs may be seen near the villages which they inhabited in life. Each tomb stands in a grove of beautiful trees and is encircled by a tall palisade of pointed stakes, covered with fine mats, like the palisade which surrounds the royal residence of a living king. Such an enclosure is sacred; the people are forbidden to enter it lest they should disturb the ghost of him who sleeps below. But the inhabitants of the nearest village are charged with the duty of keeping the tomb and the enclosure in good order, repairing the palisade, and replacing the mats when they are worn out. Once a month, at the new moon, the women sweep not only the grave and the enclosure but the whole village. The guardian of the tomb is at the same time a priest; he acts as intermediary between the god and the people who come to pray to the deity. He bears the title of Ngomboti; he alone has the right to enter the sacred enclosure; the profane multitude must stand at a respectful distance. Even the king himself, when he comes to consult one of his ancestors, is forbidden to set foot on the holy ground. In presence of the god, or, as they call him, the Master of the Tomb, the monarch must bear himself like a slave in the presence of his lord. He kneels down near the entrance, claps his hands, and gives the royal salute; and from within the enclosure the priest solemnly returns the salute, just as the king himself, when he holds his court, returns the salute of his subjects. Then the suppliant, whether king or commoner, makes his petition to the deity and deposits his offering; for no man may pray to the god with empty hands. Inside the enclosure, close to the entrance, is a hole which is supposed to serve as a channel of communication with the spirit of the deified king. In it the offerings are placed. Often they consist of milk which is poured into the hole; and the faster it drains away, the more favourably inclined is the god thought to be to the petitioner. More solid offerings, such as flesh, clothes, and glass beads, become the property of the priest after they have been allowed to lie for a decent time beside the sacred [pg 195] aperture of the tomb. The spirits of dead kings are thus consulted on matters of public concern as well as by private individuals touching their own affairs. If a war is to be waged, if a plague is raging among the people or a murrain among the cattle, if the land is parched with drought, in short, if any danger threatens or any calamity has afflicted the country, recourse is had to these local gods, dwelling each in his shady grove, not far from the abodes of the living. They are near, but the great god in heaven is far away. What wonder, therefore, that their help is often sought while he is neglected? They are national heroes as well as gods; their history is remembered; men tell of the doughty deeds they did in their lifetime; why should they not be able to succour their votaries now that they have put on immortality? All over the country these temple-tombs may be seen. They serve as historical monuments to recall to the people the names of their former kings and the annals of their country. One of the most popular of the royal shrines is near Senanga at the southern end of the great plain of the Barotse. Voyagers who go down the Zambesi do not fail to pay their devotions at the shrine, that the god of the place may make their voyage to prosper and may guard the frail canoe from shipwreck in the rush and roar of the rapids; and when they return in safety they repair again to the sacred spot to deposit a thank-offering for the protection of the deity.[498]

rship of dead kings has been an important element in the religion of many African tribes.

The foregoing examples suffice to prove that the worship of dead chiefs and kings has been an important, perhaps we may even say, the most important element in the religion of many African tribes. Regarded from the native point of view nothing could be more natural. The king rules over his people in life; and since all these tribes entertain a firm and unquestioning belief not only in the existence but in the power of the spirits of the dead, they necessarily conclude that of all the departed spirits none can be so potent for good or evil, none therefore need to be propitiated so earnestly by prayer and sacrifice, as the souls of dead kings. Thus while every family worships privately the [pg 196] spirits of its own ancestors, the whole tribe worships publicly the spirits of its departed monarchs, paying to each of these invisible potentates, whose reality they never dream of doubting, a homage of precisely the same sort as that which they render to his living successor on the throne. Such a religion of the dead is by no means incompatible with the recognition of higher spiritual powers who may have an origin quite independent of the worship of ancestors. We have seen in point of fact that many tribes, whose practical religion is concentrated chiefly on their dead, nevertheless acknowledge the existence of a supreme god, the creator of man and of all things, whom they do not regard as a glorified ghost. The Baganda, the most progressive and advanced of all the Bantu tribes, had a whole pantheon of gods whom they sharply distinguished from the worshipful spirits of their forefathers.

e African gods, who are now distinguished from ghosts, were once dead men.

Yet in spite of this distinction we may suspect that in many cases the seeming line of division between gods and worshipful ghosts is deceptive; and that the magic touch of time, which distorts and magnifies the past, especially among peoples who see it only through the haze of oral tradition, has glorified and transfigured many a dead man into a deity. This at all events seems to have been the history of some of the Baganda gods. On this subject our best authority says that "the principal gods appear to have been at one time human beings, noted for their skill and bravery, who were afterwards deified by the people and invested with supernatural powers."[499] "Mukasa held the highest rank among the gods of Uganda. He was a benign god; he never asked for the life of any human being, but animals were sacrificed to him at the yearly festivals, and also at other times when the king, or a leading chief, wished to consult him. He had nothing to do with war, but sought to heal the bodies and minds of men. He was the god of plenty; he gave the people an increase of food, cattle, and children. From the legends still current it seems to be almost certain that he was a human being who, because of his benevolence, came to be regarded as a god.... The legends about Mukasa are of great interest; they show how the human element [pg 197] has been lost in the divine, how the natural has been effaced by the supernatural, until, in the minds of the common people, only the supernatural remains."[500]

emains of Kibuka, the war-god of the Baganda.

If we cannot prove that the great god Mukasa himself was once a man, we have very tangible evidence that his brother the war-god Kibuka was so. For like the dead kings of Uganda, Kibuka was worshipped in a great conical hut resembling the huts which living people inhabit: like them, his spirit was supposed to enter from time to time into the body of his priest and to give oracles through him; and like them he was represented in his temple by his personal relics, his jawbone and his navel-string, which were rescued from the ruins of his temple and now rest in the Ethnological Museum at Cambridge. In face of this complete parallelism between the god and the kings whose personal existence is not open to question, it seems difficult to doubt that Kibuka was once like them a real man, and that he spoke with the jawbone and made bodily use of the other corporeal organs which were preserved in his temple.[501]

ssible that Osiris and Isis may have been a real king and queen of Egypt, perhaps identical with King
is queen.

These analogies lend some support to the theory that in ancient Egypt, where the kings were worshipped by their people both in life and death, Osiris may have been originally nothing but one of these deified monarchs whose worship gradually eclipsed that of all the rest and ended by rivalling or even surpassing that of the great sun-god himself. We have seen that at Abydos, one of the principal centres of his worship, the tomb of Osiris was identified with the tomb of King Khent, one of the earliest monarchs of the first Egyptian dynasty, and that in this tomb were found a woman's richly jewelled arm and a human skull lacking the lower jawbone, which may well be the head of the king himself and the arm of his queen. The carved monument of Osiris which was found in the sepulchral chamber appears indeed to be a [pg 198] work of late Egyptian art, but it may have replaced an earlier sarcophagus. Certainly we may reasonably suppose that the identification of the tomb of Osiris with the tomb of King Khent was very ancient; for though the priests may have renewed the sculptured effigy of the dead god, they would hardly dare to shift the site of the Holy Sepulchre.[502] Now the sepulchre is distant about a mile and a half from the temple in which Osiris was worshipped as a god. There is thus a curious coincidence, if there is nothing more, between the worship of Osiris and the worship of the dead kings of Uganda. As a dead king of Uganda was worshipped in a temple, while his headless body reposed at some distance in a royal tomb, and his head, without the lower jawbone, was buried by itself near the grave, so Osiris was worshipped in a temple not far from the royal tomb which tradition identified with his grave. Perhaps after all tradition was right. It is possible, though it would be very rash to affirm, that Osiris was no other than the historical King Khent of the first dynasty;[503] that the skull found in the tomb is the skull of Osiris himself; and that while it reposed in the grave the missing jawbone was preserved, like the jawbone of a dead king of Uganda, as a holy and perhaps [pg 199] oracular relic in the neighbouring temple. If that were so, we should be almost driven to conclude that the bejewelled woman's arm found in the tomb of Osiris is the arm of Isis.

arallel between Osiris and Charlemagne.

In support of the conclusion that the myth and religion of Osiris grew up round the revered memory of a dead man we may quote the words in which the historian of European morals describes the necessity under which the popular imagination labours of embodying its cherished ideals in living persons. He is referring to the dawn of the age of chivalry, when in the morning twilight the heroic figure of Charlemagne rose like a bright star above the political horizon, to be thenceforth encircled by a halo of romance like the nimbus that shone round the head of Osiris. "In order that the tendencies I have described should acquire their full force, it was necessary that they should be represented or illustrated in some great personage, who, by the splendour and the beauty of his career, could fascinate the imaginations of men. It is much easier to govern great masses of men through their imagination than through their reason. Moral principles rarely act powerfully upon the world, except by way of example or ideals. When the course of events has been to glorify the ascetic or monarchical or military spirit, a great saint, or sovereign, or soldier will arise, who will concentrate in one dazzling focus the blind tendencies of his time, kindle the enthusiasm and fascinate the imagination of the people. But for the prevailing tendency, the great man would not have arisen, or would not have exercised his great influence. But for the great man, whose career appealed vividly to the imagination, the prevailing tendency would never have acquired its full intensity."[504]

of the historical reality of Osiris left open.

Whether the parallel thus suggested between Charlemagne, the mediaeval ideal of a Christian knight, and Osiris, the ancient Egyptian ideal of a just and beneficent monarch, holds good or not, it is now impossible to determine. For while Charlemagne stands near enough to allow us clearly to discern his historical reality, Osiris is so remote that we can no longer discriminate with any certitude between the [pg 200] elements of history and fable which appear to have blended in his traditional character. I am content to indicate bare possibilities: dogmatism on such points would be in the highest degree rash and unbecoming. Whether Osiris and Isis were from first to last purely imaginary beings, the ideal creations of a primitive philosophy, or whether they were originally a real man and woman about whom after death the myth-making fancy wove its gossamer rainbow-tinted web, is a question to which I am not bold enough to give a decided answer.

Chapter XII. Mother-Kin And Mother Goddesses.

§ 1. Dying Gods and Mourning Goddesses.

We have now concluded our inquiry into the nature and worship of the three Oriental deities Adonis, Attis, and Osiris. The substantial similarity of their mythical character justifies us in treating of them together. All three apparently embodied the powers of fertility in general and of vegetation in particular. All three were believed to have died and risen again from the dead; and the divine death and resurrection of all three were dramatically represented at annual festivals, which their worshippers celebrated with alternate transports of sorrow and joy, of weeping and exultation. The natural phenomena thus mythically conceived and mythically represented were the great changes of the seasons, especially the most striking and impressive of all, the decay and revival of vegetation; and the intention of the sacred dramas was to refresh and strengthen, by sympathetic magic, the failing energies of nature, in order that the trees should bear fruit, that the corn should ripen, that men and animals should reproduce their kinds.

But the three gods did not stand by themselves. The mythical personification of nature, of which all three were in at least one aspect the products, required that each of them should be coupled with a goddess, and in each case it appears that originally the goddess was a more powerful and important personage than the god. At all events it is always the god rather than the goddess who comes to a sad end, and whose death is annually mourned. Thus, whereas Osiris was slain by Typhon, his divine spouse Isis survived [pg 202] and brought him to life again. This feature of the myth seems to indicate that in the beginning Isis was, what Astarte and Cybele always continued to be, the stronger divinity of the pair. Now the superiority thus assigned to the goddess over the god is most naturally explained as the result of a social system in which maternity counted for more than paternity, descent being traced and property handed down through women rather than through men. At all events this explanation cannot be deemed intrinsically improbable if we can show that the supposed cause has produced the very same effect among existing peoples, about whose institutions we possess accurate information. This I will now endeavour to do.

§ 2. Influence of Mother-Kin on Religion.

and father-kin. The Khasis of Assam have mother-kin, and among them goddesses predominate over
estesses over priests.

The social system which traces descent and transmits property through the
mother alone may be called mother-kin, while the converse system which
traces descent and transmits property through the father alone may be called
father-kin.[505] A good example of the influence which mother-kin may exert on
religion is furnished by the Khasis of Assam, whose customs and beliefs have
lately been carefully recorded by a British officer specially charged with the
study of the native races of the province.[506] Like the ancient Egyptians and the
Semites of Syria and Mesopotamia, the Khasis live in settled villages and
maintain themselves chiefly by the cultivation of the ground; yet "their social
organization presents one of the most perfect examples still surviving of
matriarchal institutions, carried out with a logic and thoroughness which, to
those accustomed to regard the status and authority of the father as the
foundation of society, are exceedingly remarkable. Not only is the mother the
head and source, and only bond of union, of the family: in the most primitive
part of the hills, the Synteng country, she is the only owner of real property,
and through her alone is [pg 203] inheritance transmitted.[507] The father has no
kinship with his children, who belong to their mother's clan; what he earns
goes to his own matriarchal stock, and at his death his bones are deposited in
the cromlech of his mother's kin. In Jowai he neither lives nor eats in his
wife's house, but visits it only after dark. In the veneration of ancestors,
which is the foundation of the tribal piety, the primal ancestress (*Ka Iāwbei*)
and her brother are the only persons regarded. The flat memorial stones set up
to perpetuate the memory of the dead are called after the woman who
represents the clan (*māw kynthei*), and the standing stones ranged behind
them are dedicated to the male kinsmen on the mother's side. In harmony
with this scheme of ancestor worship, the other spirits to whom propitiation is
offered are mainly female, though here male personages also figure. The
powers of sickness and death are all female, and these are those most
frequently worshipped. The two protectors of the household are goddesses,
though with them is also revered the first father of the clan, *U Thāwlang*.
Priestesses assist at all sacrifices, and the male officiants are only their
deputies; in one important state, Khyrim, the High Priestess and actual head
of the State is a woman, who combines in her person sacerdotal and regal
functions."[508] Thus amongst the Khasis of the present day the [pg 204]
superiority of the goddess to the god, and especially of the revered ancestress
to the revered ancestor, is based directly on the social system which traces

descent and transmits property through women only. It is not unreasonable therefore to suppose that in Western Asia the superiority of the Mother Goddess to the Father God originated in the same archaic system of mother-kin.

elew Islanders have mother-kin, and the deities of their clans are all goddesses.

Another instance of the same cause producing the same effect may be drawn from the institutions of the Pelew Islanders, which have been described by an accurate observer long resident in the islands. These people, who form a branch of the Micronesian stock, are divided into a series of exogamous families or clans with descent in the female line,[509] so that, as usually happens under such a system, a man's heirs are not his own children but the children of his sister or of his maternal aunt.[510] Every family or clan traces its descent from a woman, the common mother of the whole kin,[511] and accordingly the members of the clan worship a goddess, not a god.[512] These families or clans, with female descent and a worship of goddesses rather than of gods, are grouped together in villages, each village comprising [pg 205] about a score of clans and forming with its lands a petty independent state.[513] Every such village-state has its special deity or deities, generally a god and a goddess. But these political deities of the villages are said to be directly derived from the domestic deities of the families or clans,[514] from which it seems to follow that among these people gods are historically later than goddesses and have been developed out of them.[515] The late origin of the gods as compared with the goddesses is further indicated by the nature of their names.[516]

nce for goddesses is to be explained by the importance of women in the social system of the Pelew

This preference for goddesses over gods in the clans of the Pelew Islanders has been explained, no doubt rightly, by the high importance of women in the social system of the people.[517] For the existence of the clan depends entirely on the life of the women, not at all upon the life of the men. If the women survive, it is no matter though every man of the clan should perish; for the women will, as usual, marry men of another clan, and their offspring will inherit their mother's clan, thereby prolonging its existence. Whereas if the women of the clan all die out, the clan necessarily becomes extinct, even though every man of it should survive; for the men must, as usual, marry women of another clan, and their offspring will inherit their mothers' clan, not the clan of their fathers, which accordingly, with the death of the fathers, is wiped out from the community. Hence in these islands women bear the titles of *Adhalál a pelú*, "Mothers of the Land," and *Adhalál a blay*, "Mothers of the Clan," and they are said to enjoy complete equality with the men in every respect.[518] Indeed, in one passage our principal authority speaks of "the predominance of feminine influence in the social condition of the people," and asserts without qualification that the women are politically and [pg 206] socially superior to the men.[519] The eldest women of the clan exercise, he tells us, the most decisive influence on the conduct of its affairs, and the headman does nothing without full consultation with them, a consultation which in the great houses extends to affairs of state and foreign politics.[520] Nay, these elder women are even esteemed and treated as equal to the deities in their lifetime.[521]

sition of women in the Pelew Islands has also an industrial basis; for they alone cultivate the taro, the f the people.

But the high position which women thus take in Pelew society is not a result of mother-kin only. It has an industrial as well as a kinship basis. For the Pelew Islanders subsist mainly on the produce of their taro fields, and the cultivation of this, their staple food, is the business of the women alone. "This cardinal branch of Pelew agriculture, which is of paramount importance for the subsistence of the people, is left entirely in the hands of the women. This fact may have contributed materially to the predominance of female influence in the social condition of the people. The women do not merely bestow life on the people, they also do that which is most essential for the preservation of life, and therefore they are called *Adhalál a pelú*, the 'Mothers of the Land,' and are politically and socially superior to men. Only their offspring enjoy the privilege of membership of the state (the children of the men are, strictly speaking, strangers destitute of rights), and the oldest women of the families are esteemed and treated as equal to deities even in their lifetime, and they exercise a decisive influence on the conduct of affairs of state. No chief would venture to come to a decision without first consulting with the *Adhalál a blay*, the 'Mothers of the Family.' From this point of view it is impossible to regard the assignment of the taro cultivation to women as a consequence of their subordinate position in society: the women themselves do not so regard it. The richest woman of the village looks with pride on her taro patch, and although she has female followers enough to allow her merely to superintend the work without taking part in it, she nevertheless prefers to lay aside her fine apron and to betake herself to the deep [pg 207] mire, clad in a small apron that hardly hides her nakedness, with a little mat on her back to protect her from the burning heat of the sun, and with a shade of banana leaves for her eyes. There, dripping with sweat in the burning sun and coated with mud to the hips and over the elbows, she toils to set the younger women a good example. Moreover, as in every other occupation, the *kaliths*, the gods, must also be invoked, and who could be better fitted for the discharge of so important a duty than the Mother of the House?"[522] It seems clear that in any agricultural people who, like the Pelew Islanders, retain mother-kin and depute the labours of husbandry to women, the conception of a great Mother

137

Goddess, the divine source of all fertility, might easily originate. Perhaps the same social and industrial conditions may have combined to develop the great Mother Goddesses of Western Asia and Egypt.

But in the Pelew Islands women have yet another road to power. For some of them are reputed to be the wives of gods, and act as their oracular mouthpieces. Such prophetesses are called *Amlaheys*, and no surprise is felt when one of them is brought to bed. Her child passes for the offspring of the god, her divine husband, and goes about with his hair hanging loose in token of his superhuman parentage. It is thought that no mortal man would dare to intrigue with one of these human wives of a god, since the jealous deity would surely visit the rash culprit with deadly sickness and a lingering decline.[523] But in these islands men as well as women are often possessed by a deity and speak in his name. Under his inspiration they mimic, often with great histrionic skill, the particular appearance and manner which are believed to be characteristic of the indwelling divinity. These inspired men (*Korongs*) usually enjoy great consideration and exert a powerful influence over the whole community. They always acquire wealth in the exercise of their profession. When they are not themselves chiefs, they are treated as chiefs or even preferred to them. In not a few places the deity whom [pg 208] they personate is also the political head of the land; and in that case his inspired priest, however humble his origin, ranks as a spiritual king and rules over all the chiefs. Indeed we are told that, with the physical and intellectual decay of the race, the power of the priests is more and more in the ascendant and threatens, if unchecked, to develop before long into an absolute theocracy which will swallow up every other form of government.[524]

Thus the present, or at least the recent, state of society and religion in the Pelew Islands presents some interesting parallels to the social and religious condition of Western Asia and Egypt in early days, if the conclusions reached in this work are correct. In both regions we see a society based on mother-kin developing a religion in which goddesses of the clan originally occupied the foremost place, though in later times, as the clans coalesced into states, the old goddesses have been rivalled and to some extent supplanted by the new male gods of the enlarged pantheon. But in the religion of the Pelew Islanders, as in that of the Khasis and the ancient Egyptians, the balance of power has never wholly shifted from the female to the male line, because society has never passed from mother-kin to father-kin. And in the Pelew Islands as in the ancient East we see the tide of political power running strongly in the direction of theocracy, the people resigning the conduct of affairs into the hands of men who claimed to rule them in the name of the gods. In the Pelew Islands such men might have developed into divine kings like those of Babylon and Egypt, if the natural course of evolution had not been cut short by the intervention of Europe.[525]

does not imply that the government is in the hands of women.

The evidence of the Khasis and the Pelew Islanders, two peoples very remote and very different from each other, suffices to prove that the influence which mother-kin may exert on religion is real and deep. But in order [pg 209] to dissipate misapprehensions, which appear to be rife on this subject, it may be well to remind or inform the reader that the ancient and widespread custom of tracing descent and inheriting property through the mother alone does not by any means imply that the government of the tribes which observe the custom is in the hands of women; in short, it should always be borne in mind that mother-kin does not mean mother-rule. On the contrary, the practice of mother-kin prevails most extensively amongst the lowest savages, with whom woman, instead of being the ruler of man, is always his drudge and often little better than his slave. Indeed, so far is the system from implying any social superiority of women that it probably took its rise from what we should regard as their deepest degradation, to wit, from a state of society in which the relations of the sexes were so loose and vague that children could not be fathered on any particular man.[526]

nce of property, especially of landed property, through the mother certainly tends to raise the social f women, but this tendency is never carried so far as to subordinate men politically to women.

When we pass from the purely savage state to that higher plane of culture in which the accumulation of property, and especially of landed property, has become a powerful instrument of social and political influence, we naturally find that wherever the ancient preference for the female line of descent has been retained, it tends to increase the importance and enhance the dignity of woman; and her aggrandizement is most marked in princely families, where she either herself holds royal authority as well as private property, or at least transmits them both to her consort or her children. But this social advance of women has never been carried so far as to place men as a whole in a position of political subordination to them. Even where the system of mother-kin in regard to descent and property has prevailed most fully, the actual government has generally, if not invariably, remained in the hands of men. Exceptions have no doubt occurred; women have occasionally arisen [pg 210] who by sheer force of character have swayed for a time the destinies of their people. But such exceptions are rare and their effects transitory; they do not affect the truth of the general rule that human society has been governed in the past and, human nature remaining the same, is likely to be governed in the future, mainly by masculine force and masculine intelligence.

To this rule the Khasis, with their elaborate system of mother-kin, form no exception. For among them, while landed property is both transmitted through women and held by women alone, political power is transmitted indeed through women, but is held by men; in other words, the Khasi tribes are, with a single exception, governed by kings, not by queens. And even in the one tribe, which is nominally ruled by women, the real power is delegated by the reigning queen or High Priestess to her son, her nephew, or a more distant male relation. In all the other tribes the kingship may be held by a woman only on the failure of all male heirs in the female line.[527] So far is mother-kin from implying mother-rule. A Khasi king inherits power in right of his mother, but he exercises it in his own. Similarly the Pelew Islanders, in spite of their system of mother-kin, are governed by chiefs, not by chieftainesses. It is true that there are chieftainesses, and that they indirectly exercise much influence; but their direct authority is limited to the affairs of women, especially to the administration of the women's clubs or associations, which [pg 211] answer to the clubs or associations of the men.[528] And to take another example, the Melanesians, like the Khasis and the Pelew Islanders, have the system of mother-kin, being similarly divided into exogamous clans with descent in the female line; "but it must be understood that the mother is in no way the head of the family. The house of the family is the father's, the garden is his, the rule and government are his."[529]

We may safely assume that the practice has been the same among all the many peoples who have retained the ancient system of mother-kin under a monarchical constitution. In Africa, for example, the chieftainship or kingship often descends in the female line, but it is men, not women, who inherit it.[530] The theory of a gynaecocracy is in truth a dream of visionaries and pedants. And equally chimerical is the idea that the predominance of goddesses under a system of mother-kin like that of the Khasis is a creation of the female mind. If women ever created gods, they would be more likely to give them masculine than feminine features. In point of fact the great religious ideals which have permanently impressed themselves on the world seem always to have been a product of the male imagination. Men make gods and women worship them. The combination of ancestor-worship with mother-kin furnishes a simple and sufficient explanation of the superiority of goddesses over gods in a state of society where these conditions prevail. Men naturally assign the first place in their devotions to the ancestress from whom they trace their descent. We need not resort to a fantastic hypothesis of the preponderance of the feminine fancy in order to account for the facts.

The theory that under a system of mother-kin the women rule the men and set up goddesses for them to [pg 212] worship is indeed so improbable in itself, and so contrary to experience, that it scarcely deserves the serious attention which it appears to have received.[531] But when we have brushed aside these cobwebs, as we must do, we are still left face to face with the solid fact of the wide prevalence of mother-kin, that is, of a social system which traces descent and transmits property through women and not through men. That a social system so widely spread and so deeply rooted should have affected the religion of the peoples who practise it, may reasonably be inferred, especially when we remember that in primitive communities the social relations of the gods commonly reflect the social relations of their worshippers. How the system of mother-kin may mould religious ideas and customs, creating goddesses and assigning at least a nominal superiority to priestesses over priests, is shown with perfect lucidity by the example of the Khasis, and hardly less clearly by the example of the Pelew Islanders. It cannot therefore be rash to hold that what the system has certainly done for these peoples, it may well have done for many more. But unfortunately through lack of documentary evidence we are seldom able to trace its influence so clearly.

§ 3. Mother-Kin and Mother Goddesses in the Ancient East.

While the combination of mother-kin in society with a preference for goddesses in religion is to be found as a matter of fact among the Khasis and Pelew Islanders of to-day, the former prevalence of mother-kin in the lands where the great goddesses Astarte and Cybele were worshipped is a matter of inference only. In later times father-kin had certainly displaced mother-kin among the Semitic worshippers of Astarte, and probably the same change had taken place among the Phrygian worshippers of Cybele. Yet the older [pg 213] custom lingered in Lycia down to the historical period;[532] and we may conjecture that in former times it was widely spread through Asia Minor. The secluded situation and rugged mountains of Lycia favoured the survival of a native language and of native institutions long after these had disappeared from the wide plains and fertile valleys which lay on the highroads of war and commerce. Lycia was to Asia Minor what the highlands of Wales and of Scotland have been to Britain, the last entrenchments where the old race stood at bay. And even among the Semites of antiquity, though father-kin finally prevailed in matters of descent and property, traces of an older system of mother-kin, with its looser sexual relations, appear to have long survived in the sphere of religion. At all events one of the most learned and acute of Semitic scholars adduced what he regarded as evidence sufficient to prove "that in old Arabian religion gods and goddesses often occurred in pairs, the goddess being the greater, so that the god cannot be her Baal, that the goddess is often a mother without being a wife, and the god her son, and that the progress of things was towards changing goddesses into gods or lowering them beneath the male deity."[533]

In Egypt the archaic system of mother-kin, with its preference for women over men in matters of property and inheritance, lasted down to Roman times, and it was traditionally [pg 214] based on the example of Isis, who had avenged her husband's murder and had continued to reign after his decease, conferring benefits on mankind. "For these reasons," says Diodorus Siculus, "it was appointed that the queen should enjoy greater power and honour than the king, and that among private people the wife should rule over her husband, in the marriage contract the husband agreeing to obey his wife in all things."[534] A corollary of the superior position thus conceded to women in Egypt was that the obligation of maintaining parents in their old age rested on the daughters, not on the sons, of the family.[535]

brothers with sisters in ancient Egypt.

The same legal superiority of women over men accounts for the most remarkable feature in the social system of the ancient Egyptians, to wit, the marriage of full brothers with full sisters. That marriage, which to us seems strange and unnatural, was by no means a whim of the reigning Ptolemies; on the contrary, these Macedonian conquerors appear, with characteristic prudence, to have borrowed the custom from their Egyptian predecessors for the express purpose of conciliating native prejudice. In the eyes of the Egyptians "marriage between brother and sister was the best of marriages, and it acquired an ineffable degree of sanctity when the brother and sister who contracted it were themselves born of a brother and sister, who had in their turn also sprung from a union of the same sort."[536] Nor did the principle apply only to gods and kings. The common people acted on it in their daily life. They regarded marriages between brothers and sisters as the most natural and reasonable of all.[537] The evidence of legal documents, [pg 215] including marriage contracts, tends to prove that such unions were the rule, not the exception, in ancient Egypt, and that they continued to form the majority of marriages long after the Romans had obtained a firm footing in the country. As we cannot suppose that Roman influence was used to promote a custom which must have been abhorrent to Roman instincts, we may safely assume that the proportion of brother and sister marriages in Egypt had been still greater in the days when the country was free.[538]

ges were based on a wish to keep the property in the family.

It would doubtless be a mistake to treat these marriages as a relic of savagery, as a survival of a tribal communism which knew no bar to the intercourse of the sexes. For such a theory would not explain why union with a sister was not only allowed, but preferred to all others. The true motive of that preference was most probably the wish of brothers to obtain for their own use the family property, which belonged of right to their sisters, and which otherwise they would have seen in the enjoyment of strangers, the husbands of their sisters. This is the system which in Ceylon is known as *beena* marriage. Under it the daughter, not the son, is the heir. She stays at home, and her husband comes and lives with her in the house; but her brother goes away and dwells in his wife's home, inheriting nothing from his parents.[539] Such a system could not fail in time to prove irksome. Men would be loth to quit the old home, resign the ancestral property to a stranger, and go out to seek their fortune empty-handed in the world. The remedy was obvious. A man had nothing to do but to marry his sister himself instead of handing her over to another. Having done so he stayed at home and enjoyed the family estate in virtue of his marriage with the heiress. This simple and perfectly

143

effective expedient for keeping the property in the [pg 216] family most probably explains the custom of brother and sister marriage in Egypt.[540]

Thus the union of Osiris with his sister Isis was not a freak of the story-teller's fancy: it reflected a social custom which was itself based on practical considerations of the most solid kind. When we reflect that this practice of mother-kin as opposed to father-kin survived down to the latest times of antiquity, not in an obscure and barbarous tribe, but in a nation whose immemorial civilization was its glory and the wonder of the world, we may without being extravagant suppose that a similar practice formerly prevailed in Syria and Phrygia, and that it accounts for the superiority of the goddess over the god in the divine partnerships of Adonis and Astarte, of Attis and Cybele. But the ancient system both of society and of religion had undergone far more change in these countries than in Egypt, where to the last the main outlines of the old structure could be traced in the national institutions to which the Egyptians clung with a passionate, a fanatical devotion. Mother-kin, the divinity of kings and queens, a sense of the original connexion of the gods with nature—these things outlived the Persian, the Macedonian, the Roman conquest, and only perished under the more powerful solvent of Christianity. But the old order did not vanish at once with the official establishment of the new religion. In the age of Constantine the Greeks of Egypt still attributed the rise of the Nile to Serapis, the later form of Osiris, alleging [pg 217] that the inundation could not take place if the standard cubit, which was used to measure it, were not deposited according to custom in the temple of the god. The emperor ordered the cubit to be transferred to a church; and next year, to the general surprise, the river rose just as usual.[541] Even at a later time Athanasius himself had to confess with sorrow and indignation that under his own eyes the Egyptians still annually mourned the death of Osiris.[542] The end came with the destruction of the great Serapeum at Alexandria, the last stronghold of the heathen in Egypt. It perished in a furious and bloody sedition, in which Christians and pagans seem to have vied with each other in mutual atrocities. After its fall the temples were levelled with the ground or converted into churches, and the images of the old gods went to the melting-pot to be converted into base uses for the rabble of Alexandria.[543]

The singular tenacity with which the Egyptian people maintained their traditional beliefs and customs for thousands of years sprang no doubt from the stubborn conservatism of the national character. Yet that conservatism was itself in great measure an effect of geographical and climatic conditions and of the ways of life which they favoured. Surrounded on every side by deserts or almost harbourless seas, the Egyptians occupied a position of great natural strength which for long ages together protected them from invasion and allowed their native habits to set and harden, undisturbed by the subversive influence of foreign conquest. The wonderful regularity of nature in Egypt also conduced to a corresponding stability in the minds of the people. Year in, year out, the immutable succession of the seasons brought with it the same unvarying round of agricultural toil. What the fathers had done, the sons did in the same manner at the same season, and so it went on from [pg 218] generation to generation. This monotonous routine is common indeed to all purely agricultural communities, and everywhere tends to beget in the husbandman a settled phlegmatic habit of mind very different from the mobility, the alertness, the pliability of character which the hazards and uncertainties of commerce and the sea foster in the merchant and the sailor. The saturnine temperament of the farmer is as naturally averse to change as the more mercurial spirit of the trader and the seaman is predisposed to it. But the stereotyping of ideas and of customs was carried further in Egypt than in most lands devoted to husbandry by reason of the greater uniformity of the Egyptian seasons and the more complete isolation of the country.

of Osiris better preserved than those of Adonis and Attis.

The general effect of these causes was to create a type of national character which presented many points of resemblance to that of the Chinese. In both we see the same inflexible strength of will, the same astonishing industry, the same strange blend of humanity and savagery, the same obstinate adherence to tradition, the same pride of race and of ancient civilization, the same contempt for foreigners as for upstarts and barbarians, the same patient outward submission to an alien rule combined with an unshakeable inward devotion to native ideals. It was this conservative temper of the people, bred in great measure of the physical nature of their land, which, so to say, embalmed the memory of Osiris long after the corresponding figures of Adonis and Attis had suffered decay. For while Egypt enjoyed profound repose, the tides of war and conquest, of traffic and commerce, had for centuries rolled over Western Asia, the native home of Adonis and Attis; and if the shock of nationalities in this great meeting-ground of East and West was favourable to the rise of new faiths and new moralities, it was in the same measure unfavourable to the preservation of the old.

[pg 219]

Notes.

I. Moloch The King.

I cannot leave the evidence for the sacred character of Jewish kings[544] without mentioning a suggestion which was made to me by my friend and teacher the Rev. Professor R. H. Kennett. He thinks that Moloch, to whom first-born children were burnt by their parents in the valley of Hinnom, outside the walls of Jerusalem,[545] may have been originally the human king regarded as an incarnate deity. Certainly the name of Moloch, or rather Molech (for so it is always written in the Massoretic text[546]), is merely a slightly disguised [pg 220] form of *melech*, the ordinary Hebrew word for "king," the scribes having apparently given the dreadful word the vowels of bosheth, "shameful thing."[547] But it seems clear that in historical times the Jews who offered these sacrifices identified Molech, not with the human king, but with Jehovah, though the prophets protested against the custom as an outrage on the divine majesty.[548]

If, however, these sacrifices were originally offered to or in behalf of the human king, it is possible that they were intended to prolong his life and strengthen his hands for the performance of those magical functions which he was expected to discharge for the good of his people. The old kings of Sweden answered with their heads for the fertility of the ground,[549] and we read that one of them, Aun or On by name, sacrificed nine of his sons to Odin at Upsala in order that his own life might be spared. After the sacrifice of his second son he received from the god an oracle that he should live as long as he gave him one of his sons every tenth year. When he had thus sacrificed seven sons, the ruthless father still lived, but was so feeble that he could no longer walk and had to be carried in a chair. Then he offered up his eighth son and lived ten years more, bedridden. After that he sacrificed his ninth son, and lived ten years more, drinking out of a horn like a weaned child. He now wished to sacrifice his last remaining son to Odin, but the Swedes would not let him, so he died and was buried in a mound at Upsala.[550] In this Swedish tradition the king's children seem to have been looked upon as substitutes offered to the god in place of their father, and apparently this was also the current explanation of the slaughter of the first-born in the later times of Israel.[551] On that view the sacrifices were vicarious, and therefore purely religious, being intended to propitiate a stern and exacting deity. Similarly we read that when Amestris, wife of Xerxes, was grown old, she sacrificed on her

147

behalf twice seven noble children to the [pg 221] earth god by burying them alive.[552] If the story is true—and it rests on the authority of Herodotus, a nearly contemporary witness—we may surmise that the aged queen acted thus with an eye to the future rather than to the past; she hoped that the grim god of the nether-world would accept the young victims in her stead, and let her live for many years. The same idea of vicarious suffering comes out in a tradition told of a certain Hova king of Madagascar, who bore the sonorous name of Andriamasinavalona. When he had grown sickly and feeble, the oracle was consulted as to the best way of restoring him to health. "The following result was the consequence of the directions of the oracle. A speech was first delivered to the people, offering great honours and rewards to the family of any individual who would freely offer himself to be sacrificed, in order to the king's recovery. The people shuddered at the idea, and ran away in different directions. One man, however, presented himself for the purpose, and his offer was accepted. The sacrificer girded up his loins, sharpened his knife, and bound the victim. After which, he was laid down with his head towards the east, upon a mat spread for the purpose, according to the custom with animals on such occasions, when the priest appeared, to proceed with all solemnity in slaughtering the victim by cutting his throat. A quantity of red liquid, however, which had been prepared from a native dye, was spilled in the ceremony; and, to the amazement of those who looked on, blood seemed to be flowing all around. The man, as might be supposed, was unhurt; but the king rewarded him and his descendants with the perpetual privilege of exemption from capital punishment for any violation of the laws. The descendants of the man to this day form a particular class, called *Tay maty manota*, which may be translated, 'Not dead, though transgressing.' Instances frequently occur, of individuals of this class appropriating bullocks, rice, and other things belonging to the sovereign, as if they were their own, and escaping merely with a reprimand, while a common person would have to suffer death, or be reduced to slavery."[553]

ces for prolonging the king's life appear to be magical rather than religious. Custom in the Niger delta.

Sometimes, however, the practices intended to prolong the king's life seem to rest on a theory of nutrition rather than of substitution; in other words, the life of the victims, instead of being offered vicariously to a god, is apparently supposed to pass directly into the body of the sacrificer, thus refreshing his failing strength and prolonging his existence. So regarded, the custom is magical rather than religious in character, since the desired effect is thought to follow directly without the intervention of a deity. At all events, it can be shown that sacrifices of this sort have been offered to prolong the life of kings in other parts of the world. Thus in regard to [pg 222] some of the negroes who inhabit the delta of the Niger we read that: "A custom which formerly was practised by the Ibani, and is still prevalent among all the interior tribes, consists in prolonging the life of a king or ancestral representative by the daily, or possibly weekly, sacrifice of a chicken and egg. Every morning, as soon as the patriarch has risen from his bed, the sacrificial articles are procured either by his mother, head wife, or eldest daughter, and given to the priest, who receives them on the open space in front of the house. When this has been reported to the patriarch, he comes outside and, sitting down, joins in the ceremony. Taking the chicken in his hand, the priest first of all touches the patriarch's face with it, and afterwards passes it over the whole of his body. He then cuts its throat and allows the blood to drop on the ground. Mixing the blood and the earth into a paste, he rubs it on the old man's forehead and breast, and this is not to be washed off under any circumstances until the evening. The chicken and the egg, also a piece of white cloth, are now tied on to a stick, which, if a stream is in the near vicinity, is planted in the ground at the water-side. During the carriage of these articles to the place in question, all the wives and many members of the household accompany the priest, invoking the deity as they go to prolong their father's life. This is done in the firm conviction that through the sacrifice of each chicken his life will be accordingly prolonged."[554]

erved by the Zulus and Caffres to prolong the king's life.

The ceremony thus described is, like so many other rites, a combination of magic and religion; for whereas the prayers to the god are religious, the passing of the victim over the king's body and the smearing of him with its blood are magical, being plainly intended to convey to him directly, without the mediation of any deity, the life of the fowl. In the following instances the practices for prolonging the king's life seem to be purely magical. Among the Zulus, at one of the annual feasts of first-fruits, a bull is killed by a particular regiment. In slaughtering the beast they may not use spears or sticks, but must break its neck or choke it with their bare hands. "It is then burned, and the strength of the bull is supposed to enter into the king, thereby prolonging his life."[555] Again, in an early Portuguese historian we read of a Caffre king of East Africa that "it is related of this Monomotapa that he has a house where he commands bodies of men who have died at the hands of the law to be hung up, and where thus hanging all the humidity [pg 223] of their bodies falls into vases placed underneath, and when all has dropped from them and they shrink and dry up he commands them to be taken down and buried, and with the fat and moisture in the vases they say he makes ointments with which he anoints himself in order to enjoy long life—which is his belief—and also to be proof against receiving harm from sorcerers."[556]

erved by the Baganda to prolong the king's life. Human victims killed in order to invigorate the king.

The Baganda of Central Africa used to kill men on various occasions for the purpose of prolonging the king's life; in all cases it would seem to be thought that the life of the murdered man was in some mysterious fashion transferred to the king, so that the monarch received thereby a fresh accession of vital energy. For example, whenever a particular royal drum had a new skin put on it, not only was a cow killed to furnish the skin and its blood run into the drum, but a man was beheaded and the spouting blood from the severed neck was allowed to gush into the drum, "so that, when the drum was beaten, it was supposed to add fresh life and vigour to the king from the life of the slain man."[557] Again, at the coronation of a new king, a royal chamberlain was chosen to take charge of the king's inner court and to guard his wives. From the royal presence the chamberlain was conducted, along with eight captives, to one of the human shambles; there he was blindfolded while seven of the men were clubbed to death, only the dull thud and crashing sound telling him of what was taking place. But when the seven had been thus despatched, the bandages were removed from the chamberlain's eyes and he witnessed the death of the eighth. As each man was killed, his belly was ripped open and his bowels pulled out and hung round the chamberlain's neck. These deaths were said to add to the King's vigour and to make the chamberlain strong and faithful.[558] Nor were these the only human sacrifices offered at a king's coronation for the purpose of strengthening the new monarch. When the king had reigned two or three months, he was expected to hunt first a leopard and then a bushbuck. On the night after the hunt of the bushbuck, one of the ministers of State caught a man and brought him before the king in the dark; the king speared him slightly, then the man was strangled and the body thrown into a papyrus swamp, that it might never be found again. Another ceremony performed about this time to confirm the king in his kingdom was to catch a man, bind him, and bring him before the king, who wounded him slightly with a spear. Then the man was put to death. These men were killed to invigorate the king.[559]

[pg 224]

killed to provide the king with anklets.

When a king of Uganda had reigned some time, apparently several years, a ceremony was performed for the sake of prolonging his life. For this purpose the king paid a visit—a fatal visit—to a chief of the Lung-fish clan, who bore the title of Nankere and resided in the district of Busiro, where the tombs and temples of the kings were situated. When the time for the ceremony had been appointed, the chief chose one of his own sons, who was to die that the king might live. If the chief had no son, a near relation was compelled to serve as a substitute. The hapless youth was fed and clothed and treated in all respects like a prince, and taken to live in a particular house near the place where the king was to lodge for the ceremony. When the destined victim had been feasted and guarded for a month, the king set out on his progress from the capital. On the way he stopped at the temple of the great god Mukasa; there he changed his garments, leaving behind him in the temple those which he had been wearing. Also he left behind him all his anklets, and did not put on any fresh ones, for he was shortly to receive new anklets of a remarkable kind. When the king arrived at his destination, the chief met him, and the two exchanged a gourd of beer. At this interview the king's mother was present to see her son for the last time; for from that moment the two were never allowed to look upon each other again. The chief addressed the king's mother informing her of this final separation; then turning to the king he said, "You are now of age; go and live longer than your forefathers." Then the chief's son was introduced. The chief took him by the hand and presented him to the king, who passed him on to the body-guard; they led him outside and killed him by beating him with their clenched fists. The muscles from the back of the body of the murdered youth were removed and made into two anklets for the king, and a strip of skin cut from the corpse was made into a whip, which was kept in the royal enclosure for special feasts. The dead body was thrown on waste land and guarded against wild beasts, but not buried.[560]

ame.

When that ceremony was over, the king departed to go to another chief in Busiro; but on the way thither he stopped at a place called Baka and sat down under a great tree to play a game of spinning fruit-stones. It is a children's game, but it was no child's play to the man who ran to fetch the fruit-stones for the king to play with; for he was caught and speared to death on the spot for the purpose of prolonging the king's life. After the game had been played the king with his train passed on and lodged with a certain princess till the anklets made from the muscles of the chief's murdered son were ready for him to wear; [pg 225] it was the princess who had to superintend the making of these royal ornaments.[561]

human skin.

When all these ceremonies were over, the king made a great feast. At this feast a priest went about carrying under his mantle the whip that had been made from the skin of the murdered young man. As he passed through the crowd of merrymakers, he would flick a man here and there with the whip, and it was believed that the man on whom the lash lighted would be childless and might die, unless he made an offering of either nine or ninety cowrie shells to the priest who had struck him. Naturally he hastened to procure the shells and take them to the striker, who, on receiving them, struck the man on the shoulder with his hand, thus restoring to him the generative powers of which the blow of the whip had deprived him. At the end of the feast the drummers removed all the drums but one, which they left as if they had forgotten it. Somebody in the crowd would notice the apparent oversight and run after the drummers with the drum, saying, "You have left one behind." The thanks he received was that he was caught and killed and the bones of his upper arm made into drumsticks for that particular drum. The drum was never afterwards brought out during the whole of the king's reign, but was kept covered up till the time came to bring it out on the corresponding feast of his successor. Yet from time to time the priest, who had flicked the revellers with the whip of human skin, would dress himself up in a mantle of cow-hide from neck to foot, and concealing the drumstick of human bones under his robe would go into the king's presence, and suddenly whipping out the bones from his bosom would brandish them in the king's face. Then he would as suddenly hide them again, but only to repeat the manoeuvre. After that he retired and restored the bones to their usual place. They were decorated with cowrie shells and little bells, which jingled as he shook them at the king.[562]

ich the strength of the human victims was thought to pass into the king.

The precise meaning of these latter ceremonies is obscure; but we may suppose that just as the human blood poured into a drum was thought to pass into the king's veins in the booming notes of the drum, so the clicking of the human bones and the jingling of their bells were supposed to infuse into the royal person the vigour of the murdered man. The purpose of flicking commoners with the whip made of human skin is even more obscure; but we may conjecture that the life or virility of every man struck with the whip was supposed to be transmitted in some way to the king, who thus recruited his vital, and especially his reproductive, energies at this solemn feast. If I am right in my interpretation, all these Baganda [pg 226] modes of strengthening the king and prolonging his life belonged to the nutritive rather than to the vicarious type of sacrifice, from which it will follow that they were magical rather than religious in character.

erpetrated when a king of Uganda was ill.

The same thing may perhaps be said of the wholesale massacres which used to be perpetrated when a king of Uganda was ill. At these times the priests informed the royal patient that persons marked by a certain physical peculiarity, such as a cast of the eye, a particular gait, or a distinctive colouring, must be put to death. Accordingly the king sent out his catchpoles, who waylaid such persons in the roads and dragged them to the royal enclosure, where they were kept until the tale of victims prescribed by the priest was complete. Before they were led away to one of the eight places of execution, which were regularly appointed for this purpose in different parts of the kingdom, the victims had to drink medicated beer with the king out of a special pot, in order that he might have power over their ghosts, lest they should afterwards come back to torment him. They were killed, sometimes by being speared to death, sometimes by being hacked to pieces, sometimes by being burned alive. Contrary to the usual custom of the Baganda, the bodies, or what remained of the bodies, of these unfortunates were always left unburied on the place of execution.[563] In what way precisely the sick king was supposed to benefit by these massacres of his subjects does not appear, but we may surmise that somehow the victims were believed to give their lives for him or to him.

fices of children to Moloch may be otherwise explained.

Thus it is possible that in Israel also the sacrifices of children to Moloch were in like manner intended to prolong the life of the human king (*melech*) either by serving as substitutes for him or by recruiting his failing energies with their vigorous young life. But it is equally possible, and perhaps more probable, that the sacrifice of the first-born children was only a particular application of the ancient law which devoted to the deity the first-born of every womb, whether of cattle or of human beings.[564]

[pg 227]

―――――――――――――――――――――――

II. The Widowed Flamen.

§ 1. The Pollution of Death.

A different explanation of the rule which obliged the Flamen Dialis to resign the priesthood on the death of his wife[565] has been suggested by my friend Dr. L. R. Farnell. He supposes that such a bereavement would render the Flamen ceremonially impure, and therefore unfit to hold office.[566] It is true that the ceremonial pollution caused by death commonly disqualifies a man for the discharge of sacred functions, but as a rule the disqualification is only temporary and can be removed by seclusion and the observance of purificatory rites, the length of the seclusion and the nature of the purification varying with the degree of relationship in which the living stand to the dead. Thus, for example, if one of the sacred eunuchs at Hierapolis-Bambyce saw the dead body of a stranger, he was unclean for that day and might not enter the sanctuary of the goddess; but next day after purifying himself he was free to enter. But if the corpse happened to be that of a relation he was unclean for thirty days and had to shave his head before he might set foot within the holy precinct.[567] Again, in the Greek island of Ceos persons who had offered the annual sacrifices to their departed friends were unclean for two days afterwards and might not enter a sanctuary; they had to purify themselves with water.[568] Similarly no one might go into the shrine of Men Tyrannus for ten days after being in contact with the dead.[569] Once more, at Stratonicea in Caria a chorus of thirty noble boys, clad in white and holding branches in their hands, used to sing a hymn daily in honour of Zeus and Hecate; but if one of them were sick or had suffered a domestic bereavement, he was for the time being excused, not permanently excluded, from the [pg 228] performance of his sacred duties.[570] On the analogy of these and similar cases we should expect to find the widowed Flamen temporarily debarred from the exercise of his office, not permanently relieved of it.

However, in support of Dr. Farnell's view I would cite an Indian parallel which was pointed out to me by Dr. W. H. R. Rivers. Among the Todas of the Neilgherry Hills in Southern India the priestly dairyman (*palol*) is a sacred personage, and his life, like that of the Flamen Dialis, is hedged in by many taboos. Now when a death occurs in his clan, the dairyman may not attend any of the funeral ceremonies unless he gives up office, but he may be re-elected after the second funeral ceremonies have been completed. In the interval his place must be taken by a man of another clan. Some eighteen or nineteen years ago a man named Karkievan resigned the office of dairyman when his wife died, but two years later he was re-elected and has held office ever since. There have meantime been many deaths in his clan, but he has not attended a funeral, and has not therefore had to resign his post again. Apparently in old times a more stringent rule prevailed, and the dairyman was obliged to vacate office whenever a death occurred in his clan. For, according to tradition, the clan of Keadrol was divided into its two existing divisions for the express purpose of ensuring that there might still be men to undertake the office of dairyman when a death occurred in the clan, the men of the one division taking office whenever there was a death in the other.[571]

At first sight this case may seem exactly parallel to the case of the Flamen Dialis and the Flaminica on Dr. Farnell's theory; for here there can be no doubt whatever that it is the pollution of death which disqualifies the sacred dairyman from holding office, since, if he only avoids that pollution by not attending the funeral, he is allowed at the present day to retain his post. On this analogy we might suppose that it was not so much the death of his wife as the attendance at her funeral which compelled the Flamen Dialis to resign, especially as we know that he was expressly forbidden to touch a dead body or to enter the place where corpses were burned.[572]

ction the analogy breaks down.

But a closer inspection of the facts proves that the analogy breaks down at some important points. For though the Flamen Dialis was forbidden to touch a dead body or to enter a place where corpses were burned, he was permitted to attend a funeral;[573] so that there could hardly be any objection to his attending the funeral of [pg 229] his wife. This permission clearly tells against the view that it was the mere pollution of death which obliged him to resign office when his wife died. Further, and this is a point of fundamental difference between the two cases, whereas the Flamen Dialis was bound to be married, and married too by a rite of special solemnity,[574] there is no such obligation on the sacred dairyman of the Todas; indeed, if he is married, he is bound to live apart from his wife during his term of office.[575] Surely the obligation laid on the Flamen Dialis to be married of itself implies that with the death of his wife he necessarily ceased to hold office: there is no need to search for another reason in the pollution of death which, as I have just shown, does not seem to square with the permission granted to the Flamen to attend a funeral. That this is indeed the true explanation of the rule in question is strongly suggested by the further and apparently parallel rule which forbade the Flamen to divorce his wife; nothing but death might part them.[576] Now the rule which enjoined that a Flamen must be married, and the rule which

155

forbade him to divorce his wife, have obviously nothing to do with the pollution of death, yet they can hardly be separated from the other rule that with the death of his wife he vacated office. All three rules are explained in the most natural way on the hypothesis which I have adopted, namely, that this married priest and priestess had to perform in common certain rites which the husband could not perform without his wife. The same obvious solution of the problem was suggested long ago by Plutarch, who, after asking why the Flamen Dialis had to lay down office on the death of his wife, says, amongst other things, that "perhaps it is because she performs sacred rites along with him (for many of the rites may not be performed without the presence of a married woman), and to marry another wife immediately [pg 230] on the death of the first would hardly be possible or decent."[577] This simple explanation of the rule seems quite sufficient, and it would clearly hold good whether I am right or wrong in further supposing that the human husband and wife in this case represented a divine husband and wife, a god and goddess, to wit Jupiter and Juno, or rather Dianus (Janus) and Diana;[578] and that supposition in its turn might still hold good even if I were wrong in further conjecturing that of this divine pair the goddess (Juno or rather Diana) was originally the more important partner.

he Kota and Jewish priests.

However it is to be explained, the Roman rule which forbade the Flamen Dialis to be a widower has its parallel among the Kotas, a tribe who, like the Todas, inhabit the Neilgherry Hills of Southern India. For the higher Kota priests are not allowed to be widowers; if a priest's wife dies while he is in office, his appointment lapses. At the same time priests "should avoid pollution, and may not attend a Toda or Badaga funeral, or approach the seclusion hut set apart for Kota women."[579] Jewish priests were specially permitted to contract the pollution of death for near relations, among whom father, mother, son, daughter, and unmarried sister are particularly enumerated; but they were forbidden to contract the pollution for strangers. However, among the relations for whom a priest might thus defile himself a wife is not mentioned.[580]

§ 2. The Marriage of the Roman Gods.

hat the Roman gods were celibate is contradicted by Varro and Seneca.

The theory that the Flamen Dialis and his wife personated a divine couple, whether Jupiter and Juno or Dianus (Janus) and Diana, supposes a married relation between the god and goddess, and so far it would certainly be untenable if Dr. Farnell were right in assuming, on the authority of Mr. W. Warde Fowler, that the Roman gods were celibate.[581] On that subject, however, Varro, the [pg 231] most learned of Roman antiquaries, was of a contrary opinion. He not only spoke particularly of Juno as the wife of Jupiter,[582] but he also affirmed generally, in the most unambiguous language, that the old Roman gods were married, and in saying so he referred not to the religion of his own day, which had been modified by Greek influence, but to the religion of the ancient Romans, his ancestors.[583] Seneca ridiculed the marriage of the Roman gods, citing as examples the marriages of Mars and Bellona, of Vulcan and Venus, of Neptune and Salacia, and adding sarcastically that some of the goddesses were spinsters or widows, such as Populonia, Fulgora, and Rumina, whose faded charms or unamiable character had failed to attract a suitor.[584]

e of Orcus.

Again, the learned Servius, whose commentary on Virgil is a gold mine of Roman religious lore, informs us that the pontiffs celebrated the marriage of the infernal deity Orcus with very great solemnity;[585] and for this statement he would seem to have had the authority of the pontifical books themselves, for he refers to them in the same connexion only a few lines before. As it is in the highest degree unlikely that the pontiffs would solemnize any foreign rites, we may safely assume that the marriage of Orcus was not borrowed from Greek mythology, but was a genuine old Roman ceremony, and this is all the more probable because Servius, our authority for the custom, has recorded some curious and obviously ancient taboos which were observed at the marriage and in the ritual of Ceres, the goddess who seems to have been joined in wedlock to Orcus. One of these taboos forbade the use of wine, the other forbade persons to name their father or daughter.[586]

[pg 232]

Aulus Gellius as to the marriage of the Roman gods. Paternity and maternity of Roman deities.

Further, the learned Roman antiquary Aulus Gellius quotes from "the books of the priests of the Roman people" (the highest possible authority on the subject) and from "many ancient speeches" a list of old Roman deities, in which there seem to be at least five pairs of males and females.[587] More than that he proves conclusively by quotations from Plautus, the annalist Cn. Gellius, and Licinius Imbrex that these old writers certainly regarded one at least of the pairs (Mars and Nerio) as husband and wife;[588] and we have good ancient evidence for viewing in the same light three others of the pairs. Thus the old annalist and antiquarian L. Cincius Alimentus, who fought against Hannibal and was captured by him, affirmed in his work on the Roman calendar that Maia was the wife of Vulcan;[589] and as there was a Flamen of

157

Vulcan, who sacrificed to Maia on May Day,[590] it is reasonable to suppose that he was assisted in the ceremony by a Flaminica, his wife, just as on my hypothesis the Flamen Dialis was assisted by his wife the Flaminica. Another old Roman historian, L. Calpurnius Piso, who wrote in the second century B.C., said that the name of Vulcan's wife was not Maia but [pg 233] Majestas.[591] In saying so he may have intended to correct what he believed to be a mistake of his predecessor L. Cincius. Again, that Salacia was the wife of Neptune is perhaps implied by Varro,[592] and is positively affirmed by Seneca, Augustine, and Servius.[593] Again, Ennius appears to have regarded Hora as the wife of Quirinus, for in the first book of his Annals he declared his devotion to that divine pair.[594] In fact, of the five pairs of male and female deities cited by Aulus Gellius from the priestly books and ancient speeches the only one as to which we have not independent evidence that it consisted of a husband and wife is Saturn and Lua; and in regard to Lua we know that she was spoken of as a mother,[595] which renders it not improbable that she was also a wife. However, according to some very respectable authorities the wife of Saturn was not Lua, but Ops,[596] so that we have two independent lines of proof that Saturn was supposed to be married.

Lastly, the epithets "father" and "mother" which the Romans bestowed on many of their deities[597] are most naturally understood [pg 234] to imply paternity and maternity; and if the implication is admitted, the inference appears to be inevitable that these divine beings were supposed to exercise sexual functions, whether in lawful marriage or in unlawful concubinage. As to Jupiter in particular his paternity is positively attested by Latin inscriptions, one of them very old, which describe Fortuna Primigenia, the great goddess of Praeneste, as his daughter.[598] Again, the rustic deity Faunus, one of the oldest and most popular gods of Italy,[599] was represented by tradition in the character of a husband and a father; one of the epithets applied to him expressed in a coarse way his generative powers.[600] Fauna or the Good Goddess (*Bona Dea*), another of the oldest native Italian deities, was variously called his wife or his daughter, and he is said to have assumed the form of a snake in order to cohabit with her.[601] Again, the most famous of all Roman myths represented the founder [pg 235] of Rome himself, Romulus and his twin brother Remus, as begotten by the god Mars on a Vestal Virgin;[602] and every Roman who accepted the tradition thereby acknowledged the fatherhood of the god in the physical, not in a figurative, sense of the word. If the story of the birth of Romulus and Remus should be dismissed as a late product of the mythical fancy working under Greek influence, the same objection can hardly be urged against the story of the birth of another Roman king, Servius Tullius, who is said to have been a son of the fire-god and a slave woman; his mother conceived him beside the royal hearth, where she was impregnated by a flame that shot out from the fire in the shape of the male organ of generation.[603] It would scarcely be possible to express the physical fatherhood of the fire-god in more unambiguous terms. Now a precisely similar story was told of the birth of Romulus himself;[604] and we may suspect that this was an older form of the story than the legend which fathered the twins on Mars. Similarly, Caeculus, the founder of Praeneste, passed for a son of the fire-god Vulcan. It was said that his mother was impregnated by a spark which leaped from the fire and struck her as she sat by the hearth. In later life, when Caeculus boasted of his divine parentage to a crowd, and they refused to believe him, he prayed to his father to give the unbelievers a sign, and straightway a lambent flame surrounded the whole multitude. The proof was conclusive, and henceforth Caeculus passed for a true son of the fire-god.[605] Such tales of kings or heroes begotten by the fire-god on mortal women appear to be genuine old Italian myths, which may well go back far beyond the foundation of Rome to the common fountain of Aryan mythology; for the marriage customs observed by various branches of the Aryan family point clearly to a belief in the power of fire to impregnate women.[606]

clude that the Roman gods were thought to be married and to beget children.

On the whole, if we follow the authority of the ancients themselves, we seem bound to conclude that the Roman gods, like those of many other early peoples, were believed to be married and to beget children. It is true that, compared with the full-blooded gods of Greece, the deities of Rome appear to us shadowy creatures, pale abstractions garbed in little that can vie with the gorgeous pall of myth and story which Grecian fancy threw around its divine creations. Yet the few specimens of Roman mythology which have survived the wreck of antiquity[607] [pg 236] justify us in believing that they are but fragments of far more copious traditions which have perished. At all events the comparative aridity and barrenness of the Roman religious imagination is no reason for setting aside the positive testimony of learned Roman writers as to a point of fundamental importance in their own religion about which they could hardly be mistaken. It should never be forgotten that on this subject the ancients had access to many sources of information which are no longer open to us, and for a modern scholar to reject their evidence in favour of a personal impression derived from a necessarily imperfect knowledge of the facts seems scarcely consistent with sound principles of history and criticism.[608]

§ 3. Children of Living Parents in Ritual.

k and Roman ritual that certain offices could only be held by boys whose parents were both alive.

But Dr. Farnell adduces another argument in support of his view that it was the pollution of death which obliged the widowed Flamen Dialis to resign the priesthood. He points to what he considers the analogy of the rule of Greek ritual which required that certain sacred offices should be discharged only by a boy whose parents were both alive.[609] This rule he would explain in like manner by supposing that the death of one or both of his parents would render a boy ceremonially impure and therefore unfit to perform religious functions. Dr. Farnell might have apparently strengthened his case by observing that the Flamen Dialis and the Flaminica Dialis were themselves assisted in their office, the one by a boy, the other by a girl, both of whose parents must be alive.[610] At first sight this fits in [pg 237] perfectly with his theory: the Flamen, the Flaminica, and their youthful ministers were all rendered incapable of performing their sacred duties by the taint or corruption of death.

e which excludes orphans from certain sacred offices cannot be based on a theory that they are unclean through the death of their parents.

But a closer scrutiny of the argument reveals a flaw. It proves too much. For observe that in these Greek and Roman offices held by boys and girls the disqualification caused by the death of a parent is necessarily lifelong, since the bereavement is irreparable. Accordingly, if Dr. Farnell's theory is right, the ceremonial pollution which is the cause of the disqualification must also be lifelong; in other words, every orphan is ceremoniously unclean for life and thereby excluded for ever from the discharge of sacred duties. So sweeping a rule would at a stroke exclude a large, if not the larger, part of the population of any country from the offices of religion, and lay them permanently under all those burdensome restrictions which the pollution of death entails among many nations; for obviously a large, if not the larger, part of the population of any country at any time has lost one or both of its parents by death. No people, so far as I know, has ever carried the theory of the ceremonial pollution of death to this extremity in practice. And even if it were supposed that the taint wore off or evaporated with time from common folk so as to let them go about their common duties in everyday life, would it not still cleave to priests? If it incapacitated the Flamen's minister, would it not incapacitate the Flamen himself? In other words, would not the Flamen Dialis be obliged to vacate office on the death of his father or mother? There is no hint in ancient writers that he had to do so. And while it is generally unsafe to argue from the silence of our authorities, I think that we may do so in this case without being rash; for Plutarch not only mentions but discusses the rule which obliged the Flamen Dialis to resign office on the death of his wife,[611] and if he had known of a parallel rule which compelled him to retire on the death of a parent, he would surely have mentioned it. But if the ceremonial pollution which would certainly be caused by the death of a parent did not compel the Flamen Dialis to vacate office, we may safely conclude that neither did the similar pollution caused by the death of his wife. Thus the argument adduced by Dr. Farnell in favour of his view proves on analysis to tell strongly against it.

the exclusion of orphans from sacred offices.

But if the rule which excluded orphans from certain sacred offices cannot with any probability be explained on the theory of their ceremonial pollution, it may be worth while to inquire whether another and better explanation of the rule cannot be found. For that purpose I shall collect all the cases of it known to me. The collection is doubtless far from complete: I only offer it as a starting-point for research.

[pg 238]

ls of living parents employed in Greek rites at the vintage, harvest-home, and sowing.

At the time of the vintage, which in Greece falls in October, Athenian boys chosen from every tribe assembled at the sanctuary of Dionysus, the god of the vine. There, branches of vines laden with ripe grapes were given to them, and holding them in their hands they raced to the sanctuary of Athena Sciras. The winner received and drained a cup containing a mixture of olive-oil, wine, honey, cheese, and barley-groats. It was necessary that both the parents of each of these boy-runners should be alive.[612] At the same festival, and perhaps on the same day, an Athenian boy, whose parents must both be alive, carried in procession a branch of olive wreathed with white and purple wool and decked with fruits of many kinds, while a chorus sang that the branch bore figs, fat loaves, honey, oil, and wine. Thus they went in procession to a temple of Apollo, at the door of which the boy deposited the holy bough. The ceremony is said to have been instituted by the Athenians in obedience to an oracle for the purpose of supplicating the help of the god in a season of dearth.[613] Similar boughs similarly laden with fruits and loaves were hung up on the doors of every Athenian house and allowed to remain there a year, at the end of which they were replaced by fresh ones. While the branch was being fastened to the door, a boy whose parents were both alive recited the same verses about the branch bearing figs, fat loaves, honey, oil, and wine. This custom also is said to have been instituted for the sake of putting an end to a dearth.[614] The people of Magnesia on the Maeander vowed a bull every year to Zeus, the Saviour of the City, in the month of Cronion, at the beginning of sowing, and after maintaining the animal at the public expense throughout the winter they sacrificed it, apparently at harvest-time, in the following summer. Nine boys and nine girls, whose fathers and mothers were all living, took part in the religious services of the consecration and the sacrifice of the bull. At the consecration public prayers were offered for the safety of the city and the land, for the safety of the citizens and their wives and children, for the safety of all that dwelt in the city and the land, for peace and wealth and abundance of corn and all other fruits, and for the cattle. A herald led the prayers, and the priest and priestess, the boys and girls, the high officers and magistrates, all [pg 239] joined in these solemn petitions for the welfare of their country.[615] Among the Karo-Bataks of Central Sumatra the threshing of the rice is the occasion of various ceremonies, and in these a prominent part is played by a girl, whose father and mother must be both alive. Her special duty is to take care of the sheaf of rice in which the soul of the rice is believed to reside. This sheaf usually consists of the first rice cut and bound in the field; it is treated exactly like a person.[616]

g parents employed in the rites of the Arval Brothers.

The rites thus far described, in which boys and girls of living parents took part, were clearly ceremonies intended specially to ensure the fertility of the soil. This is indicated not merely by the nature of the rites and of the prayers or verses which accompanied them, but also by the seasons at which they were observed; for these were the vintage, the harvest-home, and the beginning of sowing. We may therefore compare a custom practised by the Roman Brethren of the Ploughed Fields (*Fratres Arvales*), a college of priests whose business it was to perform the rites deemed necessary for the growth of the corn. As a badge of office they wore wreaths of corn-ears, and paid their devotions to an antique goddess of fertility, the Dea Dia. Her home was in a grove of ancient evergreen oaks and laurels out in the Campagna, five miles from Rome. Hither every year in the month of May, when the fields were ripe or ripening to the sickle, reaped ears of the new corn were brought and hallowed by the Brethren with quaint rites, that a blessing might rest on the coming harvest. The first or preliminary consecration of the ears, however, took place, not in the grove, but in the house of the Master of the Brethren at Rome. Here the Brethren were waited upon by four free-born boys, the children of living fathers and mothers. While the Brethren reclined on couches, the boys were allowed to sit on chairs and partake of the feast, and when it was over they carried the rest of the now hallowed corn and laid it on the altar.[617]

[pg 240]

tes the employment of such children is intelligible on the principle of sympathetic magic.

In these and all other rites intended to ensure the fertility of the ground, of cattle, or of human beings, the employment of children of living parents seems to be intelligible on the principle of sympathetic magic; for such children might be deemed fuller of life than orphans, either because they "flourished on both sides," as the Greeks put it, or because the very survival of their parents might be taken as a proof that the stock of which the children came was vigorous and therefore able to impart of its superabundant energy to others.

g parents employed to cut the olive-wreath at Olympia and the laurel-wreath at Tempe.

But the rites in which the children of living parents are required to officiate do not always aim at promoting the growth of the crops. At Olympia the olive-branches which formed the victors' crowns had to be cut from a sacred tree with a golden sickle by a lad whose father and mother must be both alive.[618] The tree was a wild olive growing within the holy precinct, at the west end of the temple of Zeus. It bore the name of the Olive of the Fair Crown, and near it was an altar to the Nymphs of the Fair Crowns.[619] At Delphi every eighth year a sacred drama or miracle-play was acted which drew crowds of spectators from all parts of Greece. It set forth the slaying of the Dragon by Apollo. The principal part was sustained by a lad, the son of living parents, who seems to have personated the god himself. In an open space the likeness of a lordly palace, erected for the occasion, represented the Dragon's den. It was attacked and burned by the lad, aided by women who carried blazing torches. When the Dragon had received his deadly wound, the lad, still acting the part of the god, fled far away to be purged of the guilt of blood in the beautiful Vale of Tempe, where the Peneus flows in a deep wooded gorge between the snowy peaks of Olympus and Ossa, its smooth and silent tide shadowed by overhanging trees and tall white cliffs. In places these great crags rise abruptly from the stream and approach each other so near that only a narrow strip of sky is visible overhead; but where they recede a little, the meadows at their foot are verdant with evergreen shrubs, among which Apollo's own laurel may still be seen. In antiquity the god himself, stained with the Dragon's blood, is said to have come, a haggard footsore wayfarer, to this wild secluded glen and there plucked branches from one of the laurels that grew in its green thickets beside the rippling river. Some of them he used to twine a wreath for his brows, one of them he carried in his hand, doubtless in order that, guarded by the sacred plant, he might escape the hobgoblins which [pg 241] dogged his steps. So the boy, his human representative, did the same, and brought back to Delphi wreaths of laurel from the same tree to be awarded to the victors in the Pythian games. Hence the whole festival of the Slaying of the Dragon at Delphi went by the name of the Festival of Crowning.[620] From this it appears that at Delphi as well as at Olympia the boughs which were used to crown the victors had to be cut from a sacred tree by a boy whose parents must be both alive.

g parents acted as Laurel-bearers at Thebes.

At Thebes a festival called the Laurel-bearing was held once in every eight years, when branches of laurel were carried in procession to the temple of Apollo. The principal part in the procession was taken by a boy who held a laurel bough and bore the title of the Laurel-bearer: he seems to have personated the god himself. His hair hung down on his shoulders, and he wore a golden crown, a bright-coloured robe, and shoes of a special shape: both his parents must be alive.[621] We may suppose that the golden crown which he wore was fashioned in the shape of laurel leaves and replaced a wreath of real laurel. Thus the boy with the laurel wreath on his head and the laurel bough in his hand would resemble the traditional equipment of Apollo when he purified himself for the slaughter of the dragon. We may conjecture that at Thebes the Laurel-bearer originally personated not Apollo but the local hero Cadmus, who slew the dragon and had like Apollo to purify himself for the slaughter. The conjecture is confirmed by vase-paintings which represent Cadmus crowned with laurel preparing to attack the dragon or actually in combat with the monster, while goddesses bend over him holding out wreaths of laurel as the meed of victory.[622] On this hypothesis the octennial Delphic Festival of Crowning and the octennial Theban Festival of Laurel-bearing were closely akin: in both the prominent part played by the laurel was purificatory or expiatory.[623] Thus at Olympia, Delphi, and Thebes a boy whose [pg 242] parents were both alive was entrusted with the duty of cutting or wearing a sacred wreath at a great festival which recurred at intervals of several years.[624]

ere originally amulets, we could understand why children of living parents were chosen to cut and wear

Why a boy of living parents should be chosen for such an office is not at first sight clear; the reason might be more obvious if we understood the ideas in which the custom of wearing wreaths and crowns had its origin. Probably in many cases wreaths and crowns were amulets before they were ornaments; in other words, their first intention may have been not so much to adorn the head as to protect it from harm by surrounding it with a plant, a metal, or any other thing which was supposed to possess the magical virtue of banning baleful influences. Thus the Arabs of Moab will put a circlet of copper on the head of a man who is suffering from headache, for they believe that this will banish the pain; and if the pain is in an arm or a leg, they will treat the ailing limb in like manner. They think that red beads hung before the eyes of children who are afflicted with ophthalmia will rid them of the malady, and that a red ribbon tied to the foot will prevent it from stumbling on a stony path.[625] Again, the Melanesians of the Gazelle Peninsula in New Britain often deck their dusky bodies with [pg 243] flowers, leaves, and scented herbs not only at festivals but on other occasions which to the European might seem inappropriate for such gay ornaments. But in truth the bright blossoms and verdant foliage are not intended to decorate the wearer but to endow him with certain magical virtues, which are supposed to inhere in the flowers and leaves. Thus one man may be seen strutting about with a wreath of greenery which passes round his neck and droops over his shoulders, back, and breast. He is not a mere dandy, but a lover who hopes that the wreath will work as a charm on a woman's heart. Again, another may be observed with a bunch of the red dracaena leaves knotted round his neck and the long stalk hanging down his back. He is a soldier, and these leaves are supposed to make him invulnerable. But if the lover should fail to win the affections of his swarthy mistress, if the warrior should be wounded in battle, it never occurs to either of them to question the magical virtue of the charm; they ascribe the failure either to the more potent charm of another magician or to some oversight on their own part.[626] On the theory that wreaths and garlands serve as amulets to protect the wearer against the powers of evil we can understand not only why in antiquity sacred persons such as priests and kings wore crowns, but also why dead bodies, sacrificial victims, and in certain circumstances even inanimate objects such as the implements of sacrifice, the doors of houses, and so forth, were decorated or rather guarded by wreaths.[627] Further, on this hypothesis we may perhaps perceive why children of living parents were specially chosen to cut or wear sacred wreaths. Since such children were apparently supposed to be endowed with a more than common share of vital energy, they might be deemed peculiarly fitted to make or wear amulets which were designed to protect the wearer from injury and death: the current of life which circulated in their own veins overflowed, as it were, and reinforced the magic virtue of the wreath. For the same reason such children would naturally be chosen to personate gods, as they seemingly were at Delphi and Thebes.

living parents acting as priest and priestess of Apollo and Artemis. At Rome the Vestals and the Salii children of parents who were alive at the date of the election. Children of living parents employed in es at Rome.

At Ephesus, if we may trust the evidence of the Greek romance-writer, Heliodorus, a boy and girl of living parents used to hold for a year the priesthood of Apollo and Artemis respectively. When their [pg 244] period of office was nearly expired, they led a sacred embassy to Delos, the birthplace of the divine brother and sister, where they superintended the musical and athletic contests and laid down the priesthood.[628] At Rome no girl might be chosen a Vestal Virgin unless both her father and mother were living;[629] yet there is no evidence or probability that a Vestal vacated office on the death of a parent; indeed she generally held office for life.[630] This alone may suffice to prove that the custom of entrusting certain sacred duties to children of living parents was not based on any notion that orphans as such were ceremonially unclean. Again, the dancing priests of Mars, the Salii, must be sons of living parents;[631] but as in the case of the Vestals this condition probably only applied at the date of their election, for they seem like the Vestals to have held office for life. At all events we read of a lively old gentleman who still skipped and capered about as a dancing priest with an agility which threw the efforts of his younger colleagues into the shade.[632] Again, at the public games in Rome boys of living parents had to escort the images of the gods in their sacred cars, and it was a dire omen if one of them relaxed his hold on the holy cart or let a strap slip from his fingers.[633] And when the stout Roman heart was shaken by the appalling news that somebody had been struck by lightning, that the sky had somewhere been suddenly overcast, or that a she-mule had been safely delivered of a colt, boys and girls whose fathers and mothers were still alive used to be sought out and employed to help in expiating the terrific prodigy.[634] Again, when the Capitol had been sacked and burned by the disorderly troops of Vitellius, solemn preparations were made to rebuild it. The whole area was enclosed by a cordon of fillets and wreaths. Then soldiers chosen for their auspicious names entered within the barriers holding branches of lucky trees in their hands; and afterwards the Vestal Virgins, aided by boys and girls of living parents, washed the foundations with water drawn from springs and rivers.[635] In this ceremony the choice of such children seems to be based on the same idea as the choice of such water; for as running water is deemed to [pg 245] be especially alive,[636] so the vital current might be thought to flow without interruption in the children of living parents but to stagnate in orphans. Hence the children of living parents rather than orphans would naturally be chosen to pour the living water over the foundations, and so to lend something of their own vitality or endurance to a building that was designed to last for ever.

iving parents employed at marriage ceremonies in Greece, Italy, Albania, Bulgaria, and Africa.

On the same principle we can easily understand why the children of living parents should be especially chosen to perform certain offices at marriage. The motive of such a choice may be a wish to ensure by sympathetic magic the life of the newly wedded pair and of their offspring. Thus at Roman marriages the bride was escorted to her new home by three boys whose parents were all living. Two of the boys held her, and the third carried a torch of buckthorn or hawthorn in front of her,[637] probably for the purpose of averting the powers of evil; for buckthorn or hawthorn was credited with this magical virtue.[638] At marriages in ancient Athens a boy whose parents were both living used to wear a wreath of thorns and acorns and to carry about a winnowing-fan full of loaves, crying, "I have escaped the bad, I have found the better."[639] In modern Greece on the Sunday before a marriage the bridegroom sends to the bride the wedding cake by the hands of a boy, both of whose parents must be living. The messenger takes great care not to stumble or to injure the cake, for to do either would be a very bad omen. He may not enter the bride's house till she has taken the cake from him. For this purpose he lays it down on the threshold of the door, and then both of them, the boy and the bride, rush at it and try to seize the greater part of the cake. And when cattle are being slaughtered for the marriage festivities, the first beast killed for the bride's house must be killed by a youth whose parents are both alive. Further, a son of living parents must solemnly fetch the water with which the bridegroom's head is ceremonially washed by women before marriage. And on the day after the marriage bride and bridegroom go in procession to the well or spring from which they are henceforth to fetch their water. The bride greets the spring, drinks of the water from the hollow of her hand, and throws money and food into it. Then follows a dance, accompanied by a song, round about the spring. Lastly, a lad whose parents are both living draws water from the spring in a special vessel and carries it to the house of the bridal pair without speaking a word: this "unspoken water," as it is called, is regarded [pg 246] as peculiarly holy and wholesome. When the young couple return from the spring, they fill their mouths with the "unspoken water" and try to spirt it on each other inside the door of the house.[640] In Albania, when women are baking cakes for a wedding, the first to put hand to the dough must be a maiden whose parents are both alive and who has brothers, the more the better; for only such a girl is deemed lucky. And when the bride has dismounted from her horse at the bridegroom's door, a small boy whose parents are both alive (for only such a boy is thought to bring luck) is passed thrice backwards and forwards under the horse's belly, as if he would girdle the beast.[641] Among the South Slavs of Bulgaria a little child whose father and mother are both alive helps to bake the two bridal cakes, pouring water and salt on the meal and stirring the mixture with a spurtle of a special shape; then a girl lifts the child in her arms, and the little one touches the roof-beam thrice with the spurtle, saying, "Boys and girls." And when the bride's hair is to be dressed for the wedding day, the work of combing and plaiting it must be begun by a child of living parents.[642] Among the Eesa and Gadabursi, two Somali tribes, on the morning after a marriage "the bride's female relations bring presents of milk, and are accompanied by a young male child whose parents are living. The child drinks some of the milk before any one else tastes it; and after him the bridegroom, if his parents are living; but if one or both of his parents are dead, and those of the bride living, she drinks after the child. By doing this they believe that if the newly-married woman bears a child the father will be alive at the time."[643] A slightly different application of the same principle appears in the old Hindoo rule that when a bride reached the house of her husband, she should be made to descend from the chariot by women of good character whose husbands and sons were living, and that afterwards these women should seat the bride on a bull's hide, while her husband recited the verse, "Here ye cows, bring forth calves."[644] Here the ceremony of seating the young wife on a bull's hide seems plainly intended to make her fruitful through the generative virtue of the bull; while the attendance of women, whose husbands and sons are living, is no doubt a device for ensuring, by sympathetic magic, the life both of the bride's husband and of her future offspring.

[pg 247]

living parents apparently supposed to impart life and longevity. Child of living parents employed in

In the Somali custom just described the part played by the child of living parents is unambiguous and helps to throw light on the obscurer cases which precede. Such a child is clearly supposed to impart the virtue of longevity to the milk of which it partakes, and so to transmit it to the newly married pair who afterwards drink of the milk. Similarly, we may suppose that in all marriage rites at least, if not in religious rites generally, the employment of children of living parents is intended to diffuse by sympathy the blessings of life and longevity among all who participate in the ceremonies. This intention seems to underlie the use which the Malagasy make of the children of living parents in ritual. Thus, when a child is a week old, it is dressed up in the finest clothes that can be got, and is then carried out of the house by some person whose parents are both still living; afterwards it is brought back to the mother. In the act of being carried out and in, the infant must be twice carefully lifted over the fire, which is placed near the door. If the child is a boy, the axe, knife, and spear of the family, together with any building tools that may be in the house, are taken out of it at the same time. "The implements are perhaps used chiefly as emblems of the occupations in which it is expected the infant will engage when it arrives at maturer years; and the whole may be regarded as expressing the hopes cherished of his activity, wealth, and enjoyments."[645] On such an occasion the service of a person whose parents are both alive seems naturally calculated to promote the longevity of the infant. For a like reason, probably, the holy water used at the Malagasy ceremony of circumcision is drawn from a pool by a person whose parents are both still living.[646] The same idea may explain a funeral custom observed by the Sihanaka of Madagascar. After a burial the family of the deceased, with their near relatives and dependents, meet in the house from which the corpse was lately removed "to drink rum and to undergo a purifying and preserving baptism called *fàfy rànom-bóahàngy*. Leaves of the lemon or lime tree, and the stalks of two kinds of grass, are gathered and placed in a vessel with water. A person, both of whose parents are living, is chosen to perform the rite, and this 'holy water' is then sprinkled upon the walls of the house and upon all assembled within them, and finally around the house outside."[647]

Here a person whose parents are both living appears to be credited with a more than common share of life and longevity; from which it naturally follows that he is better fitted than any one else to perform a ceremony intended to avert the danger of death from the household.

hildren of living parents in ritual may be explained by a notion that they are fuller of life and therefore orphans.

The notion that a child of living parents is endowed with a [pg 248] higher degree of vitality than an orphan probably explains all the cases of the employment of such a child in ritual, whether the particular rite is designed to ensure the fertility of the ground or the fruitfulness of women, or to avert the danger of death and other calamities. Yet it might be a mistake to suppose that this notion is always clearly apprehended by the persons who practise the customs. In their minds the definite conception of superabundant and overflowing vitality may easily dissolve into a vague idea that the child of living parents is luckier than other folk. No more than this seems to be at the bottom of the Masai rule that when the warriors wish to select a chief, they must choose "a man whose parents are still living, who owns cattle and has never killed anybody, whose parents are not blind, and who himself has not a discoloured eye."[648] And nothing more is needed to explain the ancient Greek custom which assigned the duty of drawing lots from an urn to a boy under puberty whose father and mother were both in life.[649] At Athens it would appear that registers of these boys were kept, perhaps in order that the lads might discharge, as occasion arose, those offices of religion which required the service of such auspicious youths.[650] The atrocious tyrant Heliogabalus, one of the worst monsters who ever disgraced the human form, caused search to be made throughout Italy for noble and handsome boys whose parents were both alive, and he sacrificed them to his barbarous gods, torturing them first and grabbling among their entrails afterwards for omens. He seems to have thought that such victims would be peculiarly acceptable to the Syrian deities whom he worshipped; so he encouraged the torturers and butchers at their work, and thanked the gods for enabling him to ferret out "their friends."[651]

[pg 249]

III. A Charm To Protect a Town.

nas use the hide of a sacrificial ox at founding a new town.

The tradition that a Lydian king tried to make the citadel of Sardes impregnable by carrying round it a lion[652] may perhaps be illustrated by a South African custom. When the Bechuanas are about to found a new town, they observe an elaborate ritual. They choose a bull from the herd, sew up its eyelids with sinew, and then allow the blinded animal to wander at will for four days. On the fifth day they track it down and sacrifice it at sunset on the spot where it happens to be standing. The carcase is then roasted whole and divided among the people. Ritual requires that every particle of the flesh should be consumed on the spot. When the sacrificial meal is over, the medicine-men take the hide and mark it with appropriate medicines, the composition of which is a professional secret. Then with one long spiral cut they convert the whole hide into a single thong. Having done so they cut up the thong into lengths of about two feet and despatch messengers in all directions to peg down one of those strips in each of the paths leading to the new town. "After this," it is said, "if a foreigner approaches the new town to destroy it with his charms, he will find that the town has prepared itself for his coming."[653] Thus it would seem that the pastoral Bechuanas attempt to place a new town under the protection of one of their sacred cattle[654] by distributing pieces of its hide at all points where an enemy could approach it, just as the Lydian king thought to place the citadel of his capital under the protection of the lion-god by carrying the animal round the boundaries.

may explain the legend of the foundation of Carthage and similar tales.

Further, the Bechuana custom may throw light on a widespread legend which relates how a wily settler in a new country bought from the natives as much land as could be covered with a hide, and how he then proceeded to cut the hide into thongs and to claim as much land as could be enclosed by the thongs. It was thus, [pg 250] according to the Hottentots, that the first European settlers obtained a footing in South Africa.[655] But the most familiar example of such stories is the tradition that Dido procured the site of Carthage in this fashion, and that the place hence received the name of Byrsa or "hide."[656] Similar tales occur in the legendary history of Saxons and Danes,[657] and they meet us in India, Siberia, Burma, Cambodia, Java, and Bali.[658] The wide diffusion of such stories confirms the conjecture of Jacob Grimm that in them we have a reminiscence of a mode of land measurement which was once actually in use, and of which the designation is still retained in the English *hide*.[659] The Bechuana custom suggests that the mode of measuring by a hide may have originated in a practice of encompassing a piece of land with thongs cut from the hide of a sacrificial victim in order to place the ground under the guardianship of the sacred animal.

e hide is used is blinded in order that the new town may be invisible to its enemies.

But why do the Bechuanas sew up the eyelids of the bull which is to be used for this purpose? The answer appears to be given by the ceremonies which the same people observe when they are going out to war. On that occasion a woman rushes up to the army with her eyes shut and shakes a winnowing-fan, while she cries out, "The army is not seen! The army is not seen!" And a medicine-man at the same time sprinkles medicine over the spears, crying out in like manner, "The army is not seen! The army is not seen!" After that they seize a bull, sew up its eyelids with a hair of its tail, and drive it for some distance along the road which the army is to take. When it has preceded the army a little way, the bull is sacrificed, roasted whole, and eaten by the warriors. All the flesh must be consumed on the spot. Such parts as cannot be eaten are burnt with fire. Only the contents of the stomach are carefully preserved [pg 251] as a charm which is to lead the warriors to victory. Chosen men carry the precious guts in front of the army, and it is deemed most important that no one should precede them. When they stop, the army stops, and it will not resume the march till it sees that the men with the bull's guts have gone forward.[660] The meaning of these ceremonies is explained by the cries of the woman and the priest, "The army is not seen! The army is not seen!" Clearly it is desirable that the army should not be perceived by the enemies until it is upon them. Accordingly on the principles of homoeopathic magic the Bechuanas apparently imagine that they can make themselves invisible by eating of the flesh of a blind bull, blindness and invisibility being to their simple minds the same thing. For the same reason the bowels of the blind ox are carried in front of the army to hide its advance from hostile eyes. In like manner the custom of sacrificing and eating a blind ox on the place where a new town is to be built may be intended to render the town invisible to enemies. At all events the Bawenda, a South African people who belong to the same Bantu stock as the Bechuanas, take great pains to conceal their kraals from passers-by. The kraals are built in the forest or bush, and the long winding footpaths which lead to them are often kept open only by the support of a single pole here and there. Indeed the paths are so low and narrow that it is very difficult to bring a horse into such a village. In time of war the poles are removed and the thorny creepers fall down, forming a natural screen or bulwark which the enemy can neither penetrate nor destroy by fire. The kraals are also surrounded by walls of undressed stones with a filling of soil; and to hide them still better from the view of the enemy the tops of the walls are sown with Indian corn or planted with tobacco. Hence travellers passing through the country seldom come across a Bawenda kraal. To see where the Bawenda dwell you must climb to the tops of mountains and look down on the roofs of their round huts peeping out of the surrounding green like clusters of mushrooms in the woods.[661] The object which the Bawenda attain by these perfectly rational means, the Bechuanas seek to compass by the sacrifice and consumption of a blind bull.

tion of the use of a blinded ox is confirmed by a Caffre custom.

This explanation of the use of a blinded ox in sacrifice is confirmed by the reasons alleged by a Caffre for the observance of a somewhat similar custom in purificatory ceremonies after a battle. On these occasions the Bechuanas and other Caffre tribes of South Africa kill a black ox and cut out the tip of its tongue, an eye, a piece of the ham-string, and a piece of the principal sinew of the [pg 252] shoulder. These parts are fried with certain herbs and rubbed into the joints of the warriors. By cutting out the tongue of the ox they think to prevent the enemy from wagging his tongue against them; by severing the sinews of the ox they hope to cause the enemy's sinews to fail him in the battle; and by removing the eye of the ox they imagine that they prevent the enemy from casting a covetous eye on their cattle.[662]

[pg 253]

IV. Some Customs Of The Pelew Islanders.

We have seen that the state of society and religion among the Pelew Islanders in modern times presents several points of similarity to the condition of the peoples about the Eastern Mediterranean in antiquity.[663] Here I propose briefly to call attention to certain other customs of the Pelew Islanders which may serve to illustrate some of the institutions discussed in this volume.

§ 1. Priests dressed as Women.

Islands a man who is inspired by a goddess wears female attire and is treated as a woman. This hange of sex under the inspiration of a female spirit may explain a widespread custom whereby men e like women.

In the Pelew Islands it often happens that a goddess chooses a man, not a woman, for her minister and inspired mouthpiece. When that is so, the favoured man is thenceforth regarded and treated as a woman. He wears female attire, he carries a piece of gold on his neck, he labours like a woman in the taro fields, and he plays his new part so well that he earns the hearty contempt of his fellows.[664] The pretended change of sex under the inspiration of a female spirit perhaps explains a custom widely spread among savages, in accordance with which some men dress as women and act as women through life. These unsexed creatures often, perhaps generally, profess the arts of sorcery and healing, they communicate with spirits, and are regarded sometimes with awe and sometimes with contempt, as beings of a higher or lower order than common folk. Often they are dedicated and trained to their vocation from childhood. Effeminate sorcerers or priests of this sort are found among the Sea Dyaks of Borneo,[665] the Bugis of South [pg 254] Celebes,[666] the Patagonians of South America,[667] and the Aleutians and many Indian tribes of North America.[668] In the island of Rambree, off the coast of Aracan, a set of vagabond "conjurors," who dressed and lived as women, used to dance round a tall pole, invoking the aid of their favourite idol on the occasion of any calamity.[669] Male members of the Vallabha sect in India often seek to win the favour of the god Krishna, whom they specially revere, by wearing their hair long and assimilating themselves to women; even their spiritual chiefs, the so-called Maharajas, sometimes simulate the appearance of women when they lead the worship of their followers.[670] In Madagascar we hear of effeminate men who wore female attire and acted as women, thinking thereby to do God service.[671] In the kingdom of Congo there was a sacrificial

173

priest who commonly dressed as a woman and [pg 255] gloried in the title of the Grandmother. The post of Grandmother must have been much coveted, for the incumbent might not be put to death, whatever crimes or rascalities he committed; and to do him justice he appears commonly to have taken full advantage of this benefit of clergy. When he died, his fortunate successor dissected the body of the deceased Grandmother, extracting his heart and other vital organs, and amputating his fingers and toes, which he kept as priceless relics, and sold as sovereign remedies for all the ills that flesh is heir to.[672]

rmations seem to have been often carried out in obedience to intimations received in dreams or in sformed medicine-men among the Sea Dyaks and Chukchees.

We may conjecture that in many of these cases the call to this strange form of the religious life came in the shape of a dream or vision, in which the dreamer or visionary imagined himself to be a woman or to be possessed by a female spirit; for with many savage races the disordered fancies of sleep or ecstasy are accepted as oracular admonitions which it would be perilous to disregard. At all events we are told that a dream or a revelation of some sort was the reason which in North America these men-women commonly alleged for the life they led; it had been thus brought home to them, they said, that their medicine or their salvation lay in living as women, and when once they had got this notion into their head nothing could drive it out again. Many an Indian father attempted by persuasion, by bribes, by violence, to deter his son from obeying the mysterious call, but all to no purpose.[673] Among the Sauks, an Indian tribe of North America, these effeminate beings were always despised, but sometimes they were pitied "as labouring under an unfortunate destiny which they cannot avoid, being supposed to be impelled to this course by a vision from the female spirit that resides in the moon."[674] Similarly the Omahas, another [pg 256] Indian tribe of North America, "believe that the unfortunate beings, called *Min-qu-ga*, are mysterious or sacred because they have been affected by the Moon Being. When a young Omaha fasted for the first time on reaching puberty, it was thought that the Moon Being appeared to him, holding in one hand a bow and arrows and in the other a pack strap, such as the Indian women use. When the youth tried to grasp the bow and arrows the Moon Being crossed his hands very quickly, and if the youth was not very careful he seized the pack strap instead of the bow and arrows, thereby fixing his lot in after life. In such a case he could not help acting the woman, speaking, dressing, and working just as Indian women used to do."[675] Among the Ibans or Sea Dyaks of Borneo the highest class of sorcerers or medicine-men (*manangs*) are those who are believed to have been transformed into women. Such a man is therefore called a "changed medicine-man" (*manang bali*) on account of his supposed change of sex. The

174

call to transform himself into a woman is said to come as a supernatural command thrice repeated in dreams; to disregard the command would mean death. Accordingly he makes a feast, sacrifices a pig or two to avert evil consequences from the tribe, and then assumes the garb of a woman. Thenceforth he is treated as a woman and occupies himself in feminine pursuits. His chief aim is to copy female manners and habits as accurately as possible. He is employed for the same purposes as an ordinary medicine-man and his methods are similar, but he is paid much higher fees and is often called in when others have been unable to effect a cure.[676] Similarly among the Chukchees of North-Eastern Asia there are shamans or medicine-men who assimilate themselves as far as possible to women, and who are believed to be called to this vocation by spirits in a dream. The call usually comes at the critical age of early youth when the shamanistic inspiration, as it is called, first manifests itself. But the call is much dreaded by the youthful adepts, and some of them prefer death to obedience. There are, however, various stages or degrees of transformation. In the first stage the man apes a woman only in the manner of braiding and arranging the hair of his head. In the second he dons female attire; in the third stage he adopts as far as possible the life and characteristics of the female sex. A young man who is undergoing this final transformation abandons all masculine occupations and manners. He throws away the rifle and the lance, the lasso of the reindeer herdsman, and the harpoon of the seal-hunter, and betakes himself to the needle and the skin-scraper instead. He learns the use of them quickly, [pg 257] because the spirits are helping him all the time. Even his pronunciation changes from the male to the female mode. At the same time his body alters, if not in outward appearance, at least in its faculties and forces. He loses masculine strength, fleetness of foot, endurance in wrestling, and falls into the debility and helplessness of a woman. Even his mental character undergoes a change. His old brute courage and fighting spirit are gone; he grows shy and bashful before strangers, fond of small talk and of dandling little children. In short he becomes a woman with the appearance of a man, and as a woman he is often taken to wife by another man, with whom he leads a regular married life. Extraordinary powers are attributed to such transformed shamans. They are supposed to enjoy the special protection of spirits who play the part of supernatural husbands to them. Hence they are much dreaded even by their colleagues in the profession who remain mere men; hence, too, they excel in all branches of magic, including ventriloquism.[677] Among the Teso of Central Africa medicine-men often dress as women and wear feminine ornaments, such as heavy chains of beads and shells round their heads and necks.[678]

ired by a god dress as men.

And just as a man inspired by a goddess may adopt female attire, so conversely a woman inspired by a god may adopt male costume. In Uganda the great god Mukasa, the deity of the Victoria Nyanza Lake and of abundance, imparted his oracles through a woman, who in ordinary life dressed like the rest of her sex in a bark cloth wrapped round the body and fastened with a girdle, so as to leave the arms and shoulders bare; but when she prophesied under the inspiration of the god, she wore two bark cloths knotted in masculine style over her shoulders and crossing each other on her breast and back.[679] When once the god had chosen her, she retained office for life; she might not marry or converse with any man except one particular priest, who was always present when she was possessed by the deity.[680]

of inspiration by a female spirit perhaps explains the legends of the effeminate Sardanapalus and the ercules, both of whom may have been thought to be possessed by the great Asiatic goddess Astarte or nt.

Perhaps this assumed change of sex under the inspiration of a goddess may give the key to the legends of the effeminate Sardanapalus and the effeminate Hercules,[681] as well as to the practice of the effeminate priests of Cybele and the Syrian goddess. In all [pg 258] such cases the pretended transformation of a man into a woman would be intelligible if we supposed that the womanish priest or king thought himself animated by a female spirit, whose sex, accordingly, he felt bound to imitate. Certainly the eunuch priests of Cybele seem to have bereft themselves of their manhood under the supposed inspiration of the Great Goddess.[682] The priest of Hercules at Antimachia, in Cos, who dressed as a woman when he offered sacrifice, is said to have done so in imitation of Hercules who disguised himself as a woman to escape the pursuit of his enemies.[683] So the Lydian Hercules wore female attire when he served for three years as the purchased slave of the imperious Omphale, Queen of Lydia.[684] If we suppose that Queen Omphale, like Queen Semiramis, was nothing but the great Asiatic goddess,[685] or one of her Avatars, it becomes probable that the story of the womanish Hercules of Lydia preserves a reminiscence of a line or college of effeminate priests who, like the eunuch priests of the Syrian goddess, dressed as women in imitation of their goddess and were supposed to be inspired by her. The probability is increased by the practice of the priests of Hercules at Antimachia, in Cos, who, as we have just seen, actually wore female attire when they were engaged in their sacred duties. Similarly at the vernal mysteries of Hercules in Rome the men were draped in the garments of women;[686] and in some of the rites and processions of Dionysus also men wore female attire.[687] In [pg 259] legend and art there are clear traces of an effeminate Dionysus, who perhaps figured in a strange ceremony for the artificial fertilization of the fig.[688] Among the Nahanarvals, an ancient German tribe, a priest garbed as a woman presided over a sacred grove.[689] These and similar practices[690] need not necessarily have any connexion with the social system of mother-kin. Wherever a goddess is revered and the theory of inspiration is held, a man may be thought to be possessed by a female spirit, whether society be organized on mother-kin or on father-kin. Still the chances of such a transformation of sex will be greater under mother-kin than under father-kin if, as we have found reason to believe, a system of mother-kin is more favourable to the development and multiplication of goddesses than of gods. It is therefore, perhaps, no mere accident that we meet with these effeminate priests in regions like the Pelew Islands and Western Asia, where the system of mother-kin either actually prevails or has at least left traces of it behind in tradition and custom. Such traces, for example, are to be found in Lydia and Cos,[691] in both of which the effeminate Hercules had his home.

[pg 260]

hange of costume between men and women has probably been practised also from other motives, for m a wish to avert the Evil Eye. This motive seems to explain the interchange of male and female ween bride and bridegroom at marriage.

But the religious or superstitious interchange of dress between men and women is an obscure and complex problem, and it is unlikely that any single solution would apply to all the cases. Probably the custom has been practised from many different motives. For example, the practice of dressing boys as girls has certainly been sometimes adopted to avert the Evil Eye;[692] and it is possible that the custom of changing garments at marriage, the bridegroom disguising himself as a woman, or the bride disguising herself as a man, may have been resorted to for the same purpose. Thus in Cos, where the priest of Hercules wore female attire, the bridegroom was in like manner dressed as a woman when he received his bride.[693] Spartan brides had their hair shaved, and were clad in men's clothes and booted on their wedding night.[694] Argive brides wore false beards when they slept with their husbands for the first time.[695] In Southern Celebes a bridegroom at a certain point of the long and elaborate marriage ceremonies puts on the garments which his bride has just put off.[696] Among the Jews of Egypt in the Middle Ages the bride led the wedding dance with a helmet on her head and a sword in her hand, while the bridegroom adorned himself as a woman and put on female attire.[697] At a Brahman marriage in Southern India "the bride is dressed up as a boy, and another girl is dressed up to represent the bride. They are taken in procession through the street, and, on returning, the pseudo-bridegroom is made to speak to the real bridegroom in somewhat insolent tones, and some mock play is indulged in. The real bridegroom is addressed as if he was the syce (groom) or gumasta (clerk) of the pseudo-bridegroom, and is sometimes treated as a thief, and judgment passed on him by the latter."[698] Among the Bharias [pg 261] of the Central Provinces of India "the bridegroom puts on women's ornaments and carries with him an iron nut-cutter or dagger to keep off evil

177

spirits."[699] Similarly among the Khangars, a low Hindustani caste of the same region, "the bridegroom is dressed in a yellow gown and overcloth, with trousers of red chintz, red shoes, and a marriage crown of date-palm leaves. He has the silver ornaments usually worn by women on his neck, as the *khang-wāri* or silver ring and the *hamel* or necklace of rupees. In order to avert the evil eye he carries a dagger or nut-cracker, and a smudge of lampblack is made on his forehead to disfigure him and thus avert the evil eye, which, it is thought, would otherwise be too probably attracted by his exquisitely beautiful appearance in his wedding garments."[700] These examples render it highly probable that, like the dagger or nut-cracker which he holds in his hand, the woman's ornaments which he wears are intended to protect the bridegroom against demons or the evil eye at this critical moment of his life, the protection apparently consisting in a disguise which enables him to elude the unwelcome attentions of malignant beings.[701]

xplanation may account for the interchange of male and female costume between other persons at

A similar explanation probably accounts for the similar exchange of costume between other persons than the bride and bridegroom at marriage. For example, after a Bharia wedding, "the girl's mother gets the dress of the boy's father and puts it on, together with a false beard and moustaches, and dances holding a wooden ladle in one hand and a packet of ashes in the other. Every time she approaches the bridegroom's father on her rounds she spills some of the ashes over him and occasionally gives him a crack on the head with her ladle, these actions being accompanied by bursts of laughter from the party and frenzied playing by the musicians. When the party reach the bridegroom's house on their return, his mother and the other women come out, and burn a little mustard and human hair in a lamp, the unpleasant smell emitted by these articles being considered potent to drive away evil spirits."[702] Again, after a Khangar wedding the father of the bridegroom, dressed in women's clothes, dances with the mother of the bride, while the two throw turmeric mixed with water on each other.[703] Similarly after a [pg 262] wedding of the Bharbhunjas, another Hindustani caste of the Central Provinces, the bridegroom's father dances before the family in women's clothes which have been supplied by the bride's father.[704] Such disguises and dances may be intended either to protect the disguised dancer himself against the evil eye or perhaps rather to guard the principal personages of the ceremony, the bride and bridegroom, by diverting the attention of demons from them to the guiser.[705] However, when at marriage the bride alone assumes the costume and appearance of the other sex, the motive for the disguise may perhaps be a notion that on the principle of homoeopathic magic she thereby ensures the birth of a male heir. Similarly in Sweden there is a popular superstition that "on the night preceding her nuptials the bride should have a baby-boy to sleep with her, in which case her first-born will be a son";[706] and among the Kabyles, when a bride dismounts from her mule at her husband's house, a young lad leaps into the saddle before she touches the ground, in order that her first child may be a boy.[707]

ess assumed by men for the purpose of deceiving demons and ghosts.

Be that as it may, there is no doubt that the assumption of woman's dress is sometimes intended to disguise a man for the purpose of deceiving a demon. Thus among the Boloki or Bangala on the Upper Congo a man was long afflicted with an internal malady. When all other remedies had failed, a witch-doctor informed the sufferer that the cause of his trouble was an evil spirit, and that the best thing he could do was to go far away where the devil could not get at him, and to remain there till he had recovered his health. The patient followed the prescription. At dead of night he left his house, taking only two of his wives with him and telling no one of his destination, lest the demon should hear it and follow him. So he went far away from his town, donned a woman's dress, and speaking in a woman's voice he pretended to be other than he was, in order that the devil should not be able to find him at his new address. Strange to say, these sage measures failed to [pg 263] effect a cure, and wearying of exile he at last returned home, where he continued to dress and speak as a woman.[708] Again, the Kuki-Lushai of Assam believe that if a man kills an enemy or a wild beast, the ghost of the dead man or animal will haunt him and drive him mad. The only way of averting this catastrophe is to dress up as a woman and pretend to be one. For example, a man who had shot a tiger and was in fear of being haunted by the animal's ghost, dressed himself up in a woman's petticoat and cloth, wore ivory earrings, and wound a mottled cloth round his head like a turban. Then smoking a woman's pipe, carrying a little basket, and spinning a cotton spindle, he paraded the village followed by a crowd roaring and shrieking with laughter, while he preserved the gravity of a judge, for a single smile would have been fatal. To guard against the possibility of unseasonable mirth, he carried a porcupine in his arms, and if ever, tickled beyond the pitch of endurance, he burst into a guffaw, the crowd said, "It was the porcupine that laughed." All this was done to mortify the pride of the tiger's ghost by leading him to believe that he had been shot by a woman.[709]

costume between the sexes at circumcision.

The same dread of attracting the attention of dangerous spirits at critical times perhaps explains the custom observed by some East African tribes of wearing the costume of the opposite sex at circumcision. Thus, when Masai boys have been circumcised they dress as women, wearing earrings in their ears and long garments that reach to the ground. They also whiten their swarthy faces with chalk. This costume they retain till their wounds are healed, whereupon they are shaved and assume the skins and ornaments of warriors.[710] Among the Nandi, a tribe of British East Africa, before boys are circumcised they receive a visit from young girls, who give them some of their own garments and ornaments. These the boys put on and wear till the operation of circumcision is over, when they exchange the girls' clothes for the garments of women, which, together with necklaces, are provided for them by their mothers; and these women's garments the newly circumcised lads must continue to wear for months afterwards. Girls are also circumcised among the Nandi, and before they submit to the operation they attire themselves in men's garments and carry clubs in their hands.[711]

of the interchange of male and female costume.

If such interchange of costume between men and women is [pg 264] intended to disguise the wearers against demons, we may compare the practice of the Lycian men, who regularly wore women's dress in mourning;[712] for this might be intended to conceal them from the ghost, just as perhaps for a similar reason some peoples of antiquity used to descend into pits and remain there for several days, shunning the light of the sun, whenever a death had taken place in the family.[713] A similar desire to deceive spirits may perhaps explain a device to which the Loeboes, a primitive tribe of Sumatra, resort when they wish to obtain male or female offspring. If parents have several sons and desire that the next child shall be a girl, they dress the boys as girls, cut their hair after the girlish fashion, and hang necklaces round their necks. On the contrary, when they have many daughters and wish to have a son, they dress the girls up as boys.[714]

On the whole we conclude that the custom of men dressing as women and of women dressing as men has been practised from a variety of superstitious motives, among which the principal would seem to be the wish to please certain powerful spirits or to deceive others.

§ 2. Prostitution of Unmarried Girls.

tic prostitution of unmarried girls for hire in the Pelew Islands seems to be a form of sexual communism -marriage.

Like many peoples of Western Asia in antiquity, the Pelew Islanders systematically prostitute their unmarried girls for hire. Hence, just as in Lydia and Cyprus of old, the damsels are a source of income to their family, and women wait impatiently for the time when their young daughters will be able to help the household by their earnings. Indeed the mother regularly anticipates the time by depriving the girl of her virginity with her own hands.[715] Hence the theory that the prostitution of unmarried girls is a device to destroy their virginity without risk to their husbands is just as inapplicable to the Pelew Islanders as we have seen it to be to the peoples of Western Asia in antiquity. When a Pelew girl has thus been prepared for her vocation by her mother, she sells her favours to all the men of her village who can pay for them and who do not belong to her own exogamous clan; but she never grants her favours to the same man twice. Accordingly in every village of the Pelew Islands it may be taken as certain that the men and women know each other carnally, except that members of the same clan are debarred from each other by the rule of exogamy.[716] Thus a well-marked form of sexual communism, limited only by the exogamous prohibitions which attach to the clans, prevails among these people. Nor is this communism restricted to the inhabitants [pg 265] of the same village, for the girls of each village are regularly sent away to serve as prostitutes (*armengols*) in another village. There they live with the men of one of the many clubs or associations (*kaldebekels*) in the clubhouse (*blay*), attending to the house, consorting freely with the men, and receiving pay for their services. A girl leading this life in the clubhouse of another village is well treated by the men: a wrong done to her is a wrong done to the whole club; and in her own village her value is increased, not diminished, by the time she thus spends as a prostitute in a neighbouring community. After her period of service is over she may marry either in the village where she has served or in her own. Sometimes many or all of the young women of a village go together to act as prostitutes (*armengols*) in a neighbouring village, and for this they are well paid by the community which receives them. The money so earned is divided among the chiefs of the village to which the damsels belong. Such a joint expedition of the unmarried girls of a village is called a *blolobol*. But the young women never act as *armengols* in any clubhouse of their own village.[717]

supports by analogy the derivation of the similar Asiatic custom from a similar state of society.

Thus, while the Pelew custom of prostituting the unmarried girls to all the men of their own village, but not of their own clan, is a form of sexual communism practised within a local group, the custom of prostituting them to men of other villages is a form of sexual communism practised between members of different local groups; it is a kind of group-marriage. These customs of the Pelew Islanders therefore support by analogy the hypothesis that among the ancient peoples of Western Asia also the systematic prostitution of unmarried women may have been derived from an earlier period of sexual communism.[718]

milar custom observed in Yap, one of the Caroline Islands.

A somewhat similar custom prevails in Yap, one of the western group of the Caroline Islands, situated to the north of the Pelew group. In each of the men's clubhouses "are kept three or four unmarried girls or *Mespil*, whose business it is to minister to the pleasures of the men of the particular clan or brotherhood to which the building belongs. As with the Kroomen on the Gold Coast, each man, married or single, takes his turn by rotation in the rites through which each girl must pass before she is deemed ripe for marriage. The natives say it is an ordeal or preliminary trial to fit them for the cares and burden of maternity. She is rarely a girl of the same village, and, of course, must be sprung from a different sept. Whenever she wishes to become a *Langin* or respectable married woman, she may, and is thought none the less of for her frailties as a *Mespil*.... But I believe this self-immolation before marriage is confined to the daughters of the inferior chiefs and [pg 266] commons. The supply of *Mespil* is generally kept up by the purchase of slave girls from the neighbouring districts."[719] According to another account a *mespil* "must always be stolen, by force or cunning, from a district at some distance from that wherein her captors reside. After she has been fairly, or unfairly, captured and installed in her new home, she loses no shade of respect among her own people; on the contrary, have not her beauty and her worth received the highest proof of her exalted perfection, in the devotion, not of one, but of a whole community of lovers?"[720] However, though the girl is nominally stolen from another district, the matter is almost always arranged privately with the local chief, who consents to wink hard at the theft in consideration of a good round sum of shell money and stone money, which serves "to salve the wounds of a disrupted family and dispel all thoughts of a bloody retaliation. Nevertheless, the whole proceeding is still carried out with the greatest possible secrecy and stealth."[721]

§ 3. Custom of slaying Chiefs.

Islands the heir to the chieftainship of a clan has a formal right to slay his predecessor.

In the Pelew Islands when the chief of a clan has reigned too long or has made himself unpopular, the heir has a formal right to put him to death, though for reasons which will appear this right is only exercised in some of the principal clans. The practice of regicide, if that word may be extended to the assassination of chiefs, is in these islands a national institution regulated by exact rules, and every high chief must lay his account with it. Indeed so well recognized is the custom that when the heir-apparent, who under the system of mother-kin must be a brother, a nephew, or a cousin on the mother's side, proves himself precocious and energetic, the people say, "The cousin is a grown man. The chief's *tobolbel* is nigh at hand."[722]

eath and its execution.

In such cases the plot of death is commonly so well hushed up that it seldom miscarries. The first care of the conspirators is to discover where the doomed man keeps his money. For this purpose an old woman will sleep for some nights in the house and make inquiries quietly, till like a sleuth-hound she has nosed the hoard. Then the conspirators come, and the candidate for the chieftainship despatches his predecessor either with his own hand or by the hand of a young cousin. Having done the deed he takes possession of the official residence, and applies to the widow [pg 267] of the deceased the form of persuasion technically known as *meleket*. This consists of putting a noose round her neck, and drawing it tighter and tighter till she consents to give up her late husband's money. After that the murderer and his friends have nothing further to do for the present, but to remain quietly in the house and allow events to take their usual course.

observed before the assassin is recognized as chief in room of his victim.

Meantime the chiefs assemble in the council-house, and the loud droning notes of the triton-shell, which answers the purpose of a tocsin, summon the whole population to arms. The warriors muster, and surrounding the house where the conspirators are ensconced they shower spears and stones at it, as if to inflict condign punishment on the assassins. But this is a mere blind, a sham, a legal fiction, intended perhaps to throw dust in the eyes of the ghost and make him think that his death is being avenged. In point of fact the warriors take good care to direct their missiles at the roof or walls of the house, for if they threw them at the windows they might perhaps hurt the murderer. After this formality has been satisfactorily performed, the regicide steps out of the house and engages in the genial task of paying the death duties to the various chiefs assembled. When he has observed this indispensable ceremony, the law is satisfied: all constitutional forms have been carried out: the assassin is now the legitimate successor of his victim and reigns in his stead without any further trouble.

alities which a chief has to observe at his accession are much more complicated and tedious if he has d his predecessor.

But if he has omitted to massacre his predecessor and has allowed him to die a natural death, he suffers for his negligence by being compelled to observe a long series of complicated and irksome formalities before he can make good his succession in the eyes of the law. For in that case the title of chief has to be formally withdrawn from the dead man and conferred on his successor by a curious ceremony, which includes the presentation of a coco-nut and a taro plant to the new chief. Moreover, at first he may not enter the chief's house, but has to be shut up in a tiny hut for thirty or forty days during all the time of mourning, and even when that is over he may not come out till he has received and paid for a human head brought him by the people of a friendly state. After that he still may not go to the sea-shore until more formalities have been fully observed. These comprise a very costly fishing expedition, which is conducted by the inhabitants of another district and lasts for weeks. At the end of it a net full of fish is brought to the chief's house, and the people of the neighbouring communities are summoned by the blast of trumpets. As soon as the stranger fishermen have been publicly paid for their services, a relative of the new chief steps across the net and solemnly splits a coco-nut in two with an old-fashioned knife made of a Tridacna shell, while at the same time he bans all the evils that might befall his kinsman. Then, without looking at the nut, he throws the pieces on the ground, and if they [pg 268] fall so that the two halves lie with the opening upwards, it is an omen that the chief will live long. The pieces of the nut are then tied together and taken to the house of another chief, the friend of the new ruler, and there they are kept in token that the ceremony has been duly performed. Thereupon the fish are divided among the people, the strangers receiving half. This completes the legal ceremonies of accession, and the new chief may now go about freely. But these tedious formalities and others which I pass over are dispensed with when the new chief has proved his title by slaying his predecessor. In that case the procedure is much simplified, but on the other hand the death duties are so very heavy that only rich men can afford to indulge in the luxury of regicide. Hence in the Pelew Islands of to-day, or at least of yesterday, the old-fashioned mode of succession by slaughter is now restricted to a few families of the bluest blood and the longest purses.[723]

ustom shows how regicide may be regarded as an ordinary incident of constitutional government.

If this account of the existing or recent usage of the Pelew Islanders sheds little light on the motives for putting chiefs to death, it well illustrates the business-like precision with which such a custom may be carried out, and the public indifference, if not approval, with which it may be regarded as an ordinary incident of constitutional government. So far, therefore, the Pelew custom bears out the view that a systematic practice of regicide, however strange and revolting it may seem to us, is perfectly compatible with a state of society in which human conduct and human life are estimated by a standard very different from ours. If we would understand the early history of institutions, we must learn to detach ourselves from the prepossessions of our own time and country, and to place ourselves as far as possible at the standpoint of men in distant lands and distant ages.